"You are an infuriating, exasperating, crazy woman."

"Thank you."

Marcus tried his best to look annoyed, but he knew he really wasn't. "I didn't mean it as a compliment."

Annie could read the look in his eyes. He was weakening. "Yes, you did."

He shook his head. "There you go again, putting words into my mouth."

"If I were to put anything into your mouth—" she raised herself on her tiptoes again "—or near your mouth—" her arms were on his for balance "—it would be this." She tilted her head back, her eyes half shut, her mouth inviting, inches away from his.

It wasn't an invitation he could refuse, especially with the impression of her last kiss still blazing hot on his lips. But he hoped he was in control enough to just kiss her this time and break free.

He was wrong. He would never be able to break free.

Dear Reader,

Welcome to Silhouette **Special Edition** . . . welcome to romance. Each month, Silhouette **Special Edition** publishes six novels with you in mind—stories of love and life, tales that you can identify with— romance with that little "something special" added in.

And this month is no exception to the rule—June 1991 brings *The Gauntlet* by Lindsay McKenna—the next thrilling WOMEN OF GLORY tale. Don't miss this story, or *Under Fire,* coming in July.

And to round out June, stories by Marie Ferrarella, Elizabeth Bevarly, Gina Ferris, Pat Warren and Sarah Temple are coming your way.

In each Silhouette **Special Edition,** we're dedicated to bringing you the romances that you dream about— the type of stories that delight as well as bring a tear to the eye. And that's what Silhouette **Special Edition** is all about—special books by special authors for special readers!

I hope that you enjoy this book and all the stories to come.

Sincerely,

Tara Gavin
Senior Editor

MARIE FERRARELLA

Blessing In Disguise

Silhouette Special Edition

Published by Silhouette Books New York

America's Publisher of Contemporary Romance

To my brother Mark,
who is finally learning
that being optimistic
is the only way
to survive

SILHOUETTE BOOKS
300 East 42nd St., New York, N.Y. 10017

BLESSING IN DISGUISE

Copyright © 1991 by Marie Rydzynski-Ferrarella

ISBN: 0-373-09675-5

First Silhouette Books printing June 1991

Printed in the U.S.A.

MARIE FERRARELLA

was born in Europe, raised in New York City and now lives in Southern California. She describes herself as the tired mother of two overenergetic children and the contented wife of one wonderful man. She is thrilled to be following her dream of writing full-time.

OREGON

CALIFORNIA

NEVADA

Sacramento ★

San Francisco

Santa Cruz

Carmel-by-the-Sea

Pacific Ocean

Santa Barbara
Malibu
Hollywood
Beverly Hills
Los Angeles

SANTA BARBARA ISLANDS

N

San Diego

MEXICO

Chapter One

"But why can't I write it alone? It's based on my book."

The question echoed through Marcus Sullivan's mind as he moved restlessly around his living room. He paused briefly at the window and noted subconsciously that the early morning drizzle had evolved into a torrential downpour. The question had been posed during lunch with his agent more than a month ago. They had been discussing the production of a screenplay based on *The Treasured Few*, a book, he had pointed out with alacrity, that had been on the *New York Times* bestseller list for more than half a year.

But Richard had remained adamant. He had steepled his freckle-laced fingers together, his orange-marmalade brows rising innocently as he regarded his number one client.

"But my dear Marcus," he had intoned soothingly in his crisp British accent, "you are a novelist, and this project requires the hand of a screenwriter. A very good, talented screenwriter."

What Richard had said made sense, of course, Marcus
thought grudgingly. But it was his baby, and he didn't want
to just hand it over to someone else, no matter how good
that person was supposed to be. And he had said as much.
Very firmly. Besides, he had no use for movies. Movies
pandered to the public. Marcus Sullivan was not a pan-
derer by any stretch of the imagination.

Richard had turned a shade of light, unbecoming pink
when Marcus proceeded to threaten to turn down the lucra-
tive fee that Addison Taylor was dangling before them. Of
all the offers that had come pouring in from the various
producers, Addison's had been the most substantial. But
neither Addison nor Richard had reckoned with the possessive ardor of a writer.

Richard, after considerable effort, had devised a compromise that was just barely acceptable to Marcus. He had
convinced a doubtful Marcus to acquiesce, arguing that he
should at least give the project a chance. He could work with
the screenwriter.

After having more time to think things over, Marcus
wondered why in heaven's name he had initially agreed to
any of this. It wasn't really a compromise. He had surrendered. Lock, stock and barrel. In a moment of temporary
insanity, he had given up. It was all Richard's fault. Richard had reminded him that he was, after all, the one who
had originally seen the hidden promise of his talent in his
scattered writings when all the other agents had roundly rejected him.

Marcus owed him a little faith and trust, he went on.
Richard had a wonderful screenwriter in mind who just
happened to be under contract to him as well. Finally Marcus had agreed. And now he had a cross to bear.

The wind howled as rain pounded angry fists against the
window. The cross, he thought as he glanced at his watch,

was over forty-five minutes late. He didn't like to be kept waiting.

From where he stood in the living room, he could see the tip of a book peering out from beneath the white marble coffee table. Muttering, he stooped down to pick it up. He hated disorder. And that was just what his life had fallen into, disorder.

He glanced at the colorful book in his hand. It was a children's book worn down by the constant turning of pages. His godson's book. No, not his godson anymore. His ward. It was an antiseptic term to gloss over the fact that suddenly, terrifyingly, within the last three weeks, he had become responsible for another human being's life. A life he had absolutely no idea what to do with.

That, he supposed, thinking of Nathan, made two of them.

He set the book aside on the coffee table, its binding parallel to the edge. He made a mental note to take it into Nathan's room later.

Where *was* that screenwriter?

Collaboration. The whole thing was a damn stupid notion. It would have only taken him a little time to learn the basic fundamentals of scriptwriting, and a little longer to apply them to his own book. Instead, he was expected to greet an interloper with open arms, to allow her to put her name next to his on his work.

That was the way he viewed it. *His* work. Writing was a labor of love for Marcus, but it was first and foremost *labor*. When he was into a book, nothing else mattered, not time, not space, nor unanswered phone calls. Nothing. He gave himself totally to his work. It made up for the loneliness within his life. There were times he went for entire stretches of days in his den, writing furiously. He worked, *slaved*, until it was finished. How could he be expected to admit someone else into this most private of worlds? To share such an intimate process as that?

The simple answer was that he couldn't.

He let out a sigh and dragged his hand restlessly through the thick mane of straight black hair. Five more minutes, that was all he gave her. Just five more minutes. After that, he felt justified in calling the whole thing off. If Miss Hollywood Screenwriter couldn't even arrive on time for their first meeting, she certainly couldn't be expected to work to a schedule. They had exactly six weeks before production started. Six weeks to turn four-hundred-and-eighty-nine pages into a two-and-a-half hour movie. He doubted it could be done, and he was certain it couldn't be done if *she* was late.

Why wait five minutes? he decided. He'd call Richard now.

Marcus was halfway across the room to his telephone when the doorbell pealed.

He glanced at the door in mute disappointment, regretting that Holly, his housekeeper, wasn't here to tell the woman that he wasn't in. He thought of just not answering. The door chimes rang, and rang again. There was nothing to do but get this over with as quickly as possible.

Marcus crossed the floor and threw open the door. It was not a hospitable gesture and he knew it, but he wasn't feeling gracious at the moment.

The figure in the doorway was wrapped from head to foot in a huge electric-blue cape. "Hi, I'm Anne de Witt." The sunny, cheerful voice was a direct contrast to the weather.

"You're late," he announced. "Do all screenwriters show up late?"

Annie looked up at him, only mildly surprised at the curt, sarcastic tone he used. Richard had warned her. "They do if a truck jackknifes on their freeway."

He wasn't sure just what he had expected her to look like. But it wasn't what he saw standing in front of him now. She was about five foot two—maybe. The blond hair that was peering out from beneath the hood of her cape was plastered across her forehead, hanging into her eyes. She looked like something that the cat had dragged in, and she was standing, dripping, on his front step.

He was blocking the doorway and didn't appear ready to move. Annie stood on her toes and made an exaggerated attempt to look over his shoulder.

"You've got a very nice living room. Do I get to see any more of it?"

He saw the tiniest of dimples form on her right cheek as she grinned at him. Her fragile appearance diluted the edge of his antagonism. She looked like a child, he thought. How did Richard expect him to work with someone who probably popped gum as she talked? Nevertheless, he stepped back and allowed her to enter.

He was better-looking than the photograph on the back cover of his book, Annie thought as she walked in. And much, much bigger. For a moment, she felt a little overwhelmed. He had to be at least a foot taller than she was. She wondered if his aristocratic features appeared any softer when he was smiling. The photo on the book had captured a pensive expression, the same one he was wearing now. Well, Richard had told her it wasn't going to be easy. But that had made her all the more interested.

Annie pushed back her hood, revealing a wealth of swirling blond hair. The tips brushed against her shoulder, absorbing the moisture on her cape and turning darker. In a fluid movement, she removed her cape. She was dressed in a crisp gray skirt that fell an inch short of her knees and a soft pink blouse that struck Marcus as devastatingly feminine.

A feminine child, he mused. She wasn't getting her hands on his book, he decided firmly. She didn't look like she knew the first thing about life.

She turned her green eyes on him. They sparkled and momentarily held him in place, and he felt just the slightest bit disoriented. He realized that she was holding out her cape.

"Richard warned me that you were going to be difficult." She said it so matter-of-factly, she might have just said that Richard had told her his hat size. She raised the cape higher. "Where can I—?"

He took it from her grudgingly. "I am *not* difficult," he informed her tersely as he thrust the dripping cape onto the hook of an antique coatrack that stood sentry in the corner next to the front door.

"Terrific. Then we'll get along great."

I seriously doubt that, Marcus thought.

He turned from the coatrack, about to tell her why this temporary partnership Richard had planned didn't have a prayer of working, only to find that she had moved on to his living room.

Certainly makes herself at home.

He walked in after her. She was walking about the room, looking. And touching. It seemed almost a natural gesture, as if she were a spring breeze, passing through the room. But that was a ridiculous analogy, he thought.

Quickly his eyes washed over the petite figure. She looked as if she were there to baby-sit Nathan rather than to get acquainted and discuss the project. She was definitely too young to be any good, he thought again. Richard had mentioned that she was twenty-nine, but Marcus strongly doubted it. If she was twenty-nine, it was a damned young twenty-nine.

He felt far older at thirty-one.

For a moment, he studied her in silence. She seemed to- tally comfortable with her surroundings. Like a chameleon that could easily blend into its environment. In a way, he admitted, the ability was to be admired. He had never managed to blend in, or even attempt it. Instead, he had al- ways stood off to the side, watching. Even in the midst of the parties that he was, from time to time, obligated to at- tend, he always felt alone. It had been that way ever since he was a child.

He watched now as she moved about the room, running her slender fingers along nearly everything that came her way. What was she doing? he wondered.

"Into heavy reading?" She indicated the book on the coffee table, an amused smile lifting the corners of her mouth.

"That belongs to my godson," he answered stiffly, wish- ing he had put it away when he'd picked it up.

"Good book." She grinned. "I've read it myself."

"I'm sure it's just your speed."

His tongue was every bit as rapier sharp as Richard had told her it was. Rather than take offense, she enjoyed his retort. She'd always found pacific to be synonymous with dull.

Annie came to a halt in front of his fireplace. She looked briefly at the dying embers on the hearth. Then she turned her attention to the mantel. In one corner stood a small cluster of trophies, very precisely arranged. There was an inscription on the one closest to her heralding Marcus's prowess as a long-distance runner.

A godson who left books in his wake and a host of tro- phies. So, he does more than lock himself away and write, she mused.

She placed a tentative finger along the base of one cup. A smudge of dust marked her finger.

"Don't dust very often, do you?"

He looked at her in disbelief, half annoyed and half amused despite himself. Holly hated dusting. "Thank you for sharing that with me."

She shouldn't have said that, she thought, biting the tip of her tongue. Sometimes words just seemed to pop out before she thought them through. But it had showed her his mettle. He was going to be a challenge all right. So much the better. She worked best when challenged. Able to make herself comfortable in any given situation, she enjoyed collaboration as much as she enjoyed working on her own. Each project was an adventure, something to be savored, the same way life was. She had gotten that enthusiasm from her father, who had gotten it from his. Anne Kathleen de Witt was a third-generation screenwriter with an impressive list of credits to call her own.

She wondered if it was wariness she saw in his eyes, or something else. It was hard to decipher the message. The color of his eyes was so distracting. They were a deep, cobalt blue. And, she thought, they seemed to veil some sort of pain. He wasn't quite handsome, she decided, but there was definitely something there, something disturbing that went deep. She was going to like this assignment, she told herself. She could feel it. It was going to be difficult, but with tenacity, she knew she could turn out a movie that was even better than the book. And get to know a fascinating man in the process.

Silently Marcus removed her hand from the trophy.

She seemed unperturbed as she continued moving about. She stopped by the window. The storm was still raging. Running the drapes through her thumb and forefinger as if to get the feel, she looked over her shoulder at him and smiled innocently.

What the hell was she doing, he thought impatiently, taking inventory?

"I've never worked with anyone before," he began by way of an opening. He was going to tell her to go home. Having seen her, he knew that his initial feelings were correct. This was going to be *all wrong*.

"So Richard told me." She dropped the drapes and turned around. "It's a little like a marriage. You have to work at it a lot."

Her hand was hovering over an expensive vase that was the only tangible article he had taken from home when he finally left the East coast and the chilling aura of his family's house. It had always been the family house to him. He had never thought of it as home.

Protectively he placed himself before the vase. "Do you *have* to touch everything?"

She was a little surprised at his rebuke. She dropped her hands, and a slight flush came to her cheeks. She was doing it again, she thought. And she hadn't even been aware of it, really. It was second nature to her. "Sorry. I guess it just helps."

"Helps what?" How could he work with a woman who didn't speak English?

"Helps me to get a feeling for you."

The dimple appeared again. Even with her hair slightly disheveled by the wind and rain, she was lovely to look at. But lovely or not, she wasn't getting her hands on his book. He upbraided himself for having given in. If he had remained firm, he would have gotten his way. If not—well, he could certainly live without having his novel turned into a movie. There were far worse tragedies in life.

He was going through one now, he thought, then abruptly shut away the haunting sadness.

"And you're trying to accomplish that by touching?" His tone was nothing short of sarcastic.

It didn't faze her. "Best way I know how." Her green eyes crinkled a little as she smiled easily. "Vibrations." She was enjoying putting him on.

Marcus nearly looked up to heaven for help. "Oh, God, a renegade flower child."

"No, a people toucher."

Until she said it, he hadn't realized that she was now touching him. Her hand was on his shoulder. Not only was she moving in on his book, she was infringing on his space.

He took a step back. By nature, Marcus was a solitary creature, preferring to observe life at a distance and not get involved. This screenwriter from hell looked like the type who jumped in with both feet before she checked if the pool had any water. She might bear watching, but not when she was touching his novel.

His eye caught the gleam of a gold band on her hand as it dropped to her side. "Are you married?" He found himself voicing the question before he even clearly formed it in his mind.

"It's my mother's ring. I wear it for sentimental reasons. I've never been married." She congratulated herself for not giving in to the lump that rose in her throat. Briefly she shut her eyes, as if that would shut away the memory.

Yes, Marcus could definitely understand why she wasn't married. Who would want to say "I do" to a moving violation? "Never found anyone who could last, I presume?"

The slight edge of sarcasm tickled her. *I bet your bark is a hell of a lot worse than your bite, Marc Sullivan,* she thought. The sarcasm roused her and helped her shut away the pain.

"No, never met that Mr. Wonderful all those 1940s movies were written about," she said flippantly, mentally apologizing to Charlie's memory. It would have been two years this fall, she thought.

Purposely she turned her attention to the painting on the wall. It was a lonely seascape. So lonely it made her feel desolate for a moment. "And Jimmy Stewart is just a wee bit too old for me," she added as a postscript.

Lucky for Jimmy Stewart, he thought. He watched as she began to browse through his books that lined the wall on one side of the room. Enough was enough.

"Do you sit?" he asked in exasperation.

She turned and gave him a beguiling look. "Periodically."

His patience, never an abundant commodity, was at a low ebb. "Would it be too much to ask if one of these periods was coming soon?"

She pushed the book back on the shelf. They hardly looked touched. She wondered if he read them, or kept them for show.

"I make you nervous, don't I?" she asked. The wide grin was back. Her mouth was too large, he decided, even though it was strangely attractive. He wondered if she ever closed it completely. He'd wager that she didn't know how.

"Frankly?"

She shrugged. "Sure."

"Yes."

"I'll sit."

Annie sat down on his white couch. It was so pristine. Did he ever have company? Was he as lonely as the seascape indicated?

She discovered that the seat was too wide to accommodate her frame. If she sat flush against the back of the sofa, she couldn't bend her knees. It was a couch made for a big man, a man like Marcus Sullivan. She wondered where he let his godson sit in this room. It wasn't a room that really invited people in, especially not little boys.

She kicked off her shoes and curled her legs under her. "I hope you don't have anything against feet," she quipped impishly.

"Only if they're walking all over me."

The features of her slender face grew grave. As they did so, Marcus saw that she looked a bit older than the teenager he had first perceived her to be.

"Marc," she began.

"Marcus," he corrected her as he sat down himself, keeping a good distance between them.

"No," she countered with a firm shake of her head, "that makes you even more stuffy."

He didn't like being labeled. "And I suppose you want me to call you 'Annie'?"

She laughed. "Unless you prefer Witty."

"What?"

"Some of my friends call me Witty."

"Some of your friends obviously have a low threshold of amusement."

"It's a derivative of my last name," she pointed out, nonplussed.

And she was a derivative of he-didn't-know-what.

Marcus took a deep breath and tried again before she had a chance to say anything more. "I think there's been a mistake made."

She tilted her head slightly, the beguiling, childlike enthusiasm back. "Why?"

"I've decided not to do the screenplay."

That didn't sound like the man Richard told her about. "You're giving the whole project to me?"

He rose to his feet. "I'm giving none of the project to you. I'm withdrawing it."

Now that sounded like the man Richard had described. She pursed her lips, remaining quiet for the longest period of time since she got there. Exactly one second.

"Afraid?"

He saw something akin to mischief cross her face. "Of what?" he demanded.

"Of the fact that someone else might have some insight into your characters besides you." She saw a frown forming on his face. "I liked your book," she added easily.

"Thank you." There was ice in his response. Pure ice.

"And," she went on, undaunted, "I'd like to try my hand at bringing your people to the screen. I've got a lot of ideas."

"I bet you do." He loomed over her. "But the fact remains that—"

She propped herself up, tucking her arm around one of the embroidered cushions, totally unintimidated. "I'm really very good, you know."

"No, I don't know."

He was going to be a tough nut to crack, she thought, but challenges were what life was all about and she bit into this one with relish. "I wrote *The Wayward Children*." She set down the pillow.

"Never saw it."

"Did you see *Allison in the Morning?*"

"No."

"*Tears of a Nation?*"

"No."

Annie put her shoes back on and noticed that the action caught his eye. "How about *Casablanca?*"

The almost sensuous ritual made him lose his train of thought for a moment. He looked at her accusingly. "You didn't write that."

"No," she admitted cheerfully, "but I was beginning to wonder if you watched any movies."

"Not very often." He shoved his hands into his pockets, damning Richard for putting him in this spot. Unconsciously he moved away from her. His keen instinct of self-preservation had kicked in. "I'm too busy watching people."

"Good." She nodded as she rose and followed him. "I'll let you watch me work."

Why couldn't the woman stay put? She offended his sense of orderliness just by being. How could they possibly think of working together?

"That wasn't—" he began and got no further.

"No, probably not," she said, second-guessing him. "But it might be good for openers."

He began to wonder if he stood a chance against her rapid-fire delivery. "What's good for closers?"

She grinned impishly. "The screen credits rolling by."

He felt himself being reeled in. "You're determined, aren't you?"

"Yup."

"Why?"

"I like you, Marc Sullivan."

His eyes narrowed. "You don't even know me."

Again, she tilted her head, looking, he thought, rather vulnerable and confident at the same time. He hadn't thought that was humanly possible.

"You'd be surprised." She winked mysteriously. "I've read your book. As a matter of fact, I've read all of them."

"Now I can die a happy man." He paused. "And?" The writer within him always sought reaction to his work, even from people whose opinion didn't matter.

He expected her to spout glowing reviews just to get on his good side. He dared her.

"And," she responded thoughtfully, "I think you need to practice some of that sensitivity and emotion you pack into your books."

"What?" The word burst out before he could stop it, carrying with it the full weight of his annoyance.

"Anger's a start, of course," she said, neatly side-stepping the fact that he was being annoyed with her. "With luck, it might even lead to other emotions."

She was good with word games, he could see that, but it would take more than being clever to change his mind.

"All this collaboration will lead to," he informed her, "is trouble."

She smiled, contemplating his words. "That might be interesting, too."

He could feel himself wavering. She was intriguing in an offbeat sort of way. What did he really have to lose except a little time? Maybe, just maybe—

No, getting a screenplay accomplished with her was impossible. Still—

"All right," he heard himself saying. Shock began to set in. "I'll give it a week."

"To start." Annie took his large hand in hers, sealing the bargain.

"Or finish," he countered.

"We'll see." Her eyes laughed as she said it, but for some reason, he wasn't offended this time. Mesmerized would have been a better word.

He felt a warm sensation seeping into him despite his prophecy. A part of him warned that he was getting in over his head. Another part whispered that he'd be missing a chance to experience something unique if he turned his back on this. Curiosity was an important quality for a writer.

Curiosity won.

But even as he gave in, he got the very distinct impression that he had just allowed the storm to move into his house.

Chapter Two

"Oh, there is just one other thing about your books, Marc."

He knew it. Marcus let go of her hand and gave her a piercing look. He didn't mind constructive, intelligent criticism from people he respected. But that comprised a very small circle of people. She didn't fall into that category.

"Yes?"

Despite his defensive stance, Annie sensed that this was a man who didn't care for empty compliments. That was fortunate because she wasn't any good at them. "They could stand a dose of humor."

He had heard the horror stories that other novelists had to recount about what happened to their works in the process of being brought to the screen. He was not about to join their legion.

"Let's get one thing straight here, Miss de Witt—" He looked down at her from a vantage point of twelve-and-a-half inches.

If his height was supposed to intimidate her into silence, it didn't work. Instead, Annie just shook her head. "We're not going to get anywhere, Marc, if you keep insisting on addressing me as if I were an aging librarian out of some Victorian novel."

He was rapidly losing his patience. Using her nickname implied a degree of familiarity, and above all, he didn't want to foster that. She was already giving too freely of her thoughts. He wanted to maintain a professional distance between them. But to avoid any further discussion and digression, he decided to acquiesce, at least for the time being. Anything to get things cleared up and set straight. "All right. Annie—"

"There, that's better," she interrupted with a nod.

Marcus doubted it. If anything, it was worse. She was the kind, he was sure, who if given an inch, took a mile—and probably built a condo on it.

"Better," he informed her, summoning all the cool, aloof dignity he could, hoping to put her in her place, "would be if I were sitting in my den, working on another book." He saw no reason to tell her that right now, his creative process was running on empty.

His manner left her totally undaunted. "You will be," she assured him, once more meandering toward his neatly arranged book shelves, "as soon as you get this screenplay out of the way."

In her rambling, she had stumbled upon exactly the right words. That was the way he thought of the project. If he couldn't terminate his agreement, then he wanted to get this thing out of the way. Fast. Besides, there were other things, greater things, to occupy his mind. But they weren't going to get anywhere if she constantly kept intruding on his thoughts and flitting about. Like now.

He followed her over to the shelves, watching slender fingers slide along gilt-edged bindings. "You're changing the subject."

Pulling out a volume, Annie looked through it, then carefully placed it back. From her cursory glance, she saw that all the books were of a literary nature. Nothing frivolous or light. She wondered if he had a man's adventure story or a science fiction paperback tucked away somewhere. No, she thought, looking at him, probably not. His mind didn't seem to move in those directions. He needed to loosen up.

"I wasn't aware that there was a subject under discussion," she murmured, reading another title.

Marcus closed his eyes and sighed heavily. "Why do I get the feeling that I'm trapped inside a Burns and Allen routine?"

With a wide grin, she turned from the shelves. "Aha! Then you did watch television."

"Radio," he corrected evenly. Actually they had been tapes that were made of old radio shows. He had listened to them in college at Jason's behest. But Marcus didn't feel like explaining that to her. He didn't feel like explaining *anything* to her. The less said, the less ammunition she had to go off on another tangent. "And you're—"

"Not trapped at all, you know," she put in, crossing back to the sofa behind him.

Marcus turned around. Couldn't the woman stay put? His head was beginning to hurt. "What?"

"That's your problem, you know." Annie picked up the children's book again. The vivid cover was the brightest spot in the room. Flipping through the oversize pages, she wondered about Marcus's relationship with the boy.

He knew damn well what his problem was. Having an agent who was an idiot. How could Richard have ever dreamed this was going to work out between the two of them?

Firmly he lifted the book out of her hands and replaced it on the table. His unconscious drive for symmetry and order made him place it perfectly straight. "I don't need you to—"

"Tell you what your problem is?" Annie guessed, knowing she was right. "Of course you don't. But if you don't mind my saying so—"

"I do." He knew the protest fell on deaf ears, but he felt he had to make it, anyway.

"I think it's your attitude about this whole thing that's at the core of your discomfort." She turned her bright green eyes up to look at his face. "You're not trapped, Marc."

Yes he was. In quicksand. Up to his knees, and he felt as if he were sinking deep. For some odd reason, when he looked into her eyes he had the sensation that time had stood still, even as he was sinking. With great effort, he roused himself. Could an intelligent man be hypnotized by being assaulted with endless rhetoric? It was a definite possibility. He felt that way, dazed, hypnotized. Disoriented.

"Think of working on this screenplay as tapping unknown resources within you," she was saying. Her eyes on him, she moved the book slightly with the tip of her finger until it was askew. "This is a whole new field you're going into." Her grin challenged him. "It's different. You might even find it fun."

"Fun." Deliberately he moved Nathan's book to its original position. He wasn't about to let her gain any ground whatsoever, even with something so minor. "Like going over Niagara Falls in a barrel." He eyed her, waiting.

Hand raised to move the book again, she shrugged carelessly, letting it stay. It wasn't her wish to irritate him, just to test him. She had her answer. He resisted change. "If that's your idea of fun."

Marcus held up a hand, calling time out. He had wanted to say something at the beginning of all this. What was it? She had talked so much, everything had started swirling around in his head.

Then he remembered. "I don't want you tampering with my dialogue, or any part of the book."

"I'm not going to be tampering, Marc." Seating herself again, she raised her eyes upward, looking for all the world as if she were innocent of creating this turmoil that had suddenly appeared between them. "I'm going to be tempering." Carefully she enunciated the last word.

The hell she would. This was ridiculous. He had always been in control before, why should this be any different just because she talked faster than he could think? Firmly, he took a seat next to her and tried to take up the reins of leadership. "We need ground rules."

That got no argument from her. "Every partnership should have them."

Her choice of words sent a prophetic chill down his spine. That would be his idea of everlasting hell. "This is not a partnership, it's a temporary—" He threw up his hands as he rose. "Abomination." There was no other word to cover the situation.

Annie got up as well, her straight skirt clinging to her thighs. She had great legs, he thought unexpectedly, surprising himself. But he was not about to let her drop-kick him over her goalpost just because of that.

"Marc," she said calmly, "we're not going to get anywhere if you're going to throw tantrums."

"I'm *not* throwing a tantrum." Yes, he thought, he was doing just that. What was she *doing* to him? He was a calm, reasonable man who never even raised his voice.

"Good. Then what were the ground rules you wanted to set up?"

"I just—" Oh, what was the use? She'd debate over every word out of his mouth, and he suddenly felt very tired. He sighed, thinking that he needed some time and space before he could successfully tackle this. "We'll work it out as we go along."

"Good plan," she approved.

He felt like wringing her long, slender neck.

"Want to get started?" She turned and unzipped the large portfolio she had brought with her.

What he wanted was a stiff drink and a long cruise. Or maybe just a good lawyer to get him out of the contract he had so blindly signed in Richard's office, bonding him to this woman for the next six weeks.

But he had always managed to make the best of a bad situation before. He just needed time to reconnoiter, that was all. She had caught him completely off guard. Anticipating a problem with working with another writer, he had still naturally assumed that the other person would be a normal human being. He hadn't been prepared for a woman who made auctioneers sound as if they were speaking in slow motion.

He glanced at her. There was amusement gleaming in her eyes. He wondered if there was enough time in the world to get prepared for her.

Unfortunately time was at a premium and he knew it. "No, we'll get started tomorrow." It wasn't very much, but at least it was something.

Annie frowned and looked down at the notes she had taken out. She had read Marcus's book three times and was dying to get started. Jumping right into a project was one of the most exhilarating things in life for her. And, at one point, it had been all that had seen her through. "That doesn't make the deadline any easier."

"No," he agreed, wondering if he held the door open, would she take the hint. "But it might help my blood pressure."

Annie shoved her notes away again, then stopped as she zipped her case. "High?"

He disregarded the trace of concern in her eyes. They were strangers; why should she be concerned? That didn't make any sense. "Not until this moment."

"Oh." She laughed knowingly then closed the portfolio the rest of the way. "You're being dramatic again. You had me worried for a second."

Marcus was about to turn toward the coatrack. Her comment stopped him. "What do you mean, 'again'?"

Annie dropped her case to the sofa carelessly. Rocking forward on the balls of her feet, she placed her hands on either side of his shoulders. It was an intimate, friendly gesture that Marcus deemed should be reserved for old friends.

There was a smile in her eyes as she regarded him. "Marc, you do tend to get a little worked up, you know."

With a very deliberate movement, he removed her hands from his person. Contact between them was not quite as antiseptic as it had initially been. It was almost as if the light pressure of her hands cut through his apparel and *really* touched him. She was like some sort of an alien creature that was slowly, relentlessly infiltrating his system.

No, it was something much more down-to-earth than that. She was like a germ, he thought, liking the simile better. A cold germ to be warded off at all costs or be laid low.

"I think in this case I have just cause," he told her. "Normally I'm a very easygoing man."

Artfully, when he had removed her hands, she had turned them so that now she was holding his. "I'd say that you were a very uptight man."

He glanced down at their linked hands. How had she managed to accomplish that? Was this a sign of things to come? Her turning everything inside out? To his disadvantage? "And I'd say—"

They stopped as they heard a key in the door and the murmur of a voice. Annie couldn't quite discern if it belonged to a woman or a man.

She cocked her head at him questioningly. "Does someone else live here?"

Why was she always changing the subject before he could have his say? "No," he said in exasperation, pulling his hands free of hers. Then he realized what she was asking. "Yes."

It couldn't be both. "They live here part-time?" she prompted helpfully.

She was exhausting. More exhausting than sweating out a chapter in a book or making a character come to life. He began to think that for some unknown reason, Richard had it in for him.

He was momentarily spared the effort of answering her as the door opened. Her attention, he noticed almost gratefully, had shifted toward the two people entering.

"Hi!" she said brightly when Holly Hudson, a comfortable-looking, heavyset woman in her late fifties entered, bringing in the rain and ushering in a wide-eyed, thin little boy before her. The boy stared at Annie and didn't return her grin.

"Hello." Holly nodded at Annie. "The movie," Holly said to Marcus without any preamble, her small, sharp eyes looking Annie over quickly, "let out early, and he didn't want to stop for pizza." With a twist of her ample posterior, she shut the door behind them. Closing the umbrella, Holly tucked it into the stand.

"Not stop for pizza?" Annie crossed the room to the boy. "Don't you like pizza?"

Marcus thought it was only fair to warn his godson. After all, the boy was only seven, and that wasn't nearly old enough to be able to hold his own with someone like Anne de Witt. Thinking it over, neither was thirty-one.

"Brace yourself, Nathan. You're in for the Spanish Inquisition."

Nathan raised his brown eyes uncertainly, shifting them from Annie to Marcus and then back again. Behind him, Holly was busy removing his rain slicker. He stood as still as a mannequin until the older woman was finished. He clearly didn't understand what Marcus was telling him, though it was evident that he tried. "The what?"

Annie tossed a look over her shoulder at Marcus. There was a touch of exaggerated disappointment in her expression. "If that's your attempt at humor, it's lucky I'm here to help."

"I don't think the word 'lucky' can be stretched that far," Marcus muttered.

But she had already turned back to Nathan and was now squatting down to be on his level. "Hi, I'm Annie." She extended her hand to him.

Nathan took it solemnly and shook it, the epitome of good manners. It occurred to Annie that she had never seen a boy look so old before.

"And you're—?" Though she had heard Marcus say his name, she thought that the boy might want to introduce himself.

"Nathan Danridge."

Maybe he was shy. Taking a closer look, Annie decided that it went deeper than that. She glanced up at Marcus. Maybe the boy just took after his godfather. Marcus was probably like this as a child, she judged. "Well, I'm pleased to meet you, Nathan Danridge."

"Why?"

He *did* take after his godfather. "Because I'm hoping that someone in this household knows how to smile." There was no visible response to her words. Nathan continued to look at her with sad, serious eyes. "Do you?" Annie prodded.

The corners of the boy's thin face lifted slightly for politeness' sake, but his eyes did not follow suit. The expression drooped once more. Annie felt a pang, and if she hadn't been involved before, she knew that she was certainly involved now.

"We're going to have to work on that." It was a promise. She patted the boy's shoulder and then rose to her feet.

"Is there anything you don't plan to work on and rearrange?" Marcus's words fairly crackled in the air.

Marcus found himself thoroughly annoyed. Though he had no way of communicating with Nathan himself, never having mastered the art of conversing with children even when he was one, he still didn't want to see this capricious female hurt the boy by her mindless chatter. He knew that Nathan had more than enough reason for being the way he was.

Annie turned, her eyes on Marcus's face. This time, she gleaned, the reason for his curt remark didn't have anything to do with inflated ego or the right of possession. What had she stumbled onto?

"I'll draw up a schedule," she quipped, though there was no smile to go with it this time.

"Did you like the movie, Nathan?" Marcus asked. He had instructed Holly to take Nathan out in hopes that it would provide the boy with some badly needed diversion.

Nathan shrugged. "It was okay, I guess."

It was too soon yet, Marcus thought. He saw the housekeeper watching him, taking all this in. Privacy was at a high premium. "Holly, get Nathan into some dry clothes and see if you can't get him to eat something."

Holly nodded, taking Nathan's small hand into her own wide one. She looked like the perfect grandmother, Annie thought, but it seemed to have no effect on Nathan. He followed along obediently but with no life to his step whatsoever.

"Why is he so terribly solemn?" she asked quietly as she watched Nathan leave.

Marcus was surprised at her tone of voice. So, it could go down a few decibels and lose its wild exuberance. Maybe there was some sort of hope of being able to work with this woman after all, he thought. That still didn't give her a reason to ask personal questions. "I don't think that's any of your business, de Witt."

Annie turned to face him. Well, at least he had dropped the formal "Miss" part. Maybe she could ease him into this working relationship yet.

"Maybe not," she agreed, "but I'd still like to know."

The absolute audacity of the woman overwhelmed him. She didn't even entertain the notion that there were things out there that were out of her so-called jurisdiction, things that she had no business poking around in. He found her presumption incredible. And fascinating in an odd sort of way, just like her eyes.

"His parents were killed in a car accident on a day much like today." Marcus's voice was flat as he said the simple sentence.

He turned to watch the rain beat relentlessly against the windowpane, trying not to remember the horrible desolation he had felt when he had heard the news. Jason Danridge had been his best friend all through college, the only person Marcus had ever been able to open up to. They had studied together, shared their dreams and forged careers in two totally unrelated fields. Jason had been a football player in college. A star quarterback. He had turned pro shortly after graduation. The athlete and the scholar, that had been them. Yet there had been common ground. A lot of it. And laughter.

Sometimes Marcus missed him so much, he didn't think he could stand it, though no one ever guessed at the depth of his sorrow. As always, he kept that locked away.

Annie watched Marcus's back and saw the tension in his shoulders. Instinctively she sensed that she wasn't the cause of it right now. The death of Nathan's parents was. Another woman would have left the subject where it was, content to wait until the time was right to ask. But Annie had to have at least one answer with which to build her conception of the total man. He wasn't just a waspish-tongued egotist. There was more here. Much more. And she wanted to know.

"How long ago was that?"

Her voice was low, intruding into his private thoughts so subtly that he wasn't aware, at first, of her even asking the question. He didn't turn around. "Three weeks ago."

"And you took Nathan in?" She couldn't see the man who had snapped at her as she had first come in doing that. Obviously there was more to the man than met the eye. More than he wanted others to see. She thought of some of the almost poetic passages in his books. Perhaps they weren't accidental.

"Jason and Linda made me Nathan's guardian," he said quietly, as if that explained it all.

He remembered the day it happened. They had been drinking more than a few toasts to his first bestseller, and Jason had lifted a glass of champagne high, laughingly saying that now he could breathe easier. If anything ever happened to him and Linda, he knew that Nathan would never lack for anything, living with Marcus.

Even in the slightly hazy state that the alcohol had led him to, Marcus had hesitated. He knew that neither Linda nor Jason had any family to speak of. And Jason was like the brother he hadn't had, a friend to cherish forever. Still, he didn't feel qualified to be his son's guardian, entrusted with raising a living being. He didn't know the first thing about that.

And he had said so, but his fears were waved away by Jason. Both he and Linda had been adamant.

"There isn't anyone else I'd trust with Nathan except you," Jason had said solemnly, all deluding traces of alcohol instantly vanishing from the large, rugged face.

Deeply touched by the gesture of faith, Marcus had agreed and legal papers were drawn up the next day. Numbed by their death, Marcus had forgotten about his promise until Jason's lawyer had called him the day before the funeral to discuss Nathan's situation.

He had accepted his responsibility, but protested that he wasn't equipped for the job. Now that the boy was here, quiet and withdrawn, it didn't get any easier. Marcus hadn't the faintest idea on how to proceed.

"They must have thought a lot of you," Annie said softly, lightly placing her hand on his arm.

Marcus turned, surprised at the kindness he heard in her voice. "I suppose they did," he murmured.

But you don't, she guessed. Because she could see it made him feel awkward, she withdrew her hand. "That means they thought you were up to it."

He raised his head. He didn't need her advice. "Who says I'm not?"

She had read the troubled doubt in his eyes a second before he had shut it away. "No one," she said cheerfully.

How had they even gotten onto this subject? He didn't want to talk about Jason and Linda or Nathan. He really didn't want to talk to this woman at all.

Casually Annie crossed to the coatrack and retrieved her cape. "Did you come from a large family, Marc?"

There she was, probing again. "No, did you?" The question was purely a reflex action. He certainly didn't care.

"No." With a flourish Dracula would have envied, Marcus thought, she slipped the cape around her shoulders. "There were just two of us, my brother and me. But I had a lot of cousins," she added. A thoughtful look came into her eyes as she glanced in the direction Nathan had taken. "They're all married with kids of their own now. My brother had two children."

He was about to take her elbow and usher her toward the door when she swung around to look at him again, catching him off guard. It was getting to be a habit. "Maybe I can bring them over to play with Nathan."

God, she really did want to take over. "We'll discuss it." It was one of those throwaway lines meant to shut her up. He might have known better.

"Okay. Tomorrow. When I come back."

It was like making plans for the next attack of locusts. "About tomorrow—"

Once again, she didn't let him finish. "I thought that we'd work here, instead of my place, at least for the first week or so." She walked back into the room to pick up the portfolio she had left on the sofa. "It might make you relax a little."

He had the feeling that a handful of Valium wouldn't be enough to make him relax around her and nearly said so before he stopped himself.

"What time?" he asked wearily.

"Nine's good for me."

He usually got up at six. That would give him three hours to pull himself together before having to face her again. "Nine'll be fine."

Never, he thought as he started to close the door behind her, would be even better.

"I'll see you then," she promised.

Marcus closed the door and frowned. Maybe the world would end before tomorrow morning.

At least, he mused, he could hope.

Chapter Three

She was late again.

With an impatient oath, Marcus let the curtain at the front window drop. A feeling of déjà vu danced through him. It was yesterday all over again, except that this time, it wasn't raining.

Well, what did he expect? Of course she was late. It wasn't as if she had exactly struck Marcus as being the conscientious type. He had had her pegged right from the start.

How on earth had he managed to convince himself yesterday that this collaboration had a ghost of a chance of working? Obviously the rain must have seeped through his brain, Marcus speculated in mounting irritation.

If he were being honest with himself, he was in a worse frame of mind about this project than he had been to begin with. When he had initially agreed to give in to Richard and go along with this, Jason had been alive. There would have been someone to talk to, to unwind with. If working with a writing "partner" would have gotten to be too much, Marcus knew that he could always kick back at Jason and Linda's house, nursing a cold beer while Jason burned steaks on the grill and called them barbecued.

Marcus sighed as he dragged his hand through his hair. All that was gone now.

He moved about the living room restlessly. One quick moment in time and everything changed drastically. He didn't have that safety valve any longer. More than that, everything felt as if it didn't fit right, not his world, not his work, not his skin. Try as he might, he couldn't find his place anymore. He supposed it served him right for letting down his guard. Living with his parents had taught him how cold, how austere, life really was. How not to expect anything more. If he had remembered that, if he hadn't gotten involved with Jason, with his family, he wouldn't be going through this now.

He hadn't been able to write a single word in three weeks. Not since the accident. It just wouldn't come. He'd sit down at his desk and then just stare at the blank computer screen, feeling hollow. What was the use? his mind would taunt him, encroaching on the emptiness that was eating him alive. What the hell was the use? What was it all about, anyway?

He had no answers. Maybe there weren't any.

But there had to be. There was Nathan.

Nathan.

Marcus loosened his tie slightly and took off his jacket, draping it over the back of the sofa as he tried to rid himself of the sense of confinement that hounded him. He glanced toward the window. There was no car approaching the house. It figured.

His thoughts returned to Nathan. Lately, the orderliness in his life that had always given him peace of mind was deserting him. Even his thoughts were becoming scattered.

What in God's name was he going to do with a seven-year-old boy who didn't laugh, didn't play and only spoke when spoken to? Perhaps Nathan would have been considered a parent's dream come true, except that Marcus remembered that Nathan *had* laughed, *had* played. And it wasn't just a simple matter of sending him outside to play, either. With whom? There were no children in the neighborhood, at least, not any near Nathan's age. Besides, that wouldn't have been the answer even if there were children around.

Absently he picked up a gold lighter from the coffee table. A gift from Jason and Linda on his birthday, his twenty-ninth, he remembered with a smile. The year he had decided to give up smoking. He fingered it as he went on pacing, went on thinking. He thought too damn much, he knew, but there was nothing else.

Except for a seven-year-old boy.

The look in Nathan's eyes, a look that he knew mirrored his own, tortured Marcus, yet he had absolutely no clue how to even broach the subject of his parents' death, how to go about easing the boy's pain. Marcus knew exactly what Nathan was going through. The ache in his own heart was almost unbearable. He felt as if he had lost his brother, his kindred soul. Before Jason, there had been no one Marcus could relate to, talk to. Withdrawn, with books as his companions, he never seemed to have much in common with other young men.

As for the women, they were just names and faces and little more. Warmth for the evening. Physical warmth, not emotional. Emotionally he was withdrawn, starved, driven into himself by an uncaring, cold mother and a self-absorbed father. There was never a raised voice in his house. Never a hand raised in anger. But neither had there been a hand ready to stroke, to comfort, to hug. After a while, the boy had gotten used to it and grown into a man who thought he didn't need emotional nourishment. It had been Jason and Linda who had showed him a brief look at a world that might have been. But the curtain had dropped on that scene much too soon.

A noise had Marcus glancing over his shoulder. He thought he caught a glimpse of Nathan peeking into the room. But when he looked, there was no one there.

Marcus shrugged. Probably just his imagination. Maybe he was just remembering himself as a boy, feeling as lost as Nathan. There had been no kind words to free him of his cold cell then. Consequently Marcus had none to pass on to Nathan.

Maybe a military school, Marcus thought in desperation. He could enroll Nathan in a military school in the fall. They knew what to do with little boys there. At least it would give Nathan a sense of order, of structure. It would be the best thing that he could do for Nathan. That had been all that had seen Marcus through his own childhood. Structure was all he had to cling to. That and books. And his writing.

But writing wasn't there for him now. His ability to cocoon himself within the worlds he created had deserted him now when he needed it most. Marcus couldn't even express his anguish on paper. He needed something, a catalyst, to set him free, to make him write. It was that need, he realized now, that had made him act so out of character and continue to agree to this screenwriting project. Subconsciously he had understood that he needed something to stir him, to get him going again. Much as he hated to admit it, he needed some outside force to push him out of this dark and lonely place he found himself in.

He glanced at his watch impatiently. Abruptly he turned and, this time, saw Nathan before the boy had a chance to pull out of sight.

"Nathan." Marcus made it across the room in five quick strides.

But the boy was nowhere to be seen.

Marcus blew out an exasperated, frustrated breath. Nathan had been here at the house for almost two full weeks, and his suitcase still stood in the corner of his room, packed, ready to go at a moment's notice. It was as if he thought of this as just a transition period in his life, as if he hoped that his parents would return to take him home again.

Except that they weren't coming back.

"Not to either of us, Nathan," Marcus murmured under his breath. In his heart, Marcus wanted to be able to reach out to Nathan, to make things a little easier for him. But the words refused to come. He wasn't very good with words unless he could write them down.

And he couldn't even seem to do that right now, he thought, struggling against the clammy grasp of despair. God, he felt so helpless.

Damn it, where *was* she?

The doorbell rang in answer.

"Finally!" His annoyance flamed, red-hot. He considered being chronically late the ultimate, unprofessional insult. In the background, he heard the clatter of a pot being set down. "Don't bother, Holly," he called, reaching the foyer, "I've got it."

He threw open the door, his expression dark. This time, he planned to put the woman in her place. "Another jack-knifed truck, Miss de Witt?"

She wasn't alone. Some of his thunder faded, to be replaced by bewilderment. Flanking her on either side was a child, one boy, one girl. The boy was slightly taller than the girl, and he was clutching a brown paper sack. Both were blond and delicate-looking, although already the boy had a determined tilt to his chin. Just like Annie.

Hers?

Annie opened her mouth and then shut it, the rush of explanatory words dying on her lips in the face of Marcus's piercing, black look. She had been about to explain that her sister-in-law, Kathy, had called just as she was leaving the house and begged her to take Stevie and Erin for a few hours.

"You know I wouldn't ask if I had anywhere else to turn," Kathy had pleaded breathlessly. The woman was always breathless, always doing twelve things at once and eleven of them well.

Annie never said no to family, but she had hesitated, thinking of the flippant remark Marcus would have if she called and canceled their first work session. Then she remembered Nathan, and things just seemed to fall into place for her. There was no need to cancel. She'd take the children with her. Annie firmly believed in making lemonade out of every lemon sent her way.

"Sure," she had said to the harried voice on the telephone. "I'll swing by and pick them up on my way to my appointment."

The relief came flooding over the phone. "Annie, you're a saint."

"That's not an opinion shared by everyone," she had laughed, thinking of Marcus.

Now, facing him, she had trouble summoning some of that laughter. He looked as if he were contemplating having her drawn and quartered for being late. The man was definitely going to have to lighten up if they were going to work together.

"No, no jackknifed truck." Her hand tightened around the small hands lodged in hers. "There was a song on the radio I liked, so I stopped to listen."

He stared at her. "You can't be serious."

The little girl, frightened by his voice, hid behind Annie's legs, Marcus noticed, and he felt a tinge of guilt for scaring her. He also noticed something else. Annie wasn't wearing a skirt. Or slacks. The woman had come dressed for a picnic, wearing a pair of blue shorts with a blue-and-white button-down blouse knotted at her waist. Her legs were long and firm and tanned. She had the best calves he had ever seen.

No, this wasn't going to work.

"No, I'm not serious." She regretted her previous retort, but his attitude had annoyed her and she had answered before she thought. It was one of her failings.

Marcus shook his head. She wasn't making any sense. His best defense, he decided in mounting desperation, was a strong offense. It worked in war and he was beginning to think that there was more than a passing analogy here. He tried again.

"If we're going to—" *heaven help me,* he thought "—work together, I want you to understand that I won't put up with such laxness and unprofessionalism. You were supposed to be here thirty minutes ago."

She didn't particularly like being late, even when it couldn't be helped. She also didn't like being lectured to. Her chin rose rebelliously as she swept into the room, pulling the children along with her. "Why, did I miss something?"

Marcus pushed the door closed behind him without looking. She walked past him, her hips swaying slightly, reminding him of the woman he had envisioned as the heroine of his last novel. He tried not to concentrate on the effect it was having on him. He wasn't successful. "No, but I must be."

Annie turned to look at him. "What?"

"My sanity." There was an edge to his voice. This just wasn't working. She no sooner walked through the door than he lost his patience. He nodded towards her bookends. "Who are these children?"

"Lower your voice, you're scaring them." She raised their hands slightly as if to remind him of their presence. "And me."

Marcus arched a dubious brow. "I doubt if a raging bull would scare you."

She grinned, tickled at the comment. "Depends on how loud you bellow." She looked at the two children who were taking this in with wide-eyed interest. The boy was holding a large paper sack that was filled with his precious dinosaurs. "As for the children, they're my niece and nephew. Remember, I mentioned them yesterday."

"Yes, I remember." He remembered everything about yesterday's visit. It lived in his mind with the clarity of an overwhelming nightmare. He glanced at the children. They didn't look the least bit frightened of him anymore. Even the girl was merely staring at him curiously. "However, I didn't expect you to bring them here for show-and-tell." She was bringing out the very worst in him, he thought. Two minutes in her company and he was behaving like an ill-mannered boor. And he couldn't seem to help himself.

She bit her lower lip, wondering where Nathan was. She glanced toward the hallway, but didn't see him. "They're the reason I'm late."

He looked down at them. They were now studying him and the pristine, white room with unabashed interest. To their credit, they weren't wandering around and touching things. Unlike their aunt, he thought, remembering yesterday. Her flippant remark came back to him. "They wanted to hear the song on the radio?"

Rather than take offense, she laughed. It was a smoky, silky laugh that went straight down to the bone. He tried not to notice that, too. He was batting zero so far. "Very witty, Sullivan. There's hope for you yet."

"Not until this project is over."

Marcus looked at the boy and girl and consciously softened his expression. More children in his house. Just what he needed. He could see that the girl was staring at him with wide, slightly uncertain eyes. She was about six, he'd guess. Or perhaps a very petite seven. She reminded him of a doll. The boy was sturdier, almost a head taller. With his arms wrapped around his sack, he stood protectively next to his sister. Marcus liked that. He didn't care for people who were easily intimidated, and the child, he had often maintained, was the father of the man.

He was living proof of that.

"Why did you—?" His voice trailed off as he remembered what she had said yesterday. She had talked about bringing children over to see Nathan. He had thought he had cut her off by saying they'd discuss it later. Obviously he had thought wrong. "I don't think Nathan is really ready for this, Miss—"

Still formal, she thought. Well, she'd have to break him of that, too. She certainly had her work cut out for her, she mused. "Annie," she corrected him.

Erin looked up at her aunt, bewildered. "He calls you Miss Annie?"

Annie ruffled Erin's short blond hair, but her eyes were on Marcus. "No, I think he has another name for me, but he's not going to use it, are you?" she ended, putting the question to him.

He liked symmetry. Her grin, he realized, was lopsided. There was no reason on earth why that should be appealing. "Only when pressed," Marcus muttered. "Look—" he tried again, "I don't think that Nathan is ready for two children to descend upon him—"

A flash of a dark head in the doorway caught her eye. So, he was listening. "I think we'll let Nathan decide that." Annie put her hand out toward the empty space the slight boy had vacated. "Right, Nathan?"

Shyly Nathan reappeared in the doorway. Marcus turned in time to see him take a step inside the room.

Annie pretended not to notice how heart-wrenchingly shy Nathan was. "Nathan, I'd like you to meet Erin and Stevie." With a hand on each shoulder, she ushered the two toward the boy. She smiled at him encouragingly. "I think the three of you might have a lot in common."

The awkward look on Nathan's face had Marcus remembering another time, another place. "And what makes you think that?" Marcus wanted to know, a protective feeling for Nathan springing up within him. Just who the hell did this woman think she was, rearranging lives like this? She should have asked if she could bring these children along with her. Asked so that he could have turned her down.

"Nathan, if you'd rather not—" Marcus was about to give the boy a way out. But, again, he didn't get a chance to finish.

Annie turned slowly to face Marcus, her head tilted a little. He noticed that she swallowed before speaking. The flicker of pain caught his attention, cutting short his words. "Well, for one thing," Annie told him, "they lost their dad, too."

She saw that she had startled Marcus with her words. "It was a couple of years ago, but I thought that perhaps they could talk to one another. Sometimes, talking is all we have." She turned her attention back to the children. "Nathan, is there somewhere you could take Erin and Stevie so you could play together while Mr. Sullivan and I try to get a little work done? You'd really be doing me a tremendous favor."

Hesitantly Nathan looked over his shoulder toward the stairs, and then nodded. "Sure," he answered quietly. "I'm staying upstairs if you want to come up."

Hefting up the sack with one hand, Stevie put his arm around Nathan's shoulders, having sized him up favorably.

"Got any video games?" He motioned for his sister to fall into step.

"No."

Stevie mulled the information over for a minute. "That's okay. I've got my dinosaurs. We can play with them." Because she wasn't following fast enough, Stevie let his hand drop from Nathan's shoulder, took hold of Erin's hand and pulled her along in his wake.

Annie watched the three make their way up the stairs before she turned toward Marcus. "You're going to have to get video games for him."

She would have made a hell of a drill sergeant if he were in the market for one. Which he wasn't. "Anything else?"

"Yes, a better attitude wouldn't hurt." She saw the frown and decided to take another approach. He wasn't used to her yet. "Look, Sullivan, I know I have a tendency to come on a little strong—"

Obviously the woman was given to understatements. "Nothing that can't be measured on the Richter scale."

She laughed, enjoying the joke at her expense. "Touché. But I think we'll get along much better if you don't try to thrust and parry every time I open my mouth."

"What should I do when you open your mouth?" Suddenly, precisely, he knew what he would like to do. He would like to kiss her. No, like was too tame a word. *Wanted* fitted much better.

My God, what was he thinking of? The realization startled him. He would have thought that gagging her would have been foremost in his mind. He wondered if she dabbled in witchcraft on the side. Why else would he want to kiss someone who annoyed him so completely?

She turned her face up to his, her eyes innocent. "You could try listening."

He forced air into his lungs slowly. Her green eyes had him forgetting to breathe. "You mean I have a choice in this matter?"

"No," she answered cheerfully.

"Somehow, I didn't think so." He relented, looking away for his own safety. "You really should have called about the children."

Yes, she should have, she thought. But she had been in a hurry, and besides, it was too late for that. She shrugged. "They were a last-minute surprise."

He looked at her, confused. "You didn't know you had a niece and nephew?"

"I didn't know I had a niece and nephew who were going to be coming along. Kathy, my sister-in-law," she interjected quickly, "had an emergency crop up. She didn't have any place to leave the children. I knew if she called me, she was desperate."

"People only call you when they're desperate?"

She looked up at him. What had caused all that awful, wary sadness she saw in his eyes? Was it in some way connected to the fact that he kept trying to make her keep her distance? People didn't normally react to her that way. She usually got as close to them as she chose. Not him, she thought.

"Sometimes," she told him. "Other times they call me because they enjoy it."

He had a hard time picturing someone voluntarily calling her just to talk. To listen, maybe, but not just to talk. Therein lay only frustration.

She wandered off into the hallway. "I like your house, Marc. Do I get a tour later?"

He looked at her, still debating the wisdom of all this. He kept telling himself that it wasn't too late to back out. "If there *is* a later."

She looked at him over her shoulder, amused. "Oh, there will be."

There was an inverse relationship here, he thought. The more negative he was, the more positive she became. What made her like that? Was she merely a grinning idiot, an infuriating female who meddled with everything that came in contact with her, or—

Or what? And why did knowing what she was even matter to him?

The answer was, he told himself firmly, that it didn't. They had work to do, and he had to get started if there was ever going to be a way to get this woman out of his hair and get his life—his and Nathan's—back in order.

Was there ever going to be order again? he wondered, the overbearing sadness gnawing at him again.

He thought of the children she had brought with her. "Umm, the children's father—"

"My brother?"

"Yes. How did he—?"

"Die?"

He was beginning to feel as if he was an unwilling contestant in a game show, one where he was required to speak in tandem with someone else. "Yes."

"You have trouble saying that word, don't you?" she asked sympathetically.

"I have trouble," he told her in a moment of unguarded honesty, "accepting that word."

She could appreciate that. She knew how she had felt when it had struck in her life, leaving gaps that burned into her soul.

"My brother died of leukemia. It was fast. Very fast. We didn't even know there was anything wrong until the end. He was lucky."

"Lucky?!" he cried incredulously. How could death be lucky?

"Yes," she said simply. "Usually the patient lingers and suffers a lot. Daniel had just enough time to say the things that counted—I love you and goodbye." With effort, she shut away the pain. It was never easy. Part of it, she knew, would always be there.

She skimmed her hand through her hair, looking up the stairs where the children had disappeared. "I explained about Nathan's situation to the children on the way over here. I think that talking to children his own age who've gone through the experience of losing someone close to them might help Nathan cope with this a little better."

It was something he would have liked to have done for Nathan, he thought. But he hadn't known how.

"Perhaps."

She merely grinned. "I'll take that as a thank-you."

"It wasn't meant to be."

"I know, but I'll take what I can get."

He bet she did. He just bet she did. Marcus had a very uneasy feeling that the next six weeks were going to be quite an endurance test. One he wasn't completely certain that he could pass.

Chapter Four

She was here; Nathan was occupied. There were no excuses left. He had to begin this project. Marcus realized with growing discomfort that he had no idea how to proceed. How exactly did one collaborate?

She knew. She had said as much. But it was his book and he wanted to maintain control. He didn't want to surrender the lead to her right from the outset. Permitting her to have control was tantamount to Custer asking the Indians how to shoot a gun. Hands in his pockets, staring at the multiple panes on the front window, Marcus cast about for a way to start, for something to say.

"You did read the book." It was a stupid thing for him to ask. He knew she had. Annoyed with himself, he shoved his hands deeper into his pockets. Once again, he wished he had never agreed to this.

He looked uncomfortable, restless, and it bothered her. Annie wished she could put Marcus at ease. But she was uncertain how to approach him. Being friendly, the way she always was, didn't seem to work with him. She really didn't have another approach. He looked as if he took offense at everything she said. It was as if he was intentionally fostering discord between them. She wanted to know why.

"Every golden word," she answered.

He interpreted her response as sarcasm. Adrenaline shot through his veins. "Then you have no objections to talking over the plot."

Marcus looked at Annie, daring her to voice an objection. Traces of a smile were just visible at the corners of her mouth. What was so amusing? he wondered.

It was a place to start, she thought. She had her notes and her PC in the car. She could always get them later. "None."

Stiffly he gestured toward the sofa. "All right, let's sit down and get started."

"Okay." She sat down, kicked off her sandals and tucked her feet under her the way she had done the day before. The woman looked as if she felt right at home.

Too bad he didn't, he thought.

She distracted him. Unsettled him. Suddenly he couldn't remember the details of his book. He had written it, sweated over it, made slow, deliberate love to it in a way he never had to a woman. Why then couldn't he remember the plot? This was embarrassing, frustrating. What the hell was wrong with him? Disoriented panic threaded through him as he lowered himself onto the sofa.

He came in contact with something soft, yet firm. Instinctively he jerked to the side. Without looking, he had managed to pick the exact same spot on the sofa as she had.

She was too damn soft, he thought, annoyed with himself and with her. Too soft and, if he wasn't misreading his reactions, too attractive for his own good.

He cleared his throat as he looked down into her amused eyes. She could sense his discomfort. She was enjoying it.

"Sorry," he muttered.

"Nothing to be sorry for. A simple law of physics states that two objects can't occupy the same space at the same time." She paused. "But they can try." Her dimple was prominent in the corner of her mouth as she laughed. The sound washed over him like a warm, caressing hand. "This better?" She slid over to the corner of the sofa and looked up at him, one arm carelessly hooked over the side, her toes curled beneath her.

He could have strangled her for the totally innocent look she gave him and for the fact that it had his blood warming.

If this so-called collaboration was going to work in any shape, manner or form, he had to think of her in the neuter gender. Better yet, he would think of her as some sort of a challenge from God and his agent. Under no circumstances could he think of her as a flesh-and-blood woman who was at this moment packaged in such a way as to wreak havoc on his every coherent thought.

He sat on the edge of the sofa and gave her a long, penetrating look. "Why are you wearing shorts?"

Annie glanced down at her attire. She hadn't given it a second thought when she left her house. This was the way she usually looked when she worked. She had, though, taken a little extra care with her hair.

"Because they make me feel comfortable." She looked at what he was wearing. He was dressed as if he were on his way to a formal meeting. His suit jacket was slung over the arm of the sofa. He'd probably just taken it off. "The same way I guess a shirt and tie make you comfortable." Although for the life of her, she couldn't see how.

He didn't care for the laughter he detected in her voice. "Comfort isn't the point here. We're professionals."

No one was disputing that. But what did clothes have to do with it? Just what was he driving at? "Yes?"

She was goading him on. How could he work if everything was reduced to a debate? "And I thought that we should dress the part." There was a certain way to do things, and he had always found a certain amount of solace in rituals and routines, just as he did in order. It was a poor substitute for warmth, but he had learned to live with it.

She still didn't understand what he was trying to say. "Of mannequins?"

"Are you deliberately trying to annoy me?" His formidable manner didn't intimidate her. He would have found it admirable if it didn't have a direct effect on his position.

"No, not deliberately. Look, Marc." She reached over and touched his arm. He didn't care to be touched. But he left his arm where it was. "I really think that we'll get along better if we loosen up." She used the word "we" to be polite. They both knew she meant him. If *she* were any looser, he thought, she'd come in liquid form. "Do you mind?"

"Do I mind what?" Suspicion brushed over him.

Annie leaned forward, her fingers reaching for his tie. "My father always said this was more of a noose than a fashion statement." She undid the already loosened knot, her eyes on his. "Cuts off the circulation to your brain."

Marcus put his hands over hers, intent on stopping her. Her hands felt so small under his. Small and delicate and fragile.

So much for his having an astute sense of touch, he thought.

"The circulation to my brain is just fine." *Except, perhaps, where thoughts of you are concerned,* he added silently. *There I seem to be somewhat addled.* "Can we dispense with the word play and the disruptions and just get down to work?"

She raised her hands high, fingers spread wide. The tie hung loosely about his neck. "That's why I'm here."

"Nice to know," he muttered, straightening his tie. She was right, it did suddenly feel too tight. But he wasn't about to admit it.

Annie cocked her head. "Now who's bantering?"

He wanted to wipe the grin off her face. He wanted—

He stopped himself from completing the thought. It wasn't going to end the way he would have liked.

Filling his lungs with air, he let the breath out slowly. There, that was better.

He looked straight ahead and moved back on the sofa. "The story starts—" He looked at her, about to make a point. Her eyes were wide as she prepared herself to listen. Her lips were slightly parted as if she were about to savor what he was about to say. Except that he wasn't saying anything. "The story starts," he began again.

To his horror, his mind went blank again, utterly, completely blank.

Annie leaned forward. She seemed to fill the small space around him, crowding him, her hands on her knees, her body arched forward, as if every fiber was alert, poised. Ready. How had the distance between them evaporated? He didn't remember moving closer. When had she?

"Yes?" Annie encouraged, waiting. He seemed to have gone into a holding pattern, and she wondered if this was some sort of a test on his part. He was bent on making her withdraw from the collaboration, that much she would have been sure of even if Richard hadn't warned her that this might happen.

But what Marcus didn't know was that she needed to work, that she thrived on it, for all his theories about her laxness. She had her own style, her own way of working. There were no hard-and-fast rules to slavishly adhere to, except to finish what she started and to produce the best possible product she could. When she worked, she was dedicated, but she never lost sight of the fact that for her, work was fun and she felt very, very fortunate to dearly love the thing that paid for her food and provided the luxuries in her life.

He had never had this much trouble gathering his thoughts together, had never felt this sort of an inability to concentrate on something that was basically second nature to him. It had to be her. He didn't quite understand how, but it had to be her. "Answer me a question."

"Okay. What is it you want to know?"

He was at the end of his patience. "Are you a plague from God?" He wouldn't have been the least surprised if she said yes. He had never, ever, met anyone so infuriating, so inflammatory.

"No." There was mischief in her eyes as she lifted her chin. "Were you expecting one?" If ever a man had a right to expect to be set straight by the powers that be for being so perverse, it was him.

His anger intensified. He would have had difficulty deciding who he was angrier at, her or himself for responding to her. "I was expecting another writer."

She spread her hands wide. "That's what you've got."

"No, that's not what I've got. What I've got—" What I've got is an all-consuming headache for the next six weeks.

Marcus cleared his throat again. What was the use of debating this? He glanced at her tanned legs. "Can you wear slacks tomorrow?"

She grinned, pleased. It was nice to know. "Am I distracting you?"

"No," he retorted, knowing it was useless. She saw through him. "Yes."

Annie weighed his words. "Half distracting, then. I'm glad. It makes you human."

All too human right now, he thought, and it wasn't going to do.

Lightly she placed her hand on his forearm. She felt it tense, then watched as he made a conscious effort to relax at least this much of his body. She was glad that she was having an effect on him. God knew something was humming through her own body, not giving her any peace. It had been like this, she realized, since she had met him yesterday. Something had just snapped into place for her, although what that was she wouldn't have been able to explain. Yet. "Maybe we can take that tour of your house now. Showing me around might make you feel more in control."

Marcus managed to hold on to his temper, but just barely. "I wish you'd stop analyzing me."

"I'm not analyzing," she corrected him. "I'm trying to help."

"If you really wanted to help—" He was very close to saying that she shouldn't bother coming by anymore, but knew that was impossible. He settled for second best. "You'd dress more appropriately." At least then he wouldn't keep getting distracted.

"Tomorrow—" she raised her hand "—sackcloth and ashes. I promise."

Some wars, he knew, were won by retreating and fighting another day. He needed a few minutes to regroup. "C'mon, I'll take you on that tour now."

When she raised her hand to him, he took it instinctively. Feelings and thoughts came rushing up at him when her fingers entwined around his. As she rose to stand next to him, his body tensed, a low vibration beginning in his very core. It was because of her nearness. He could smell a very light, feminine fragrance that wafted along her skin. It seemed to him as if every pore of his body opened up in the face of this unabashed radiance that was emanating from Annie. Disjointed, lax, with a mind that he knew was probably as scattered as the four winds, she still radiated sexuality. More than that, she radiated sensuality, which in his book was the far more deadly of the two.

Even brooding, he was handsome. Maybe more so, Annie thought. "You know, you look kind of cute with your nostrils flaring like that."

Consciously he disengaged himself from her and dropped her hand. "I wasn't aware that they were."

"They were. They are." She placed a gentling hand on his shoulder. She wasn't used to this sort of resistance. People always liked her. She really just wanted to be friends.

No, her mind whispered, she wanted to be more. Much more. But first came friendship. And trust. Nothing was worth anything without trust. "I don't bite, Marc."

His brows drew together. Words were all he had. "It'd probably be toxic if you did."

This, she thought, was going to be very, very interesting. He was going to keep her on her toes, and she liked that, liked being stimulated. But there was more here, she thought, more than just the clash of wits. He *did* interest her, as a writer. As a man.

A slow smile curved her lips as a bittersweet feeling begged to be allowed out. She pushed it away with both hands. Now wasn't the time to think of that. Or to feel that, either.

"C'mon, show me Nathan's room," she urged, grabbing his hand again and tugging.

The look on her face told him that she was enjoying herself immensely. She was as at ease with all this as he was not. He realized suddenly that his malaise and sense of apathy were gone. At least she had done that much for him. "This way."

Holly appeared just as he walked into the foyer. She looked at Annie, and there was neither approval nor disapproval on her face. Holly was the type to reserve judgment. But she saw everything. Like their linked hands. "How many for lunch, Mr. Sullivan?"

Aware of Holly's gaze, Marcus pulled to free his hand. "Are you planning on staying, Annie?"

Lunch was only a little more than two hours away. "I thought we could work it in, yes," Annie responded, amused. "Maybe we can eat with the children." She cocked her head, waiting for his comment, a hopeful expression on her face.

The meals he had shared with Nathan in the past two weeks had been painfully quiet and formal. Perhaps eating with this woman and the children she had brought would break the ice for them. If nothing else, he and Nathan could join forces against this hurricane that had blown into their lives. He wondered how the boy was faring with the children. Better than he was with her, Marcus hoped. "There'll be five for lunch, Holly."

Holly nodded briskly and marched off to see what could be done about that.

"You know, Marc—" Annie easily slipped her arm through his "—you have definite possibilities."

She was attached to him again. The woman had more sticking power than industrial-strength glue. "Thank you for noticing."

She ignored the cool put-down. "You're welcome."

The woman was impossible. And Marcus had absolutely no idea why he found himself smiling. But it did feel good, as did the touch of her hand on his arm.

When they came to the landing, the sound of childish laughter greeted them. Marcus looked questioningly at Annie, then down the hall at the source of the sound.

"Nathan?" she asked. It was a rhetorical question. She already knew it was. Stevie laughed like a young blue jay, and Erin giggled almost silently.

"I'm not sure." Afraid to find out it wasn't, he moved slowly down the subtly wallpapered hall.

"Must be." Annie kept abreast of him. "Stevie has a very distinct, high-pitched laugh." With a nod of her head, she urged him to push open Nathan's door.

When they peered into the room, they saw the three children on the floor, playing with the dinosaurs that Stevie was never without.

"He's a meat-eater," Stevie declared, pointing to the figure Nathan held for the benefit of the two adults in the doorway, "but I can fly away."

To prove it, he moved his pterodactyl up and down, gliding it on the air.

Not to be left out, Erin quickly announced, "I'm a princess."

Stevie frowned. "There were no princesses back then," he told her authoritatively.

"She can be a princess if she wants," Nathan said softly. "Maybe a cave princess."

Annie smiled. He was a kind-hearted boy, just as she had surmised. "Destined to be some girl's knight in shining armor," she told Marcus quietly. *Are you?* she wondered.

There was a question in Annie's eyes that Marcus chose to ignore.

Nathan's solution pleased Erin greatly, and Stevie grudgingly accepted it, his interests immediately turning to staging another battle with the flying attacker.

"See you at lunch," Annie told the children. She tugged on Marcus's arm and indicated the hall with a slight incline of her head.

He followed her out, mystified and relieved at what he had witnessed. "You knew that was going to happen, didn't you?"

She nodded. "I was hoping. It's not so much that misery likes company as sadness needs a shoulder to cry on—a shoulder it can reach.'' She patted his for emphasis, indicating that she wasn't trying to criticize him. "I asked Stevie to tell Nathan about his dad and see if he could make Nathan feel a little better.'' She fell into step as Marcus led her away from Nathan's room. "It made Stevie feel important, and in turn, I was hoping that he could help Nathan. See," she said, looking up at him. "Simple."

"Right, simple.'' There was nothing simple about her mind, he thought, or the way it worked. "Well, this is my bedroom.'' Feeling uncommonly awkward, Marcus opened the double doors and watched her face as she looked inside.

Annie didn't just look; she walked in and somehow, Marcus noted, took possession just by entering. Hands on hips, she surveyed the room carefully.

She could have picked it out of a lineup, she thought. It reminded her of him. Everything was very neat, very clean, very precise. The black curtains with their bold floral pattern hung just so, each fold in place. The king-size bed with its matching bedspread was made, four pillows scattered at exactly the same distance from one another along the carved headboard. There wasn't a slipper showing, a tie left out, or any change left uncollected on the bureau. It wasn't a bedroom; it was a room out of a museum. Cheerless and dignified.

Annie thought of the jumble her own bedroom was in. "You sure you sleep here?"

He kept his post by the doorway, his arms folded across his chest. "Yes, why?"

She had an urge to open the closets and see if everything was hung in descending order. Probably. "I didn't think a human being could be this neat."

Leave it to her to make a virtue sound like a failing. "It's in the genes."

"Must be." She turned around to face him. "Me, I live in subtle chaos."

Live in it and create it around you, he thought. "Subtle?"

For the first time, Annie saw amusement highlighting his eyes. It was a change for the better. He might look sexy with smoldering moodiness, but this was devastatingly appealing.

"All right," she conceded, "not so subtle." She let him lead her out into the hall again. "But I find order within it. Not worrying about keeping things neat gives me time for other things."

"I don't have any trouble coordinating both."

He pointed out a guest room, but she hardly noticed it. She was too busy watching him. "No, I don't doubt you would." At least, not on the surface, she wanted to add.

No one could be so precise, so controlled and not be on the verge of erupting, she thought. She wondered if she'd be around when that finally happened. A shiver swept through her as she walked along beside him. She hoped she'd be there. She had a feeling that there would be a great deal of passion involved, passion and emotion when he finally let go. He was capable of passion. His works had showed her that. No one could write the way he did and not feel it somewhere, in the privacy of his own mind, his own heart.

Because she urged him on, he went through the entire house, room by room. He watched her take it all in, commenting, approving, sometimes silently nodding her head as if she were agreeing with something in her own mind. The silence proved as unsettling as the banter. He wanted to know what was going on in her mind. Forewarned, he told himself, was forearmed. And he was going to need all the forearming he could manage.

He noted that she absorbed everything like a sponge. What went on in that chaotic space she called a mind? Why did all this matter to her, how the rooms were decorated, if he had chosen the furnishings himself or if he had handed it over, carte blanche, to a decorator? He hadn't, and she had guessed that, too.

"What makes you say that?" he asked, returning to the living room.

"Easy. Because you're not the type to let anyone make decisions for you. You like being in control."

At least she understood that much, he thought. "Try to remember that." He had little hope, though, that she would.

"I'll try." The emphasis was on the last word.

He had no doubts that "try" was as far as it was going to go. "All right, we've done the tour. Now I think we should finally get down to work." He said it as if it hadn't been he who had procrastinated in the first place.

"Whatever you say." She began walking to the front door.

"Where are you going?" he called after her.

"Just to get some things."

He had scarcely assimilated her words when she was back at his side, a portfolio under one arm, her PC held in the other.

Marcus took the PC from her and led the way into the den. "You're being very agreeable," he said. Suspicion tinged his words. He knew better than to believe that she would just docilely go along with what he suggested.

The den, she noticed, was just like the rest of the house. Neat, slightly austere. The smell of leather, wood and polish blended and lent a pleasantness to the room. But it was as pristine as the rest. If there hadn't been a computer on his desk, she would have never guessed that he worked here. There were no signs of the agony of creation. Yet she had read his books and knew that he was capable of it.

Carefully placing her portfolio on the corner of the desk, she unzipped it.

"I'm always agreeable."

"News to me," he muttered. He placed her PC next to his. Hers was small, portable, almost a toy. His was a permanent fixture, massive, sturdy. They didn't blend. Yet both, he noticed, were made by the same company and had been created to complement each other. Maybe there was a message to be picked up here.

He was being unfair to her, but he was also fighting for life as he knew it. Something in the corners of his mind whispered, like an elusive melody, that things were never going to be the same again.

Marcus glanced again at the papers she had taken out and was now placing on the desk in a haphazard pile. He stifled the urge to stack them neatly.

"What are those?"

"My notes," she answered cheerfully, twisting a chair around to face his.

He no longer thought he was in danger of bidding goodbye to life as he knew it. He *knew* he was.

Chapter Five

Well, she certainly had gotten his adrenaline flowing yesterday, he'd give her that. There had been little time to become really anxious over whether he was suffering from writer's block or to mourn the fact that he might never give birth to another creative thought again.

Before the day was out, he had devised a dozen ways to do away with her. If that wasn't creativity, then he didn't know the meaning of the word.

They had sparred all afternoon. It seemed as if they just couldn't agree on anything. Strangely enough, although she made him terribly annoyed to begin with, by the end of the day he felt invigorated. It was almost as if he was beginning to enjoy the tension between them.

No, that didn't quite describe it. He wondered how he would have labeled the scene if he were writing about it. It wasn't just tension. It was *sexual* tension.

Marcus froze mentally. No, it couldn't be that. And yet, if he were being honest . . .

If he were being honest, he told himself, shifting in the passenger seat in Richard's car, he was just a man who had gone through a terrible emotional ordeal and was consequently not responsible for what he *thought* he was feeling.

He tried to concentrate on the way the session had gone yesterday and not on the participant. All things considered, it hadn't been as bad as he had expected. Of course, it hadn't gone as smoothly as it would have if he'd been working on this alone, he thought, giving his agent an intense, sidelong glance that seemed to bounce off the man as they drove toward Shalimar Studios. In her own chaotic way, Annie had raised credible points.

Given a choice, though, he still preferred working alone. It grated on Marcus that he probably wouldn't have accomplished anything if it hadn't been for her. She had been the catalyst he had unfortunately needed, the fire that had set him off.

He didn't like being in debt to anyone, especially when he had no idea how to repay the debt.

He also didn't like having to put in a command appearance before anyone. And he definitely didn't feel like having to protect his work from the "creative input" of a producer who envisioned the movie as his own. That was the problem here, he thought—too many cooks wanting to spoil *his* broth, however unintentionally.

Richard brought his Bentley to a stop at the studio gate. "I still don't see why I have to come, Richard. That's why you're getting ten percent."

Richard showed his identification and was waved onto the grounds by the guard. He slipped his wallet back into his jacket. "Dear boy, I do think you should meet the man who's putting money into your pocket. Now, make nice for my sake."

It wasn't enough of a reason. Again, Marcus shifted restlessly in his seat, wishing he was back in his den and working. "My readers put money in my pocket. I don't have a burning desire to meet every one of them."

The redheaded man parted his lips. Something that passed for a smile slipped into place for a moment, then was gone. "You would if they slipped an *obscene* amount of money into your pocket."

Marcus reflected on all his years of struggling, of making do with one meal a day. "There's nothing obscene about money, Richard."

Richard rolled his eyes heavenward. There at least they were in agreement. "Amen to that."

A blonde in a harem outfit came into Marcus's line of vision, her head inclined toward a tall, muscular man as they shared a joke. Involuntarily Marcus thought of Annie, then wondered why. It was bad enough to have to put up with her during working hours. To allow her to materialize in his thoughts was like having his mind rebel against him.

His body, it seemed, had already gone that route, but that, he felt, could be restrained with a simple act of control.

Richard carefully brought his pride and joy to a stop before an imposing one-story Spanish hacienda in the center of the studio lot. Richard angled the car across two parking spaces.

"All right." He turned to the younger man. "You haven't said a word about her since I picked you up. Don't play stoic with me. I know you far too well. How did yesterday work out?"

Marcus thought of the way their words and thoughts had kept overlapping throughout the entire day. "Does the phrase 'unorganized chaos' give you a clue?"

Richard lifted a red eyebrow. "Then I take it that things did not go well." With a shake of his head, he got out.

Marcus slammed his door and crossed to the hacienda's entrance. "That all depends."

Richard rang the bell. The first few bars of the theme song from *The Alamo* floated through the air. "On what?"

"On just how little you're expecting by the word 'well.'"

"You're exaggerating again."

Marcus gave a short laugh. "That's not possible this time."

One of Addison's assistants, a slight, scholarly-looking youth dressed in shades of brown, opened the door, mumbled a greeting and motioned them inside.

Allowing Richard in first, Marcus had just enough time to cross the threshold before someone raced up breathlessly behind him. He knew who it was before he turned around. He recognized the "whoosh."

"Hi." Annie beamed at Richard as she placed herself between the two men. "Have I missed something?" The question was for Marcus's benefit, a reminder of yesterday's lecture about punctuality.

Marcus looked accusingly over her head at Richard. "You didn't say she was going to be here."

Bony shoulders rose and fell beneath the expensive designer jacket. "You didn't ask."

Addison's assistant silently turned on his heel and began leading them down a wide hallway, the walls lined with framed photographs of all the celebrities who had ever worked on an Addison Taylor movie. Every one bore an intimate inscription.

Annie looked up at Marcus. "I'm your other half, remember?"

Marcus sighed. "Unfortunately my memory is alive and well."

"And so are you." Hurrying to keep in step, Annie looked Marcus over. He was dressed in a pearl-gray suit with a light blue shirt and tie that brought out the color of his eyes. "Nice suit," she noted. The assistant led them all past a brightly lit, windowless reception area that held a large, round desk and three secretaries. "You're looking well, too, Richard."

"As well as can be expected when my two prize clients are at each other's throats."

"Singular, Richard. I am not going for the jugular. Marc, I'm afraid, is still having trouble working out his differences."

"Wait here, please," the assistant instructed, ducking into another office. Annie noticed that he looked relieved to leave.

"My differences?" Marcus echoed incredulously. At the moment, his only difficulty seemed to be a rather short, headstrong woman.

"Well, they're not mine," she answered innocently. "I have no problems with working together. How's Nathan?" The question came quickly, forestalling the response she knew would follow.

She was good at ducking and weaving, he thought with something distantly akin to admiration. "He's fine."

"Good. Stevie and Erin would like him to come over and visit."

"All right." He looked at Addison's closed door and wondered just how long he was expected to wait before he had an excuse to leave.

"When?" Annie pressed.

Her question was unexpected. "When what?"

"When can Nathan come over?"

Marcus shrugged, pulling his thoughts together. He had surmised that she was just making aimless conversation while they waited. He should have known better. She wasn't the aimless sort. Instead, she seemed to aim straight for any available vital organ. "You need an answer now?"

"It would be nice."

Marcus threw up his hands. "I don't know." Her expression told him she wanted something more definite. "Saturday."

"Good. I'll pick him up."

"I'm sure you will. What are you grinning at?" he snapped at Richard.

Hands that were unusually wide-palmed for such a thin man went up to ward off Marcus's ire. "Nothing. I've just never seen a Hepburn and Tracy movie in action before, that's all."

"And what's that supposed to mean?" Marcus wanted to know. Had everyone gone crazy on him? Or was it him?

"Catch one and you'll understand, dear boy."

He needed another agent, Marcus thought. And if he went along with this farce any longer, he needed his head examined.

The unobtrusive assistant reappeared, leaving the door open this time. "Mr. Taylor will see you now." He motioned them into the inner sanctum.

"My prayers have been answered," Marcus muttered sarcastically, passing the young man.

Annie threaded her arm through Marcus's and entered with him. "Have you had your rabies shots, Marc?" she asked sweetly.

"Why, are you planning to bite?"

She laughed, undaunted. "Touché."

Why did the sound of her laughter have to affect him? Wasn't he dealing with enough problems as it was? Jason and Linda's deaths. Nathan. Writer's block. What in the world was he doing, collaborating with a woman who looked as if she were more suited to reclining on the beach in a bikini? A small, scarlet bikini...

He banished the image before he made a total idiot of himself.

"You're breathing harder," she murmured.

He looked straight ahead. "It's suddenly gotten very stuffy in here."

She gave Marcus a knowing look. "It's bound to get stuffier." Releasing his arm, she moved toward the thin, angular man seated behind the gleaming black desk. "Hello, Addison."

The man in the round, black-rimmed glasses rose slightly in his seat and took her hand in both of his. "Annie, you're getting more gorgeous every day." The affection in his voice sounded genuine.

Marcus stared at Annie's back. She wore an attractive white suit with a straight skirt and a vivid red silk blouse. As if she needed color to enliven her. "You know each other?"

Annie looked over her shoulder as Addison released her hands. "Sure."

"Of course." Why had he thought differently? Marcus told himself to be patient, that this too shall pass. The sooner they got this over with, the sooner he'd be back at work. He thrust his hand at Addison. For a diminutive man, he thought, Taylor had a strong grip. "I'm Marcus Sullivan."

"I know." When he smiled, Addison Taylor looked like a boy play-acting in an adult world. He didn't look anywhere near thirty-seven. "I'm paying you a lot of money to be."

Marcus raised an eyebrow in Richard's direction. In return, Richard gave him his patented, all-enduring half smile. Nothing seemed to ruffle Richard. Marcus's theory was that someday, Richard was going to explode. No one could remain continually calm. Especially, he thought glancing at Annie, with her as his client.

Addison gestured toward the blue brocade chairs before his desk. Annie took the one closest to the producer, Marcus noticed. The center of the storm. "This meeting is predominantly being held because of you, Marcus."

"And why is that?"

Marcus looked tense, on guard. Why? Annie wondered. Did he think they were going to attack him? What an awful way to face life, always being on your guard, always anticipating the worst, she thought. Had he always been like this? Or had something happened to make him this way? For a moment, she didn't hear what Addison was saying to them. She was far more interested in the man who had seated himself to her right.

"I like to meet the people I work with," Addison told Marcus. "Get to know them. Share my thoughts."

Marcus wasn't so annoyed that he didn't take note of the fact that Addison had said "people I work with," not "people working for me." He revised his opinion of the man. Slightly.

Still, Addison wanted to "share" his thoughts. "About the novel," Marcus began.

"Hell, no, about the screenplay," Addison interjected enthusiastically, unconsciously rubbing his hands together. "The novel is yours. The movie, however—" he leaned back in his well-padded chair and looked at the trio as he rocked "—is ours."

Annie could see that communal possession of his story didn't sit well with Marcus. There was a slight furrow over his brow even though his expression hadn't actually changed. It had, however, hardened. She didn't want things to rise to a head here. Although Addison had a congenial approach toward business, it only went so far. He was strong-willed. An iron hand in a velvet glove. He liked to hear the right words come his way.

"My name," Addison was saying, "appears above the title of the movie." With a sweep of his long, delicate hands, he stretched out an imaginary banner. "Therefore, you understand, I have a great deal besides money invested in this—"

"I understand," Marcus began. He understood very well. He was being led deeper and deeper into Oz by Dorothy and a misguided Scarecrow. He had no intentions of playing the part of the Cowardly Lion. Certain things had to be made clear, no matter what the consequences. "I understand quite well—"

Marcus looked down at the armrest. Annie's hand was covering his, as if that single, small gesture could keep him in his seat and the words in his mouth. It couldn't. But the surprise it generated within him could and did.

"I do have all your notes, Addison, and naturally, we will be taking them into account," Annie said quickly before horns were locked. The glance she gave Marcus warned him to keep still. "But don't you think that we should have something concrete in the way of a script before we discuss this any further?"

"Further?" Marcus echoed. "We haven't—"

"We have," Annie cut in.

"You have," he corrected her. If he disliked having his work dissected in front of him, he disliked the fact of having it dissected behind his back even more.

The pressure on his hand increased. She was pushing it into the delicately carved wood. "Right now," she reminded him calmly, wondering if she should be hitting this man between the eyes with a two-by-four to get through, "I am part of 'we.'"

But not for long, God help me, Marcus thought. "And that's another thing—"

"That he'd like to thank you for," Richard put in, taking Annie's cue. He knew the danger signs far better than she did. "Marcus had no idea what working with a partner would be like and feels—"

"That you made a splendid choice, Addison," Annie ended. "As always."

The thin lips parted into a full-bloomed smile that seemed to fill out the man's face. It emphasized his boyishness further. The product of his mind, Marcus thought, was in the hands of a teenager.

"Well, if things are going well and you have my notes, I suppose there's no reason to repeat myself. If none of you has any objections, we can conclude this meeting. I've got a comedy on Lot Six that is anything but funny." Addison rose and moved around his desk. He was hardly taller than Annie. It surprised Marcus. The producer thrust his hand toward him again. "Nice meeting you after all this time, Marcus. I've been a fan for a long while."

Marcus encircled the bony fingers in his large palm. "Thank you." He meant the words sincerely. If people stopped buying his books tomorrow, Marcus knew that he would still go on writing. He had to in order to survive. For him it was as necessary as breathing. Maybe more. But it was still gratifying to hear that people enjoyed reading his books. He never took it for granted. He had learned that nothing could be taken that way.

Addison preceded them out the door, followed by his assistant.

"What was that all about?" Marcus asked, taking Annie's arm and hustling her out of the office, toward the front door.

"All what about?" Annie nodded toward Addison's secretary as they sailed past her desk. The woman looked curiously at Marcus's hold on her arm. "It's all right. He likes to get physical," Annie told her. There was only envy shining in the older woman's eyes as she looked on.

It was a nightmare, Marcus thought as he strode out into the hallway, and it was his. "Do you really have to do that?"

"Do what?" She wondered how long he could keep up this pace.

He pushed the front door open with the flat of his hand, still holding on to her arm. "Call attention to yourself, to us?"

"Who's hustling who out the door?" Abruptly he let go of her arm and sighed. Momentarily he looked befuddled. She felt sorry for him. "You had a question earlier?" Annie prompted. Richard came out and joined them in the parking lot, standing off to the side and enjoying the fireworks.

She had gotten him so muddled, he forgot he had a question. Marcus jerked a thumb back at the building. "What was all that tap dancing you were doing in there?"

She had a strong suspicion that if she said black, he would say white. Why was he so pigheaded? Couldn't he see that she had done him a favor? "Did you want to discuss Addison's changes?"

"No." He bit off the word.

"Did you want to tell him that you'd work them in?" The dark look he gave her answered that. "Well, in case you haven't noticed, Sullivan, I just saved you the trouble. Addison softens up when he hears that people are working in harmony with him."

As far as he could see, it was only a stalling tactic, putting off the inevitable. "What happens when the script comes on his desk and his changes aren't in it?"

"He won't make a fuss as long as the story works." She smiled brilliantly. "Trust me."

That was just the trouble; he couldn't. Something told him it would be very dangerous if he began to trust her. Trust only led to disappointment. "You've been through this before, I take it?" Marcus asked, suddenly fascinated by how the sun was tangled in her hair.

Annie was aware of the way he was looking at her. She felt a momentary scramble of her pulse before she answered. "About six or seven times."

Marcus looked at his watch. It was only ten o'clock. Too early for lunch. "I guess I owe you a cup of coffee."

She grinned. "At the very least."

It was better not to answer that. Suddenly remembering Richard's presence, Marcus turned toward the agent. "Join us?"

Richard held up his hands. "Unlike the curious observers at the Battle of Bull Run, I have no desire to get a front-row seat for the beginning of the war. Besides—" he glanced at his watch "—I have an appointment at eleven. You'll take him home for me?" he asked, dropping a kiss on Annie's temple.

"If he lets me."

He was stuck. It occurred to Marcus that he had precious little control over his life lately. None where she was concerned. "Coward," Marcus called after Richard's retreating back.

"Down to the long yellow streak between my skinny shoulder blades," Richard agreed cheerfully. "Have fun, you two."

For a second, they just stood there, a moment of awkwardness shimmering between them. She pointed vaguely to the left. "There's a little restaurant just off the lot on the next block, if you were serious about the coffee. Felicity's."

He had no idea what had made him extend that invitation. Temporary insanity was becoming a way of life with him. "All right," he muttered stoically. He approached her car. "Mind if I drive?"

"I figured you'd want to." Tossing him the keys, she slid in on the passenger side.

Marcus closed the door behind her a little too firmly. "One-upmanship your specialty?" He came around the hood.

"How did you guess?"

Allowing him a few moments' grace, she watched him start the car. His were large, capable hands, hands that would always know what to do, instinctively know how to touch a woman and make her want more. She settled back, taking a deep breath, pushing aside thoughts that were coming too soon.

And then she turned toward him, her smile wider, if that was possible. "Is this a date?"

If he had been driving a standard transmission, he knew he would have stalled out. As it was, he swerved. A car honked behind him. "What?"

"The restaurant. Coffee. Is this a date?"

"No." The answer came tersely. "It's a cup of coffee." The implications of an actual social outing with this woman were far too jarring.

"Oh."

Her expression told him that she didn't believe him. Well, what did he care what she believed or didn't believe? He knew what he was thinking.

What was he doing, anyway, driving off to a restaurant to have a sociable cup of coffee with a woman who—who—

He was being polite, that's what he was doing. Nothing wrong with manners. It made up the backbone of this country. He almost believed the excuse.

The restaurant was bright and noisy, with a prominent counter that ran along the length of one wall. Almost every seat was occupied by someone in costume. He and Annie were the only ones in street clothes. He should have known.

"Felicity's is open almost all the time. It's a favorite with the extras." Annie nodded over toward the corner. There were two people whose gender he couldn't begin to guess at dressed as fruit. He looked quizzically at Annie. "They're probably shooting a commercial. Or a science fiction movie."

All of this felt like a science fiction movie, Marcus thought.

"Want to sit at the counter?" She pointed toward two vacant seats between a gunslinger and a Viking. "Or a table?"

"Table."

She was already weaving her way through the crowd toward an empty one. "I had a hunch."

A tall woman with a pink-feathered boa dripping off her shoulders deliberately brushed against Marcus as she walked by. She gave him an appreciative, come-hither look. The boa tickled his nose. He tried not to sneeze. "I wish you'd stop second-guessing me," he said to the back of Annie's head.

"I will if you do something against type."

"And just what is my type?"

She seated herself neatly, then looked up at him, innocence in her eyes. "Reticent."

She was doing it to him again, making his blood rise to its boiling point. If there hadn't been people all around them, he would have taken that moving target she called a mouth and kissed her to show her just how reticent he was.

No, it wasn't the people stopping him. It was his common sense. He knew the danger of that sort of action. He had no intentions of working without a net. He wasn't a complete fool.

Oh no? Then what was he doing here with her? Holly had plenty of coffee at home.

He had no answer for that, only an odd, sinking sense of foreboding.

Chapter Six

Marcus sat nursing his coffee and mulling over the situation he was in now. At least the coffee was good, surprisingly so. He liked his coffee strong and eye-opening. Most restaurants didn't.

He tried not to be aware of the fact that sitting so close to Annie was a problem. It shouldn't have been. But it was. She made him conscious of things that had absolutely nothing to do with writing.

"Come here often?" Coming from a bestselling novelist, Marcus thought in contempt, that was pitiful.

If it was, she didn't seem to notice. "Only when I'm in the neighborhood to see Addison."

"So, have you known him long?" He didn't like the idea much. He liked the fact that it bothered him even less. There was no reason for it, he told himself.

An actual personal question. Finally, Annie thought. The stone wall around him was beginning to wear down. It was about time. It would make working together easier. It would make a lot of things easier.

"Forever. He used to come over to the house a lot when he was first starting out. My parents' house," she clarified. The dark look in his eyes made the clarification seem necessary. "Addison was simply rabid to learn everything he could about every facet of filmmaking. He said the only thing he wanted to do was make movies, quality movies. My father liked his dedication and sort of took him under his wing, introducing him to a lot of people on the lot."

She leaned over the small, chipped table that separated them. He couldn't explain why it seemed like such an intimate movement. It just did. He was beginning to have the feeling that if she so chose, she could make reading the phone book an intimate experience.

"If Addison chose your novel to put his name to, it's going to make a great movie. He has faith in it."

Now that he had gotten over that huge blank wall in his head and had begun writing again, he felt he could take it from there. "Enough faith to leave it to me?"

"He doesn't have that much faith in God, let alone a human." She laughed, remembering. "The first film he ever made under his own name was based on one of my father's scripts. Addison was everywhere. Directing, checking cameras, props, sites, doing everything himself before the people responsible had a chance to get to it. By the time the movie was finished, he had made everyone crazy, including himself. But it was a wonderful movie."

The glow in her eyes as she spoke prompted Marcus's next question. "Are you involved with him?" Subtle, damn subtle, Marcus thought, irritated with himself.

"With Addison?" The idea tickled her. The producer was like a brother to her. "No, not in the way you mean." She couldn't resist. "What makes you ask?"

He shrugged, unusually preoccupied with his coffee. "No reason. It just came up in the conversation."

"Oh." Annie hid her smile behind the coffee cup, which she then placed back on the saucer. It took her a moment to compose herself. If she laughed now, she knew he'd get up and walk right out of her life. "But he does have very good judgment, Marc. And I'd take his suggestions—as well as mine—into consideration."

Yes, he was sure she would. But she wasn't him. "He bought my book, therefore he bought my conception of the characters."

"True," she agreed, "but you can't stuff almost five hundred pages onto the screen. At least, not without subjecting the audience to kidney problems." He was about to suggest a solution to that, but only got as far as opening his mouth. "Besides," she went on quickly, "some things just can't be translated onto the screen no matter how well they read." She knew he wasn't going to like this. "I'm afraid we're going to have to cut out whole sections of the book."

She was talking rapidly, even for her. It made him uneasy. He found it difficult to assimilate so much so fast. He should be alert, ready to defend his turf, yet he was just listening to her, practically hypnotized by the sound of her voice. He shook his head in an unconscious effort to regain control over his thoughts. "It's not going to work, you know."

"What?" For a moment, she thought she detected an inviting look in his eyes. She began to fantasize just a little. Something, possibly something very good, was going to happen between them. She wanted it to. She wasn't going to vacate his life until it did. "The screenplay, or us?"

"Us?" She read him too well. He was right in wanting to terminate this association. He had no desire to see this— whatever "this" was—through.

"Yes, us." She felt a very strong attraction to him, but knew that there was an equally strong probability that it could go nowhere, due to his resistance, his barriers. Because they both needed the safety of the lie to save face, she gave it. "Working together."

He drained his cup, then placed it down with a clatter. "Both."

"You're wrong."

He wondered if there was anything she didn't challenge. "About which part?"

"Both." She grinned. It camouflaged the shakiness she felt coursing through her body. "Everything'll work out. If you let it."

His chest felt tight. His breath struggled to escape from his lungs. Her very presence seemed to have a way of cutting off his air supply.

"And if I chose to maintain control instead of 'going with the flow'?" It would be simpler, far simpler, not to see this woman again. He didn't need this. The money and the glory were irrelevant. He had more than enough of both. Neither made him particularly happy. Instinct told him to cut bait and run. Why didn't he just go with it?

Everyone, he mused, had a self-destructive edge. This was his.

"Then you're probably in for a big legal hassle. You signed papers, my friend, and Addison may be a pussycat in some respects, but he takes his business—and his contracts—very, very seriously." She pushed aside her cup. The coffee was cold. "Why are you so against working with someone? Is it me?"

It would have been easy to say yes, but it was no longer as simple as it had been two days ago. He decided to play it safe, safe according to his definition. "I don't like sharing my thoughts with someone." He hadn't meant to be quite that honest. "I've never worked with a partner before." The creative process was far too intimate an act. To share it with someone, to let her be part of it, would leave him wide open, make him feel exposed, vulnerable. He didn't want that.

But I want you to share your thoughts with me, she mused silently. *I want to know what you're thinking and why. I want you to tell me everything.* The smile on her face hid what she was feeling. "Perhaps it's time for a new experience."

That's what she was all right. An experience. He thought of the constant arguing over interpretation yesterday. The nonstop battle of wits. The scent of her cologne that had kept wafting up to him and had preyed on his senses long after she had left with her brood.

"I'm not sure I can work with someone on a day-to-day basis." That much was honest. There was no need to add that she made his palms feel sweaty even while he contemplated strangling her.

A roar of laughter rose from the back of the restaurant, and five spacemen strode out together, their antennae bobbing as they walked. Annie gave them a cursory glance and smiled unconsciously. "We've already gone over ground rules and plot line. The rest should be easy."

Was she serious? Hadn't she been there for yesterday's session? Wasn't this the same woman who had absolutely refused to let him use the prostitute in the bar scene because she insisted that it would hurt the main character's heroic appeal? They had spent the better part of three hours on that. "Are you always this optimistic?"

His tone was sarcastic, but she was learning to ignore that. "Almost always. I cringe a little when I go to the dentist, but even then, why anticipate the worst? Most of the time, there aren't any cavities."

That's because the main cavity was in her head, he was tempted to say.

Annie rested her chin on the bridge formed by her clasped hands, her elbows leaning on the table. She barely noticed the waitress who came by with the check. Marcus made her think of a homeless puppy in need of a lot of understanding. He took a great deal of pleasure in biting off her head, but she didn't think it was just because he was being perverse. True, he was possessive of his work, but there was more to it than that.

She had to admit that she had been intrigued by the man behind the words when she had finished his first book. By the sixth, she was hooked. And if she had any doubts as to the basic nobility of his character, well, there had been a late football player who shared her belief that there was much more to this man than a frown and flashes of wit aimed at keeping people at bay.

She wasn't much for football, but she had heard of Jason Danridge. He had made all-American in college. The world had been at his feet, and he had a lot to give in return. It was a crime that his life had been cut so short. But while he lived, he could have had his pick of friends, his pick of associates. He had chosen Marcus to be his friend and to take care of his son. There had to be a reason.

She wanted to know what it was. Maybe it would tell her why she was so attracted to him. She had to know why the deeply sensitive human being who wrote stirring prose, who had such insight about people on paper, was so distant in person.

She had given up hope of ever being attracted to anyone again, not in that special, mind-spinning way that made her blood hum. Exceedingly gregarious and friendly with the world at large, Annie still held a little of herself in reserve. It had been the part she had given Charlie. The part, she had been so sure, that had died when he did. To know it didn't please her. And frightened her just a little.

"Well—" Annie began to rise. Marcus mechanically moved to her side and pulled out her chair. "Now that we're stimulated—"

It was getting to the point that every time she opened her mouth, it was to say something that befuddled him. "What?"

"The coffee." The expression on her face was nothing short of mischievous.

Once again, he hadn't understood her. He wondered if there was anyone who could accomplish that magic feat. "Oh, that." He left a few bills on the table and let her lead the way out.

"Are you game to go back and work, or are you going to have to think this through, too?" Annie stood on the curb, waiting for him to catch up.

He was never one to shrug off responsibility. "I suppose the sooner we get this over with, the sooner my life will be back in order."

Taking his arm, Annie walked over to the lot where they had left her car. "You do have a way of making a girl feel that she's the center of your world, Marc."

The sun was high overhead and the smog seemed to hang around them like a leftover witch's curse. The lot, with its gravelly terrain, seemed dustier than it should be. "Marcus," he corrected. "I'd really rather have you call me Marcus."

Annie put her key into the car door, then looked at him questioningly. "Only when I'm issuing a formal request for a duel, Marc. Do you want to drive again?"

He was surprised that she would relinquish her car to him twice in one day. He got in behind the wheel. "Don't you ever get serious?"

"Yes." The seatbelt clinked as she buckled it.

"When?"

"When I work. My work is very, very important to me."
She saw several people she knew entering the restaurant and
waved out of the window.

"And mine is to me." Marcus saw his chance and pulled
the car out onto the street.

"Fine, we're in agreement about something. The rest'll
follow."

Traffic looked annoyingly heavy, he thought as he inched
along. "Like an avalanche."

The temperature was rising. Annie rolled up her window
and turned on the air conditioner. She spared him a disap-
proving look. "We're going to have to do something about
your pessimistic attitude, Marc."

"You could tell me that this is all a bad dream. Maybe
then I'd wake up full of optimism."

"No," she said, shaking her head. "That was done on TV
once. No one bought it."

"Then we're stuck."

"Afraid so."

He managed to angle the car out from behind a truck.
Visibility improved. Traffic did not. "Not nearly as much
as I am. Not nearly as much as I am."

"Are you any good with cars?"

He looked up, startled at the sound of her voice. They had
just put in over six hours of solid work, most of which had
been spent quarreling. Exhausted, he had let her win more
than half the points. The operative word, he had told himself, was "let." He wanted to believe that if he had insisted
enough, the matter would have gone his way. Deep in his
heart, though, he had his doubts that even God could have
won an argument with her.

Five minutes ago she had bidden him goodbye and walked
out of the den. He had let out a sigh of relief and begun
looking forward to an evening listening to quiet music.

Maybe he would ask Nathan if there was something he wanted to listen to. He didn't think he had enough energy left to face her again so soon.

But then, the woman was full of surprises, as well as questions he wasn't expecting.

Rubbing the bridge of his nose, he tried to focus on her. She didn't look half as tired as he felt. "Am I what?"

"Any good with cars," she repeated. She gestured abstractly to her left, not having the vaguest sense of direction of where the driveway actually was. "My car seems to be sitting, dead, in your driveway."

He was tempted to make a remark about her joining it, but restrained himself. There was no point in being nasty, even though she deserved it.

Marcus stood up and ran his hand through his hair. "What's wrong with it?"

"If I knew that, I wouldn't be asking you if you were any good with cars." There was a touch of irritation in her voice.

Well, well, well, he thought, suddenly amused. So, something did get to her once in a while. That was encouraging. "I'm not. I'm good with phones." He picked up the receiver. "I can call someone to tow your car to my mechanic if you like."

She nodded. She didn't need to ask if his mechanic was good. She knew that if Marcus used him, the man had already been thoroughly checked out. She glanced at the pile of papers neatly stacked next to the printer while he made his call. It was a nice amount of work that they had produced today. A good start for a first draft. They might even be finished ahead of schedule. Bet that made him happy, she thought.

"He'll send someone over in the morning," he told her, about to hang up.

Annie nodded, taking the receiver from him. He surrendered it, looking at her curiously. Annie glanced around, knowing that it wouldn't be in plain sight. He was too neat for that. "Do you have a Yellow Pages around somewhere?"

He took one out of the bottom drawer and handed the hefty tome to her. "Who are you calling?"

"A cab." She flipped through the pages quickly, then found what she was looking for. "I don't think you want me camping out here until the car's fixed. Besides, I have a pregnant dog to feed."

Impulse was not something he allowed into his life very often. It had been something that he had only experienced when he was with Jason and Linda. Because he was so comfortable with them, they had brought it out. There was no reason for it flourishing now. But it did. Inexplicably he found himself putting his finger on the telephone button and cutting her off.

Annie looked at him, waiting for an explanation.

"I'll take you home."

"If it's not too much trouble," she said cautiously, enough to be polite, not enough to force him to change his mind.

"It is," he said with undue harshness because his own actions confused him.

Chivalrous to the end. "Then why—"

"Are you going to stand here, debating this with me, too?"

"Heaven forbid. I never look a gift horse in the mouth. Here." She handed him her keys. "The mechanic might want these."

He pocketed them absently, scribbled a quick note for Holly, then led the way outside. He refused to think about what he was doing or why. He was tired; he needed fresh air and a break. That's all there was to it.

He jammed the key into his car's ignition and turned it. "Where do you live?"

It took him a moment to orient himself after she gave him the Malibu address. "That's near the beach," Marcus said, heading the car in that direction.

"No, that's *on* the beach. I like listening to the waves beat against the shore at night. It's very soothing." She had contemplated moving out after Charlie had died because the memories there were so painful. But she loved the old house, and she knew that wherever she went, she'd be taking her memories with her. They would always be a part of her and would contribute to making her what she was.

"Real estate's expensive there."

She knew that. Enough realtors had knocked on her door telling her of the fantastic price she could get if she sold. "It's been in the family a long time. My grandfather bought it when he first moved out here. It was his until he died. He left it to me in his will."

He heard the fondness in her voice. "Were you close to him?"

He didn't know why he asked, except that a deep-seated hunger made him do it. He had never been close to anyone in his family. Affection was unheard of, unwelcome. Both of his parents reacted badly to such displays the few times that he had attempted them as a young child. It made them uncomfortable. Marcus eventually realized that *he* made them uncomfortable. He had left after high school graduation and he hadn't been back since. He didn't miss his parents. But he missed the idea of them sometimes, the idea of a family, of closeness. She, he thought, raising a brow, had probably been close to everyone when she was growing up, including the mailman.

When Annie thought of her grandfather, she thought of strong hands that had held her high and a robust laugh that told her to reach for the sky; not the stoop-shouldered old man he was before he died. "Very. I worshiped the ground Grandpa walked on. I thought he was next to God, or at the very least, Walt Disney. I lived a good deal of my life in Disneyland,'' she explained.

''I could have guessed that part.''

''What about you?''

He took a turn down a long, winding road. ''What about me?''

She watched as early evening shadows played hide-and-seek with the planes of his angular, aristocratic face. He had the brooding, sensitive face of a poet. Byron. No doubt about it, the man raised her pulse. ''Whose ground did you worship?''

''No one's.''

The answer was so pat, so curt, it hurt her to hear it. ''What about Jason? Did you and he—''

''We went to school together.'' His answer dismissed the subject. But as he said it, a collage of memories spun through his mind, bits and pieces feeding into one another. His parents had robbed him of love and so the person he might have been withdrew. Jason had seen what there was hidden within him and had brought it out. Marcus had allowed himself to become part of Jason's family, to be part of Jason and Linda's lives. It had felt good. But it had ended.

''And you—''

Why didn't she leave it alone? Everyone else left him alone. Everyone else knew when to back off. Everyone, he remembered, but Jason. Jason had never allowed him to pull his cloak around himself and retreat. He was always there, cajoling, pushing, daring him to try things. Jason would have understood someone like Annie. He would have been equipped to deal with her. But Marcus didn't have the faintest clue how to handle this woman.

''I'd rather not talk about Jason.''

She could appreciate the fact that the wound was still raw. To lose a friend, to lose someone who mattered, was very hard. She knew about that twice over. "Okay, what do you want to talk about?"

"I'm all talked out for tonight. Silence would be nice."

"If you say so."

"I say so."

She lasted a little over three minutes, then turned on the radio. Johnny Mathis was singing something warm and romantic. Marcus switched the station. The sound of drums and guitars vibrated through the car, melding with the cooling night air. They reached her house ten minutes later, and Marcus walked her to the front door.

"I don't suppose you want to come in?" She bit her lower lip and waited, hoping.

He almost did, just to prove her wrong, but he was tired and not up to tilting at her windmills.

"I think I'd feel a lot safer not entering your lair." The words were prompted by self-preservation. The less he knew about her, the better. It would keep the barriers up between them.

He made the fatal mistake of looking down into her eyes. There were worlds to get lost in in her eyes, teasing worlds, worlds that knew his secrets. They were the sexiest pair of eyes he had ever seen.

They matched the rest of her.

Without fully knowing or understanding, he reached for her. Another impulse had taken him over. Dangerous habit, giving in to impulses. It was totally out of character for him. He was beginning to be confused as to what was *in* character for him, or who and what he was. He had thought he knew. He had felt comfortable with that knowledge, with himself. Now he was no longer sure. He was acting strangely and he didn't know if he even liked it.

Impulse made him sample what he had been craving all day.

Framing her face, he filled his hands with waves of blond hair and brought his mouth down to hers. It was an action that he had done countless times. He couldn't remember one of them. He knew, instantly, that he would remember this no matter how long he lived.

He had thought of her as a hurricane, as mischievous. There hadn't been the slightest hint of the exotic about her. Yet she tasted exotic, electrifyingly so. She made him think of strange, mysterious foreign lands, with the scent of silks and heady perfumes.

A surprise. It was all a wondrous, unique surprise.

He had kissed her to get it out of the way and to satisfy his own curiosity, which had nagged him since the first time he had seen her standing on his doorstep, dripping wet.

But he wasn't satisfied. As the kiss deepened, as it revealed things to him that he had never known before, as he drew her body closer against his, Marcus grew only hungrier.

Hungrier for something that he knew would lead to his undoing. He grew hungrier for soothing, for passion, for the feeling of peace. Hungrier for a hundred conflicting things that swirled through his mind as his lips slanted over hers. None of that had anything to do with the woman in his arms.

It had everything to do with the woman in his arms.

Lips sought, tested, gained and retreated, leaving fiery imprints in their wake. Tongues touched hesitantly, then explored, first shyly, then boldly, sending sensations soaring, blood pumping. Neither one of them was left unchanged.

A kiss begun in curiosity rose quickly in intensity until there was no air left in his lungs and only whirling, disjointed thoughts in his head. He had the unmistakable feeling that he had just put a match to a very dangerous fuse, a fuse that was going to have lasting effects on his life somewhere down the line when it came to journey's end.

She hadn't expected this. She had hoped, but she hadn't even begun to dream that there was this waiting for her. It was every single happy experience rolled up into one. Her head filled with fireworks, and there was nothing and no one but him. The scent of the beach, the quiet night sounds, everything disappeared as if it didn't exist. The only thing that did was this man holding her, this man whose body was supporting hers, keeping her from falling. And yet she was falling, falling into a deep, dark tunnel with bright lights shining at the other end.

Shaken, Marcus let his hands drop and dragged himself away, knowing if he didn't stop now, he'd pick her up in his arms and carry her into her house, to take her just beyond the door.

She didn't know what to say. The taste of his mouth had been dark, powerful and had robbed her totally of her control. He had left her stunned. And more than convinced that the attraction she thought was there was *definitely* there.

He could apologize, he thought. He could turn on his heel and just leave. He could have himself committed. Since she thought a cup of coffee was a date, she might see this as a proposal of marriage.

"This isn't to be misconstrued, either," he warned her. Damn, even his voice sounded shaken.

"Is it all right to construe it as a kiss?" Somehow, she summoned a smile. Her impish grin belied the turmoil going on inside her. She felt like a washing machine on spin dry with all the towels tangled up and pulling against the force.

He had no words to answer her. Retreat seemed best at the moment until he could gather his thoughts together. "Yes. I'll see you tomorrow."

"Count on it." Annie hugged herself as she watched him move quickly back to the safety of his car.

Chapter Seven

Marcus stood before the multipaned windows, staring at the rainbow of colors created by the sun breaking through the prismlike thick glass. He was staring, but he wasn't seeing. His mind was elsewhere.

Behind him were the muted sounds of some golden oldie he half remembered. Annie had won that concession from him their third morning together. She worked better, she had insisted, with music. He had expected Beethoven. He had gotten Beatles.

He had gotten a hell of a lot more than that, he thought, rubbing his hand along the back of his neck, and probably more than he could safely handle.

Above the music he could hear the continuous, rhythmic clatter of computer keys. She had an idea, he knew, and was working it through. Though she could talk and write at the same time, mercifully, right now she was busy communing exclusively with the machine. Even with his back to her, but she'd come, marching undoubtedly to some inner clock the world hadn't, mercifully, tapped into yet.

She'd come not only prepared to work, but prepared to nose her way into his life the way he had never allowed anyone, except for Jason and his wife, to come into his life before. She was impervious to frost, let sarcasm roll off her back and had absolutely no idea what the word privacy meant. She was even on a first-name, friendly basis with his housekeeper, who, for the first time since Marcus had employed her, had lost some of that dour expression he had assumed had been stamped on her face at birth.

More important, Annie had an amazing effect on Nathan. She had accomplished what Marcus had wanted to do. Too timid and withdrawn at first to venture into the den, Nathan soon took advantage of the path Annie forged for him into Marcus's life. He was evolving from a quiet guest into a normal seven-year-old boy.

Because of her.

She had no idea what the word "no" meant. And nothing seemed to stop her. He longed to know what could, yet put off finding out.

She took to rearranging his life. "What in God's name is that?" he had demanded just this morning when she had arrived overloaded and fairly staggering under the combined weight of her briefcase and the rather large box she was hefting. He took the latter from her. "Did it ever occur to you to take two trips to the car?"

"Wastes too much time."

She was slightly breathless and her voice was husky and warm. He couldn't help wondering if her voice would sound that way after she made love. Something he wouldn't find out, he warned himself. Not if he was smart. This was not a lady who would pass through his life leaving no impression, no mark. This one, if he let her, would hurt. It seemed almost ridiculous to believe that, but he saw the signs, had felt it when he had kissed her. He really didn't want to get close.

"Aren't you the one who's always trying to save time?" she asked, walking into the den.

Marcus deposited the box on his side of the desk. There was no room on her side. "You don't save anything by getting a hernia."

"Why, Marc." She dropped her briefcase casually on the chair. It slid to the floor. She left it there. "You care." She fluttered her lashes at him coquettishly, then laughed.

As always, her laugh stirred him. "I care about finishing this damn screenplay on time."

The slim shoulders, gracefully bare thanks to an electric-blue halter top, moved up and down. "I'll take what I can get." Purse met briefcase on the floor. She glanced toward the hall. "Where's Nathan?"

He itched to pick up her things and put them in their proper place, but forced himself to leave them where they were. "Probably pacing up and down in the living room, waiting for you."

"Well, at least one member of the household looks forward to seeing me." She flashed Marcus a dazzling smile, then turned on her heel before he could respond to that. "Well, let's not keep him waiting."

He caught up to her at the doorway. "You didn't answer my question."

Her blond hair was pulled up in an outrageous ponytail that perched on the crown of her head and bobbed as she moved. She made him think of an ad for suntan lotion. "Oh, I thought I did. What question did I miss?"

"What did I just bring into the house?" Besides my undoing, he thought.

"A video game system."

He looked at her, his brain failing to register what she was saying. "And what am I going to do with it?"

Was he serious? What cave had he been hiding in? "You're going to hook it up for Nathan so that he can practice."

"Practice?"

"You're beginning to sound unoriginal, Marcus. We can't have that." Her eyes smiled as she patted his cheek.

Her touch made him remember the single kiss they had shared. He shifted his eyes to her mouth. It made things worse. There wasn't a part of her that he could look at safely, he thought.

"Stevie and Erin would love to see him again if it's all right with you." She had already brought Nathan to her sister-in-law's house on Saturday, as promised, and the three children were well on their way to becoming fast friends. She intended to nurture that. "And I thought they might play a few video games to keep out of your hair."

"Very thoughtful of you to try to preserve my hair." Why couldn't Richard have sent him a man to work with? Or at least someone who didn't smell so good, who didn't have creamy white shoulders that tempted him to reach out and touch. He wasn't used to not being able to concentrate, and she kept making him lose his train of thought. Just by being.

She insisted, when he proved to be all thumbs, on hooking up the video game system for the boy right then and there herself. And secretly, he had taken pleasure at the light that had risen in Nathan's eyes. She was, all in all, like a ray of sunshine in their lives.

At least, he amended, in Nathan's.

After Annie played one game with amazing dexterity, he had disengaged her from the game and led her off to the den where she attacked their screenplay with exactly the same amount of gusto.

Their screenplay.

When had it become "their" screenplay and not exclusively "his" in his mind? The line was blurred, as was most of his life in the past week and a half. A wild, exhilarating, breath-taking blur filled with arguments, regroupings and then wars over interpretations. The woman actually had the unmitigated gall to explain his characters to him.

"Women interpret things differently than men," she had told him.

He had been restrained enough to keep the reason for that to himself. He noted that no matter how heated the arguments got, they were only heated on his side. She was adamant without raising her voice, without so much as changing her expression.

It made him long to change her expression. The way he had last week. Eight days ago, precisely. When nothing less ordinary than skin touching skin, lips touching lips, had occurred.

And haunted him every night.

Finally, now, he decided to reply to her statement. "Women are more emotional than men."

Annie looked up from the screen. She had been frowning over a word. "You say that as if it's a bad thing."

"It is." He came away from the window. "Emotions are fine in books. But they get in the way of things in real life. They cloud our judgment, color our decisions."

"Color." Annie seized on the word, a poised finger raised in the air, the keyboard temporarily abandoned. "That's exactly it. Without emotion, there is no color, only shades of gray."

He was arguing with her because she seemed to constantly push that button within him, yet in his heart, he agreed with her. Where they really differed was that he thought, apart from his writing, that shades of gray were preferable to pain. And he told her so.

Annie stared at him, silent for a moment. He would have savored the silence, except that it made him uncomfortable. The look in her eyes made him uncomfortable. Inadvertently admitting to pain—he knew how her mind worked by now—had been a momentary slip on his part, and he regretted it immediately. She reached out and placed a hand on his shoulder. Because he thought he recognized pity when he saw it, he moved aside.

It was obvious that he had been hurt very badly once, she thought. They had that much in common, and the kindred ache within her reached out to him, making her want to soothe, to take away the unspeakable pain she knew he was dealing with. She had lived with it herself.

"Was it someone you loved?"

He didn't want to answer, but knew she'd only press until he did. He tried evasion. "What?"

"The pain in your eyes," she said quietly. "Did you lose someone you loved?" Whoever she was, Annie felt herself suddenly envying the woman he had loved enough to take into his life.

Maybe it would have done him good to talk about it. But reaching out to another human being had always been difficult for Marcus at best. As a child, it had been drummed into him not to let his feelings show until he found that he *couldn't* let them show even if he had wanted to.

"There's no pain in my eyes. That's a squint. The sun's too bright." As he tugged the chord, the opposite ends of the drapes flew toward each other, shutting out the daylight.

Though she was sure he thought she didn't know how, Annie retreated. If she pushed too hard, she'd only succeed in pushing him away. He'd talk about it when the time came. Everyone needed to talk, to let the hurt out. Talking heightened happiness and dissipated fears and pain. It was something she firmly believed.

"Have it your way."

A reprieve. She was something else again, he thought. "Thank you."

"You're welcome." Annie arched her back, linked her fingers and stretched her arms above her head slowly. It had been a long day and she felt it.

Marcus watched her, fascinated. If he had been in the midst of producing the great American novel, it would have evaporated from his brain.

Nothing he knew of could have competed with the utterly feminine, utterly feline, gracefulness of Annie's body. Each movement was captivating, lyrical, and brought his blood pounding through every vein in his body. The ache he felt in his loins was very real, very demanding and very difficult to shut away.

With a sigh, he put down the pages he was perusing. "I wish you wouldn't do that."

She stopped, puzzled. She was just sitting on a chair. "Do what?"

He gestured, helpless. Frustrated. "Stretch like that."

Annie relaxed, her body almost fluid in the chair now. "Does it disturb you?" Her eyes were wide with surprised amusement. And pleasure.

"Yes." What was the point in denying it? Even if he did, she could read the signs.

"Good." She rose and crossed to him. "Because I have to admit, you disturb me."

He had never met anyone like her before, which he took to be God's kindness to him. "Do you always say what you think?"

She smiled, and the smile spread across her face, moving up into her eyes. It was a smile that made him feel like smiling, although there was nothing to smile about.

"I'm not saying what I'm thinking now," she told him.

He had a thousand responses milling around in his head. Not a single one materialized on his lips. What did materialize, though it had not been far from the surface the past eight days, was his desire.

His hands slid down her back. He memorized each inch as his fingers skimmed along her spine. The sensation of her bare skin aroused him to such a point that it seriously worried him. It was as if he had no control over his own actions, his own thoughts. And he had always had control. Female companionship was pleasant, but he could take it or leave it, and he had always chosen women who didn't tax him on every level of his existence.

He seemed to have no choice whatsoever in this matter. He wanted her, and he resisted as long as he could. But it seemed hopeless to go on trying. He had only to touch her, ever so lightly, and the demands within him would begin, linking themselves to pleasures he had experienced the last time he had kissed her. He was always going to want her. It seemed hopeless.

He knew that they had absolutely no business being together, not professionally, not socially. She didn't fit into his world. She represented chaos, disorder, constant tension.

There were a thousand reasons to back away and only one not to.

Because he didn't want to.

He had always been one not to go with the odds.

Gathering her to him, he sought and found what his soul had been lacking these last few days. It was as if he were stepping into a warm haven after freezing in the darkness. He crushed his mouth against hers, cursing himself for his weakness, cursing her for making him weak.

Curses faded. All he wanted to do was go on kissing her, feeling this strange combination of being safe, yet being breathlessly swept away at the same time.

He had never known anything remotely like this sensation that held him in its grip. He knew he never would. But for now, he hung on to it with both hands, savoring it, savoring her.

Annie was surprised by the force of his kiss, by the force with which she reacted to it. He stirred up all the needs that she had swept so carefully away, under a rug somewhere in the corners of her soul.

They were back, brought to her in a misty cauldron by a man who professed not to care, not to feel. She knew better. And now she had proof. Though she had sampled the passion within his pages, to have it here, now, was beyond anything she had imagined. His kiss was hot and urgent, creating a complete meltdown within her. She had thought she could handle this, thought that whatever happened between them could be contained within ramifications that she drew up.

She was wrong.

And she was frightened. He resurrected things within the ashes in her heart that she would have sworn were forever gone. While she rejoiced that they weren't, their very existence brought new fears. She had lost someone she loved once; could she risk living with that hurt again? Should she? Especially with a man who kissed her as if he were angry with her for making him want her.

Annie drew back, her fingers still digging into his forearms, as much for strength as to push him away. She closed and then opened her eyes again, trying to refocus. ''You're going to have to warn me the next time. My supply of oxygen is gone.''

She pulled in a ragged breath and looked at him, her eyes saying things her banter couldn't. She knew they were filled with awe and wonder. She did her best to hide the fear.

There was anger in his eyes, anger amid the desire. When would it leave? *Would* it ever leave? she wondered. ''Are we going to argue about this, too?'' she asked.

''What are you talking about?'' He forced himself to let her go, even though he wanted to go on holding her, go on touching her, perhaps until the end of time.

Her stomach was all tied up in knots. She wanted her relationship with him to be perfect, effortless. The last time she had loved, it had been so easy. It wasn't like that now. "You look angry."

"I am." Caution seemed to be eluding him. He couldn't lie to her, even though it would be easier. "I don't want to want you."

"But you do?"

He didn't want to see happiness in her eyes. Didn't she know things like this were only temporary? That happiness, if it came at all, hadn't a prayer of lasting? He knew that. Why didn't she? "Yes."

"I see." Her heart was pounding, but she maintained her composure, forcing herself to keep it light. It was enough for now that she knew. She'd work out the rest as they went along. "I could come in wearing sackcloth and ashes tomorrow." She wanted to ask why he thought that wanting her was so bad, but she didn't want to hear his answer.

"You promised that once before." It wouldn't help. Underneath, she'd still be her, maddening, infuriating and incredibly desirable. But the image of her so attired brought a slight smile to his lips.

"I forgot." She wanted to touch him, to make him see that it was all right. For once, she was at a loss.

"So it would seem." He sighed. "Let's get back to work."

"Okay." She sat down again. The words she had written were still on the screen, green letters against black. She had to concentrate intently to remember what she was working on. He had completely stripped her mind. "I still think the love scene has to be moved up in the timetable in order to snare the audience's attention."

How many lovers had she had? he wondered. An annoying spark of jealousy zipped through him, but he wasn't going to ask her. It wasn't his business who she had taken to her bed, who she had touched and kissed and loved.

"Just what do you know of love scenes?" The question was not as innocently phrased as he had wanted it to be, but it was too late. Anything he said now to fix it would only make it worse.

Annie looked up at him, not seeing Marcus at all. "Enough."

Her voice had a quiet, melancholy note he had never heard before. He wanted to press and ask her questions, but asking would only open up channels that were best left closed.

Yet he couldn't shake the desire to hold her and ask who it was that she had loved. It wasn't jealousy exactly that prompted him now, although there was a shade of that, too. It was the slight flinch and flicker of pain he had seen in her eyes. She had loved someone. And lost him.

And he wanted to comfort her. Her, the woman who put his life into total chaos.

Marcus had the uncomfortable, panicky sensation that he was steadily, inevitably sinking into quicksand. And there wasn't a limb or anything that might save him in sight.

Chapter Eight

It took considerable effort, it always did, but she shut out the pain the memories generated. It would do no good to relive the past. Not when there was someone who needed her in the present. A man on the radio was singing about his girl being sweet sixteen. She hadn't been sixteen for quite a while. She hadn't felt like this about a man in quite a while.

A smile chased away any signs of sadness on her face. "You know, Sullivan, if you're trying to get me to quit, you're going to have to try harder."

Moving around him, Annie crossed to the window and tried to open it. The room needed fresh air and so did she. "I've worked with some incredibly maddening people in my life and never once walked out on a project. I've contemplated justifiable homicide a time or two, but never quitting." Try as she might, the window wouldn't budge.

Marcus stood back and watched her struggle, amused, waiting to see how long it would take before she asked for help.

"Compared to them, you're just a pussycat." Annie looked around the window casement. How did this darn thing open?

A pussycat. Did she mean he was a pushover? "I'm not sure how to take that."

"In the best possible sense, trust me." Her forearms strained, a nail broke, but the window wouldn't move an inch. Annie swallowed an expletive.

"I'm also not sure how to take you." *And I damn well know I shouldn't even try,* he thought.

"Also in the best possible sense." She half turned toward him. "Okay, what's the secret? How do you open this darn thing?"

He came up behind her. With an arm around her on either side, he grasped the sash. It wasn't the most convenient way to do it, but he wasn't looking for convenience, just excuses. "You have to jiggle it, first on one side, then the other." He demonstrated. "It's temperamental."

She felt his body brush up against hers. His warm breath whispered along her back. It was as if her very skin was sensitized to him. Any second, there'd be goose bumps. Goose bumps, for heaven's sake.

The thought made her smile to herself. She relished the small, pulsating excitement that danced through her.

"Like a lot of things here," she murmured, carefully turning around so that she faced him.

There was no room between their bodies. There wasn't meant to be.

"You do have a way of getting under a person's skin." He played with a wisp of hair at her neck that moved in the breeze from the open window. He saw the desire that rose in her eyes. It matched the fire that burned within him.

This was counterproductive. But he didn't care.

"I've been working on it." Her words feathered along his lips.

He looked down. She was standing on her toes. It made him smile. Marcus let his hands drop to her small waist. It was as if his hands were meant to fit there, his fingers dipping down slightly and resting on the feminine curve of her hips.

God, he wanted her. He had never truly wanted a woman before. When he had taken one to his bed, it was unpremeditated, just a spontaneous reaction that lasted for the pleasure of the moment. He couldn't remember his pulse scrambling like this, couldn't remember his body throbbing and aching with demands.

Annie wound her arms around his neck. "Kiss me, Marc. I can't stay on my toes forever. My calves are cramping up."

He pulled her body to him, close enough to feel every soft contour against his, close enough to feel the tempting swell of her breasts rubbing against his chest. "Can't have that." Softly, gently, he nipped at her lower lip. Then his mouth covered hers.

He went with it because she had asked him to, he told himself.

He kissed her because he would have blown apart inside if he hadn't.

Surprised, worried about the speed with which his emotions surfaced, Marcus was swept out to sea again. He had only to touch his lips to hers, only to taste the flavors that were hers alone, to lose touch with reality. His mind filled with thoughts of only her as he lost himself to the passion that consumed him.

Her lips parted invitingly beneath his as he heard her moan. It vibrated against his mouth, filled his throat. His tongue teased hers, exciting him, pushing him closer and closer to the guardrail.

She tasted wonderful, *was* wonderful. He felt as if he were drugged, spinning on the rim of the universe, having control spin away from him.

He didn't want to get involved. He didn't. It had been far better as a child. Then there had only been the pain of rejection. Before long, the barrier around his heart had hardened and he had told himself it didn't matter anymore. He didn't need love, didn't need to feel loved. It made life simpler.

It was infinitely preferable to the pain of losing someone. If he were to care about her, if it came to the point where it mattered if she left, then he would be opening himself up to devastation. He had been emotionally rejected by his parents, abandoned, in a manner of speaking, by Jason and Linda. He didn't want to risk facing the pain of opening up and then losing a third time.

He took a deep breath as his lips parted from hers. Her eyes were wide and slightly dazed, the outline of her mouth blurred from the force of his. "We can't keep doing this."

She found it difficult to think clearly. And even more difficult to deal with his barriers than she had thought. "Why?"

For a thousand reasons. Because I'm afraid. Because it won't work between us. Because I'll care too much. Better not to care at all. "Because we won't get any work done."

He would slip behind that excuse. She had no recourse but to go along with it. But she didn't have to make it easy for him. She smiled as she took a step back. "Man does not live by work alone."

He dragged his hand through his hair, wishing he could do the same through his life and have it fall into place as easily. "I do."

She studied him a moment. He was fighting too hard. "I don't think so."

His eyes narrowed. She was always presuming to know him better than he knew himself. If he could just hold onto his irritation, he'd be in the clear. "Then you think wrong."

Annie slowly shook her head. "Uh-uh."

He felt like taking her by the shoulders and shaking her. "Are you always this smug?"

"No. Only when I'm right."

He had heard of a succulent plant that shot off a poisonous substance when it was touched. Maybe he could make her a gift of it. She was always touching things. . . .

Annie continued to look at him, trying to understand. It was a nice face, even, if allowed, a kind face. But he wasn't allowing it, wasn't allowing anything to touch him or to come in, perhaps not even the boy in the next room. A boy, if she was any judge of things, who desperately needed him.

Marcus's defenses had to be broken down for more than just a fragmentary moment. *She* needed to break them down. For Nathan. For herself. Annie curbed her impatience. For now, she knew she had to retreat. If you pushed too hard, you could break something that was frail.

She turned her attention to the screenplay. There were people counting on her and Marcus. Work would go a lot faster if he'd stop arguing with her. After working with her for over a week, he still didn't think of her as an equal.

"That's part of your problem."

Now what? He found it frustrating not being able to keep up with the workings of her mind, which seemed to shift around like a sidewinder on the hot desert sand, moving ever forward but in a complex, sideways pattern.

"Part of my problem—no, *most* of my problem—is trying to follow what it is you're talking about. It's like you're feeding me bits and pieces of conversations you start in your head."

She grinned. He had found her out. "The man is absolutely right." She made her decision. Abruptly she moved over to her computer and pushed the storing sequence. Green messages flashed at her. "What I am talking about, as you so deftly put it, is that part of the problem is that you don't respect my judgment."

He was relieved that they were talking about work. At least there he had a foothold. Respect, in his book, had to be earned. He watched as her fingers flew across the keyboard. "Forgive me, but why should I?"

She typed in the segment name and pushed the key marked "return." The computer began making low, grunting noises. "Good point."

"Good point?" He looked at her suspiciously. This was too easy. She was up to something.

Annie looked up. "Yes, good point. The reason you don't respect my judgment, the reason you don't treat me as a competent equal, is because you haven't seen any of my work. I've read all your books, but by your own admission, you haven't seen any of my movies."

He'd be damned if she was going to make him feel guilty about that. "I don't see—"

She glanced at the screen. It was blank again. Satisfied, she shut the computer off. "No, but you will once you watch."

"Watch what?" Any moment now, he was going to give in to another passion and wrap his hands around her slender, tempting throat. Maybe he could squeeze something out of her that made sense. But he doubted it.

Annie looked up at him, mystified that he still didn't follow her. It was obvious. "One of my movies. *Until Tomorrow* is currently out."

"And you want me to see it?"

She smiled. "Yes."

"When?"

"Now."

"No." She never ceased to astound him.

Annie put her hands on her hips, telling herself that losing her temper wasn't going to accomplish anything. She wasn't going to let him be obstinate this time. "Once you've seen one of my movies, maybe you'll stop treating me as if you were Moses bringing down the Ten Commandments and I was a lowly goatherd allowed to witness you do it."

She was babbling again. He went for the obvious. "Goatherds are men."

"We'll quibble about gender later, now c'mon." She moved around to his side of the desk and looked at his monitor. The screen was empty. "Anything there to save?" She knew there wasn't, but if she tried to shut off his computer without asking, he'd probably take her fingers off.

"No, but—" They hadn't gotten nearly as far in the script as he had intended. In any event, he had no desire to go off and see one of her movies. He was still trying to hold on to the idea that the less he knew about her, the better he could keep her at bay.

The perverse little voice that everyone carries within them laughed at the paper-thin hope.

"Good." She switched his computer off, and a single swirl appeared on the fading green screen before it went black.

He glared at her, not knowing whether to admire her guts or have her shot for the same reason. "You take too much on yourself."

"Yes, I know," she answered cheerfully. "It's self-defense." With one efficient movement of her hip, she pushed in her chair. "Let's go get Nathan."

She was already out of the room. He had to grab her arm to get her to slow down. "Why are we dragging him into this?" Somehow, he realized, in the last minute or so she had gotten him to go along with her impetuous suggestion.

"Because he needs to do things with you." She saw by the look that came into his eyes that she had overstepped her ground. Again. "Besides, it's a very entertaining movie," she added quickly. "Rated PG because of a couple of 'damns' and a 'hell.' I'm sure Nathan's heard as much or worse from you."

"I don't swear around the boy." *Although around you it's getting to be a habit.*

"Very admirable. Do you talk around him—or to him?"

He decided that the woman couldn't help meddling. It was in her blood. "I talk *to* him." And it was, he was relieved to note, getting steadily better all the time. He looked down at Annie. "Just how long have you been a social worker?"

She could match him, flippant remark for flippant remark. "I was born in 1962."

Marcus was fighting a losing battle.

"Nathan," Annie called as she entered the foyer. There was no answer.

Going on instinct, she went to the family room. Nathan was still there, sitting cross-legged in front of the television set. She arrived in time to see a green goblin make off with the princess. Nathan maneuvered the control panel, his tongue caught between his teeth, trying to save her.

She knew he'd be hooked once he started playing. "Nathan, we're going to see a movie. Would you like to come along?"

Nathan, his fingers curled around the hand control, his eyes glued to the set, didn't look up. He gave no indication that he'd even heard her. His body swayed as he tried to make a hit and failed. The princess disappeared into the goblin's dark castle.

"I think I've created a monster," Annie confided to Marcus.

He thought of the effect she kept having on him. "In more ways than one," he muttered.

Annie gave him a curious look. She didn't know if he was being flippant, or not. For now, she let it pass. "Nathan, honey." She tapped the boy on the shoulder and he jerked as he looked up, surprised to see anyone else in the room. "I think it's time we gave that thing a rest. You don't want to beat Stevie too badly, do you?"

Nathan grinned sheepishly. He was going to be a heart-breaker when he got older, Annie thought fondly.

"No." He shook his head.

She took the control panel out of his hand and placed it on top of the television set, then switched the power off. "Marc and I are going to see one of my movies. Would you like to join us?"

Nathan scrambled to his feet. "One of your movies?" he echoed. "Like a video you own?"

"No, like a screenplay I wrote. Do you know what a screenplay is, Nathan?"

He had heard Marcus talking about it to someone named Richard over the telephone. He hadn't sounded happy about it. "A story for a movie?" he guessed.

"You're very bright." Nathan beamed at her approval. "I'd like your opinion of the movie." She draped her arm around his shoulder casually. "Got anything better planned for this afternoon?"

"Heck, no." The video game was already forgotten.

"Then it's settled. We'll let Marcus take us to the movies." She moved toward the door, her arm still around Nathan, who she could see was enjoying being included.

"Let?" Marcus repeated, following. "I think the FBI would file this particular 'outing' under the heading of kidnapping."

Annie playfully lifted her chin, a challenge twinkling in her eyes. "You're much stronger than I am, Sullivan. Nobody'd believe it."

At this angle, her chin made a very tempting target. He wondered what she'd do if he clipped her one. "That doesn't make it untrue."

"Nope." Her eyes laughed at him.

He let Nathan and Annie precede him out the door to the driveway. Nathan seemed very excited over the prospect of going out with them. The change from the withdrawn, morose child he had been just a month ago to the well-adjusted boy he now appeared to be was astounding. The only time Nathan still acted somewhat subdued was when he was alone with Marcus. But Marcus wasn't vain enough to be jealous of the fact that Hurricane Annie could evoke responses in Nathan that he couldn't. He was just glad that Jason's son was back among the living.

He made no conscious acknowledgment of the fact that Annie was working the same miracle on him.

Annie turned as he slammed the front door. "Mind if we use my car?"

He descended the three steps that it took to join her. "And if I did?"

"We'd use yours." He was halfway to his car when she added, "but I know the way better."

He preferred driving. Just one more thing he liked having control over. But it was a petty matter. There were bigger things to fight over. And he had every confidence that they would.

Resigned, Marcus nodded for Nathan to climb into her car.

Annie hid a smile when the boy settled himself in the front seat next to her, leaving the back door open for Marcus. She turned slightly to get a better view as Marcus got in. "You don't mind being chauffeured around, do you, Marc?"

He closed the door after him. "As a matter of fact," he answered truthfully, "I hate it."

"Oh, I forgot. You like to be in control." She raised her hands from the steering wheel. "I have no problem with that."

"Ha!" Marcus stayed where he was, and Annie turned on the engine. He tugged at his seatbelt, which obstinately refused to budge. It was stubborn. Like her. It was with no small satisfaction that he finally wrestled it out of its inertia.

No sooner had he buckled up than she peeled out of the driveway. His stomach lurched. "Are we in a hurry?" he wanted to know.

Annie changed lanes to get in front of another car. "Not particularly."

The woman drove like she talked. "Then why are you trying to break the sound barrier?" he asked.

"Sorry." Annie eased her foot off the gas pedal. "Habit. I drive fast when I'm alone."

"Which is why you probably drive alone," he muttered under his breath. "Just what is it we're going to see?"

He forgot. It just proved her point. He didn't think what she had to say was important enough to pay attention to. "I told you. *Until Tomorrow.* It's a comedy."

Marcus looked out the side window, watching scenery and cars whiz by. "I'd never have guessed."

Annie glanced at the boy on her right before looking back at the road. "You know him better, Nathan. Is he always this grumpy or am I special?"

"I think you're special."

Nathan's words made her throat tighten the way it did every time she watched greeting card commercials that heralded the best that life had to offer. The precious moments. This was most definitely one of them. She reached over and squeezed his hand. "I think you're special, too, Nathan."

Marcus tried hard not to feel as if he were intruding.

* * *

They didn't have far to go. She made it a practice to know the exact locations of the theaters where her films were playing. It never ceased to give her a kick. This time the closest one was at a triplex nestled within a well-frequented minimall.

Annie parked as close as she could to the triplex. *Until Tomorrow* was playing in theater number three. "We're here," she announced as she turned off the ignition.

Marcus didn't move. He had thought this through on the ride over and had decided that while he had every intention of seeing one of her movies eventually, he didn't care for the fact that she had decided that it was going to be here and now. Until she had turned up, he had made all his own decisions. Now she swept in, arguing every point, making him want her when there was no sane reason to do so, and turning everything in his world upside down. He had to take a stand somewhere before she had him crowded against a wall.

Annie closed her door and then looked into the car. Marcus was still sitting in the back seat, making no effort to get out. She looked at Nathan. The boy shrugged and shook his head. She peered into the back seat. "This isn't a drive in, Marc. You have to come inside to see the film."

"You know, it seems to me as if you always get your way."

She knew that look. There was an argument in the making. "Not always."

He knew she'd contradict him. "Then what are we doing here?"

Why was he being so stubborn? "We're here to see my movie."

"When we should be working."

Annie felt her patience draining. And she felt hurt because he didn't want to see the movie she had written.

"You wouldn't have come if you hadn't wanted to," she pointed out.

"What I really wanted to do was finish the scene we were working on. I wasn't particularly in the mood to see a movie."

She opened her mouth, flabbergasted, then thought better of it. The phrase about leading a horse to water but not making him drink ran through her mind. She couldn't make him want to see her movie, or make him like it once he had. That was up to him. She quietly closed the car door. If he wanted to be pigheaded, that was certainly his privilege.

"In that case, you really don't have to come in. But it's a shame to waste a trip. I'll go by myself."

He was fully annoyed at this point. He was through being led around by the nose. "Fine."

"Fine," she shot back

The man was insufferable. Nathan was looking at her eagerly. She wanted to take him with her, but that would mean coming between them or forcing the boy to make a choice. She had no desire to put Nathan through an ordeal. "You take care of him, okay?" She tried not to notice that his expression fell.

Stunned, Marcus watched Annie walk up to the booth, buy a ticket and walk inside without so much as a backward glance. What had started out as a bid for control had degenerated into a petulant act on his part. He didn't care to feel that he was behaving like an idiot. If he wasn't mistaken, there had been a hurt look in her eyes just as she turned away. He didn't want to hurt her. He just wanted to prove a point, a point that suddenly didn't mean that much anymore. Moreover, there was no denying one disconcerting fact. He *wanted* to be with her in the theater.

"Mr. Sullivan?"

The high voice had him looking up. He had forgotten about Nathan. "Yes?"

The boy climbed into the back seat next to him. "I think we should go in with her." He looked uncertainly at Marcus, obviously worried that he might have said the wrong thing.

So do I. "Why?" Curiosity had him asking for the boy's reasons.

Nathan struggled to put his feelings into words. "Well, she's a lady and she's all alone. Shouldn't we protect her or something?"

"It's more of a matter of protecting the world from her." Marcus laughed, then ruffled Nathan's hair. The boy smiled up at him shyly. It was, Marcus realized, the first time they had actually had any physical contact with each other. The boy had been so withdrawn, so self-contained with his hurt tightly wrapped inside him, that Marcus hadn't been able to bridge the gap. Talking about Annie was helping. It figured. He couldn't seem to get away from her influence no matter how hard he tried. What was worse, he was beginning to be at odds with himself about the problem as well. "You really want to go in and see it?" Nathan nodded. "Why?"

"Well, I like movies."

What else didn't he know about this young life that had been thrust into his? Marcus wondered. "Do you?"

Again, the dark brown head nodded up and down. "My dad and I—" Nathan's voice broke as tears suddenly sprang up into his eyes.

"Yes?" Marcus urged kindly.

Nathan cleared his throat of the tears lodged there. "My dad and I, we used to go all the time, when he was playing in town, I mean. Sometimes we used to go out real late." Remembering made him smile. "He liked science fiction best."

"Yes, he did." Marcus looked down at the small, delicate face. Nathan had Linda's soft eyes and bone structure, but the grin belonged to Jason. "He used to drag me to awful old movies all the time when we were in college. *Flash Gordon and the Mole Woman* was one of his favorites. He made me sit through it three times."

Nathan tucked his legs under his body as he sat up. "Really?"

"Really." Marcus looked at the boy, the eager expression getting to him. "Maybe you and I could see it together. They must have it at some video store."

"Sure!"

There were no science fiction movies to see now. Just a comedy by a woman whose intrusion into his life was no laughing matter. "Well," Marcus said slowly, looking toward the theater. "I guess we'd better go in there and find her, eh, Nathan?" Marcus got out and held the door open for the boy.

Nathan tumbled out. "Can we stay and watch, maybe?"

"Sure, why not?" Trying not to seem obvious, he guided the boy across the street.

"Can we have popcorn?" Nathan asked as Marcus handed the woman in the booth a ten-dollar bill.

Marcus grinned at the eager note in Nathan's voice. "What's a movie without popcorn?"

Nathan cocked his head, testing the waters a little further. "With butter?"

"Absolutely."

Nathan grinned happily as Marcus ushered him inside the theater.

Chapter Nine

Annie held the box of popcorn steady on her lap. She had bought the small container more to have something to do with her hands than because she was actually hungry. It was still full. She hadn't touched any of it. Though her eyes were on the screen, her mind was somewhere else. On the occupants of a blue car in the parking lot.

Maybe she had been a little overbearing, she thought. She did have a tendency to come on strong sometimes. A rueful smile curved her lips. More like ninety-eight percent of the time. She really didn't mean to. It just happened, especially when she cared about something. About *someone*.

Maybe she should have tried coaxing him into the theater instead of just giving him his choice. The trouble was, she didn't know how to coax gently. Her own eagerness and good intentions always got in the way. Marcus was probably hailing a cab right now, Nathan in tow, on his way home.

She was annoyed with him, with herself and with her failure to get him to open up. She was certain he liked her, and she could sense that he was coming around, but each time it looked as if there was a little headway being made between them, suddenly the antagonism was back along with that damned impregnable wall of his.

Annie plunged her hand into the container, grabbing a fistful of popcorn. She bit down on an unpopped kernel and flinched as the shaft of pain registered, radiating from her tooth through her jaw.

Pulling the kernel out, she moved the perfectly round shape back and forth, rolling it between her thumb and forefinger. It made her think of Marcus, stubbornly retaining its original shape even under considerable pressure.

She sighed. Maybe he was happy that way, but she doubted it. It was this doubt, this belief, that everyone preferred being happy to angry, integrated to isolated, that drove her on with people in general.

And Marcus in particular.

That, and the very persistent, very sensual pull she felt whenever she was around him, despite his standoffish demeanor.

"Some way, somehow," she murmured to herself, scarcely aware that she was talking out loud, "it's going to happen between us."

"What is?"

Marcus caught her container of popcorn before it hit the floor. Annie stared, surprised, as he took the seat next to her. An overwhelming sense of contentment washed over her.

"Only good things," Annie managed to answer finally. She nodded at the container Marcus handed her. "Nice catch."

"Jason used to like to throw passes. He needed a receiver."

Annie tried to imagine that—Marcus out on a field, running back as his friend threw a football toward him. It gave her a good feeling.

She leaned forward and looked past him to the boy who sat down to his right. "Did you have to twist his arm?" she asked Nathan.

"No. He thought it was a good idea."

Someone two rows in front turned and shooshed them. Annie bit her lower lip sheepishly and grinned. "I guess they want to hear this," she whispered to Marcus.

So, he had come into the theater voluntarily. Miracle number one hundred and seventy-three, Annie thought happily.

Marcus cocked a brow. He couldn't see her facial expression. The scene up on the screen was taking place on a moonless night and the theater was shrouded in darkness. She sounded smug, though, and he would have bet six months' royalties from his last book that she felt that way. She had read him right all along. Why was it he couldn't say no to her and stick to it?

"Pretty pleased with yourself, aren't you?" Marcus couldn't help whispering.

She continued to look at the screen, but he could make out the slight curve of the smile as she said, "No, I'm always this happy."

"Shh," the person directly behind them said sharply.

"He's right," Annie responded, inclining her head toward Marcus. "You don't want to miss a word of this." She indicated the screen with fingers that were filled with popcorn. Suddenly she had an appetite.

Marcus had his doubts whether he'd feel as if he were missing anything if a line or two of dialogue were lost to him, but he had ultimately come to see the movie because he believed in being fair. And because he was a firm believer that one way or another, a person was always reflected in his or her work.

For reasons that he didn't care to delve into, he decided that he wanted to scratch more than just the surface with Annie de Witt. Never mind about the less he knew about someone, the less involved he'd be. He *was* involved; there was no use in denying that any longer. And since he was, he needed to know things about her. Knowledge, after all, was power. He couldn't let her have all of it.

Besides, she seemed determined to scratch him down to his inner core. A core that hadn't been touched or disturbed before, not this way.

That was the word for it, he thought, absently taking a handful of popcorn from the container Nathan offered. Disturbed. More than anything else, she disturbed him. Disturbed him emotionally, professionally. Physically. It had to stop. But in order for it to stop, he had to know what made it happen. He had to have a key as to what it was about her that made him react so strongly.

Marcus watched Annie as much as he watched the action on the screen. She seemed completely absorbed in the movie, as if she didn't know what was going to happen next. But of course she did, he thought, fascinated by this reaction. She wrote it. If he hadn't known it before, he would have guessed by the contented glow that radiated from her when the audience laughed in all the right places. Annie's rapt attention prompted him to start watching the movie in earnest.

Without knowing exactly when it happened, Marcus became involved.

The dialogue, crisp and quick, was riveting and funny, intelligently written so that it could appeal to an adult audience and yet draw in the younger crowd as well. He had to admire her for that feat. Marcus caught himself actually wondering how the story would resolve itself and what would happen to the characters on the screen. The story made him care about the people whose lives he was watching evolve—not a small accomplishment, he silently admitted. He wasn't easily roped in.

He glanced at Annie again. At least he hadn't been until now.

When the credits finally rolled by, he heard her draw a breath as her name scrolled upward. It was little more than a soft sigh, but he heard it. His eyes narrowed. She still got a thrill out of it, he marveled, the thrill of knowing that something she had created was there for all the world to see, to enjoy. He understood that. He had felt it once, the first time a work of his had been accepted for publishing. When it had finally hit the shelves, he had haunted all the bookstores to see it, to stand back and just admire the collection of books with his name on it. Somewhere along the line, the thrill had faded, replaced by work, responsibility, contracts and details. The excitement had gotten lost, he thought, envying her the fact that she could still feel it.

Annie didn't have a clue as to whether or not he liked the movie. He hadn't laughed. She was acutely aware that all through the showing she had been waiting for the sound of his laugh, listening for it above the sound of others. It hadn't come. He didn't like the movie. Her movie.

So what? Thousands of other people did. Why should it matter that one black-hearted man didn't?

Because it did.

Falling in step with the other people as they surged out of the theater, Marcus, Annie and Nathan made their way through the lobby and out of the building. Outside, the sun was a glaring white, baking everything in sight, as if atoning for the fact that it had rained outside the perimeters of the rainy season just the week before.

Annie blinked several times as her eyes slowly became accustomed to the brightness that surrounded them. She drew a breath and found it hurt her lungs. In the last two hours, it had gotten almost unbearably hot.

"I feel like my eyelashes are going to burn off any second." She knew she was making small talk, but if he thought she was going to beg a response out of him, he had a long wait coming. "How about an ice cream?" The question was directed toward Nathan more than to Marcus.

"Sure." Nathan knew he would have said yes to anything she suggested. She was the prettiest lady he had ever seen and she made him feel good. She made him feel as if he still mattered. After his parents had died and left him, Nathan didn't think that he did. Shyly he reached for her hand.

Annie squeezed it, touched by the loving look she saw in the boy's eyes. "Never met anyone who could say no to ice cream on a hot day. C'mon." She tossed the word over her shoulder, knowing that Marcus was lagging behind. "There's this great ice-cream parlor just on the other side of the theater complex. And it's air-conditioned." She said the last words reverently.

Marcus had to walk quickly to keep up with her. Even in this heat—the weather bureau had predicted a hundred degrees for today, and he could feel that they had passed this conservative estimate—the woman had the energy to move fast. Maybe she wasn't human, just a fast-talking, over-energized android in a pair of short shorts and a skimpy halter top.

Android, hell. No android could create the kind of reactions he was experiencing around her, he thought. One did not daydream about stripping androids of their clothing slowly.

The blast of cold air that hit them when they walked into the ice-cream parlor was a welcome relief from the heat, and for Marcus, a welcome relief from his own thoughts. He needed, he decided as he followed Annie and Nathan to a table, a cold shower.

The halter dipped slightly as she sat down, giving him a fleeting glimpse of firm, small breasts that had his gut tightening and his loins following suit.

A long, cold shower, Marcus amended, taking the seat opposite her. Nathan slid in next to her with no hesitation, his allegiance clear.

After ordering something called a Kitchen Sink Sundae for herself and for Nathan, Annie settled back, her hands folded neatly on the table. She eyed Marcus expectantly. He gave no indication that he knew why. "Okay, I think I've shown restraint long enough."

"You?" Marcus nearly laughed out loud. Restraint and Annie was a contradiction in terms. "Restraint? I'm glad you told me. I would have never noticed on my own."

"There's a lot of things you don't notice on your own." She ignored the darkening look in his eyes. "Yes, I was showing restraint. I didn't ask you what you thought of the movie."

"No," he agreed, "you didn't."

She waited a beat. Nothing. She felt like hitting him. "Well?" she demanded. He was doing this on purpose, but she decided that she wasn't too proud to ask, to push. Pride was just a cumbersome, empty thing that could only get in the way of things for her. "You know, you are an infuriating man."

The water glass felt comfortingly cold against his hands as he held it. Marcus raised his eyes to her face. "Must be catching."

She wasn't about to be put off any longer. Bracing herself for his response, she forged ahead. "What did you think of the movie?"

He shrugged. "I'm not much for movies."

She gave a frustrated little huff. "We've already established that. You're not answering the question, Sullivan."

"It was better than most."

Annie clutched at her heart, rolled her eyes toward the ceiling and gasped, "A compliment. Quick, Nathan, check to see if the sky is falling."

Nathan was bright enough to laugh rather than to run outside the little shop and do as she said. He didn't even look at her oddly.

The waitress, however, did. As quickly as she could, the woman set down their order. Giving Marcus an interested glance that spoke volumes if he had only bothered to look, the waitress hurried away.

Marcus's attention wasn't on the waitress but the over-animated woman sitting opposite him. What made her tick? "Haven't you ever written anything serious?"

"Everything I write—" Annie sank her spoon into a mound of hot fudge "—is serious." Sampling, she closed her eyes and sighed. Heaven, pure heaven. When she opened her eyes she saw that Marcus was watching her. "Comedy is a very serious subject."

Was that the way she looked when she made love? As if ecstasy had touched her? It didn't seem possible that a person could take such joy in everything. He gathered his thoughts. He was drifting again. "Are you really going to eat that?" The dish in front of her was filled to overflowing with different flavors of ice cream.

She grinned. "Every last bit, or die trying."

Marcus watched her as he took a tentative lick of the single scoop of vanilla he had ordered.

"Really dig right in, don't you?" Her voice was teasing. She took another spoonful, savoring the cool feeling that the ice cream created. When she looked to her right, she saw Nathan mimicking her every move. It made her smile.

Damn, how could a woman make eating ice cream look so erotic? What the hell was wrong with him lately? Just being around her generated desire within him, made him want her in crazy, unconventional ways.

Unconventional for him. She, he had no doubts, would probably think that being covered in ice cream and having it slowly licked off her body was equal to making love in the missionary position.

He sucked in his breath, struggling to clear his mind. It was due to the heat, that was all. In an effort to put things in perspective, he tried to remember when he had been with a woman last. No woman's face came into his mind. Only hers.

Damn.

She thought he had said something. Their eyes met and held as time froze. She saw desire, hot and impatient, in his eyes. Cobalt blue and desire, an unbeatable combination, she thought.

"I like vanilla." The words were said defensively. He couldn't remember what it was he was responding to. If this kept up, he'd be declared totally senile by the end of the month.

Annie lowered her eyes, knowing enough to hide her pleasure. "I'm sure you do."

Grown-ups were strange, even nice ones, Nathan thought, watching the two with him. "Vanilla's a good flavor," he volunteered. "My dad liked it."

Annie tried not to be obvious when she looked at the boy. To her relief, there was no sign of the deadening, soul-wrenching sadness she had seen the first time she met Nathan. She put her arm around him. "Vanilla's a terrific flavor."

"He liked mint chip better," Marcus recalled.

Nathan's face lit up as he remembered, a vivid memory flashing by. "Yeah, he did."

They were sharing a moment, Annie thought. Whether they were aware of it or not, they were sharing a moment. Jason Danridge, she decided, had been one smart man. He had known who to leave his son with.

"Annie?" Nathan ventured in between mouthfuls of fudge-covered ice cream.

"Hmm?"

"Did you really write that movie?"

"Yes, I did." She watched Marcus's face as she said it. The condescending smile she expected didn't materialize. *Maybe we're making headway here, too,* she thought. Hope spun out, casting slender threads of steel that caught and held.

"I thought it was really neat. Especially when that guy's boat sank when he was in it."

Yes, that would appeal to someone his age. "That was one of my favorite parts, too." So, she was a kid at heart; there was nothing wrong with that.

"Are you really writing a movie with Mr. Sullivan?" He had heard them talking loud, when they thought he wasn't around, but it was still hard to believe that big people actually wrote what he saw.

Annie gave Marcus a long, penetrating look that he couldn't quite read. "I'm doing my best."

"Was than an insult?" Marcus wanted to know. With her, he was sure of nothing except his own confusion.

She shook her head, another tendril coming loose. "That was a statement. You'll definitely know when I insult you," she promised, taking another spoonful.

He eyed the half-eaten concoction before her. His stomach hurt just to look at it. "If you don't explode first."

She merely laughed and went on eating.

"Do you *really* enjoy writing such frivolous stuff?" He didn't even know why he felt compelled to make it sound like a put-down. She was competent in her own offbeat way, and he had to admit, if only to himself, that the movie had been well written—for what it was. But something kept goading him on, as if he were fighting for his own survival, fighting to keep her at bay. Disparaging remarks about her work could accomplish that.

She knew what he was doing and reacted accordingly. "I enjoy writing *entertainment,* Marc. If I didn't, I wouldn't do it. I never do anything I don't like."

He was silent for a moment. "You can't possibly be as happy as you let on."

She raised her eyes. It was nothing if not seductive. He wondered if she knew just how seductive. "Try me."

"If you are," he said quite seriously, "I really envy you. You're very lucky."

Lucky. If she had been lucky, she thought, truly lucky, she would have sampled more than just a taste of what real love would have been like. She almost said that to him, experiencing a sudden need to say the words aloud.

But then she buried it. The pain she carried with her was something very, very personal. It was something she didn't share. Not with anyone. She hadn't let it out even when all her family had done their best to divest her of it. They had been there for her and she had wept a little, but then she had carried on the way she always had. It was only the look that sometimes came into her eyes that gave her away.

The sudden sadness in Annie's eyes made Marcus want to reach out, made him want to ask: What? Why?

Who?

But Nathan was there, and it wasn't a subject Marcus sensed that could be shared with a child present. Meticulously Marcus folded his napkin and placed it on the table without thinking.

The woman was really getting to him. And that wasn't good. But he wouldn't have stopped it if he could, and he suspected that he couldn't.

Probably had something to do with a death wish, he thought.

For the first time, the silence growing between them felt very painful. "Have you always written for the movies?" Marcus heard himself asking.

"Always." She nodded, reinforcing her words. "My grandfather started in this business when it was just getting on its feet, right after the talkies blossomed. My dad followed because there was nothing else he wanted to do. He had different plans for me, something more stable and dependable—"

"But you wouldn't listen," Marcus put in knowingly. He felt a twinge of pity for her father, for any man who had come up against her.

"Why start a precedent?" She pushed her bangs away from her face. "I went into the business because making up stories was my whole world. It still is. Between my dad and grandpa, they garnered five Academy Awards and twelve nominations. I've got one of my own," she said with a touch of awe and pride he found strangely irresistible. In some ways, she was almost an innocent.

Annie raised her spoon and used it to emphasize her point. "And this project of ours just might net us another one."

It wasn't until later that Marcus realized he had taken the word "us" in stride.

Chapter Ten

Nathan had finished his giant sundae, although it involved a major effort on his part toward the end. But he didn't want Annie to think that he was ungrateful. The attention she gave him meant everything.

Annie maintained a cheerful stream of conversation during the drive home, receiving occasional answers from Marcus. Nathan hardly murmured at all. She cast a side glance at him as she stopped at a light. This time, she suspected, the boy's silence didn't have anything to do with his emotional state. The problem went a little lower than that. Poor thing. His hands were clasped over his stomach, his expression slightly pained. She took care to drive a lot slower returning to Marcus's house than she had leaving it.

"What's the matter, Nathan?" she asked gently as they approached the house. "You look a little peaked. The sundae not agreeing with you?"

"That sundae couldn't have agreed with anyone who doesn't have a cast-iron stomach," Marcus commented.

Annie looked up into the rearview mirror and caught a glimpse of Marcus's eyes. "I ate it."

"I rest my case." Marcus moved to the edge of his seat in order to see Nathan's face. The boy pressed his lips together and raised his eyebrows helplessly as he nodded in response to Annie's question. "You didn't have to finish it," Marcus reminded him.

"Yes, I did." Nathan felt miserable now, but the sundae had tasted good to begin with. "It was there."

"Spoken like a trouper." Annie laughed fondly. She coasted into the driveway and stopped her car next to Marcus's navy Jaguar. "A little bicarbonate of soda should have you feeling a lot better." She yanked up the emergency brake and turned off the engine. "Or, barring that, try some club soda."

"I'll see if we have any," Marcus promised Nathan. He got out first and opened the boy's door. Nathan climbed out slowly. He looked green, Marcus thought. He placed a comforting hand on Nathan's shoulder. "C'mon, fella, we'll see if we can fix you up."

She wondered if he knew how natural he seemed with the boy. The stiffness, the hesitation she had witnessed just a few short days ago, was dissipating. This was the man she wanted to get to know. Not the man who insisted on matching wits with her, although she did enjoy that. But this man, this gentle person who resided within the stern, demanding, competent writer, was the one who awakened her dormant emotions, who stirred her vulnerability at the same time that he made her feel safe.

Marcus stopped and looked over his shoulder. "In view of the situation, I think we'll call it a day. I'll see you tomorrow."

"Right." It pleased her immensely that he put a small boy's comfort ahead of his work ethic. Annie turned on the ignition again. She hadn't been wrong about him. For some reason, he just wanted to keep his better traits hidden from view. Those days were numbered.

An impish grin spread across her face. "Oh, Marcus," she called after him.

He turned, ready, he thought, for anything. "Yes?"

"This *was* a date."

She drove away before he could say anything.

"I think she likes you," Nathan mumbled, holding his stomach as if he was afraid that if he didn't, it would explode.

Marcus opened the front door. "If she does, it'll probably mean sealing my doom."

Nathan shuffled in, trying manfully not to moan. "What's doom, Mr. Sullivan?"

Marcus glanced down the street. Annie was making a U-turn. One slender hand waved jauntily out of the driver's side as Annie stepped down on the gas pedal and sped off. With a sigh, he closed the door behind them.

"Something that seems to shiver up my spine every time that woman walks into my line of vision." He led the way into the kitchen.

Nathan screwed up his face, trying to understand as he hurried to keep up. "You mean Annie?"

He tried to remember if there was any club soda in the refrigerator. "That's the one."

Nathan sat down on the first available chair he came to. "I think she's neat."

Marcus rummaged through the refrigerator. No club soda. "You, Nathan, are very young and very naive." He found a half-filled bottle of ginger ale. Holly's. Maybe that would do. "Live grenades are never 'neat.'" He reached inside the overhead cabinet for a glass. "One cure coming up."

She hummed along with the song on the radio as she drove, feeling very, very content with herself, with life in general. The screenplay was coming along, albeit slowly. And so was her campaign to break down Marcus's defenses, albeit even slower. But the bottom line was that it *was* progressing, which was all that counted.

It was really wonderful just to be alive. Annie sang out loud the rest of the way home.

She opened the front door and was assaulted by hot, almost stagnant, air. With quick strides, she crossed the living room and flipped the switch on her air conditioner. It rattled into life. An off-white dust mop on four legs scurried up to greet her.

"Hiya, Beatrice, how's my girl?" Annie bent down to scratch the small animal behind the ears. Beatrice thumped her tail madly against the floor.

Annie eyed her pet's very rounded stomach. It was almost dragging on the floor. She patted the dog gently. "How's the family coming along?" Beatrice was very much in the family way due to a very brief but passionate encounter with the feisty Scottie on the next street. Chauncey, his owner had whimsically called him. "Couldn't resist you, could he? Someday you'll have to teach me that trick. C'mon." Annie rose to her feet. "It's time to feed all of you."

The dog waddled after her mistress to the kitchen. Annie refilled Beatrice's water dish, then hunted through the refrigerator for the last of the leftover roast beef. Since she had gotten pregnant, Beatrice had demonstrated a definite fondness for roast beef.

Annie cut up the remaining meat into small bite-size pieces. "Here, this should satisfy your cravings." She set the dish in front of the dog. Crossing her arms and leaning against the refrigerator, she watched as the animal ate hungrily. "Well, we have that much in common. We both love food. And we've both thrown our lots in with men who are poles apart from us in temperament."

As she listened, Annie could hear the faint sound of barking. The Scottish terrier had a bark that could have belonged to a dog three or four times larger than he was. It really carried in the daytime when everyone else in the area was at work or school.

Sighing, Annie shoved her hands in her pockets and wandered into the living room. Beneath her contentment a bittersweet feeling gnawed at her. She knew she was saying goodbye to something, finally letting go. Her eyes wandered to the piano that dominated the room, a beautiful white baby grand that had been a housewarming gift from her father. She hadn't touched it in over a year. Not since Charlie had died.

Annie sat down and slowly lifted the cover from the keyboard. He had loved to pick out tunes on the piano. Sometimes he had composed things for her, silly, nonsensical songs that had touched her heart and made them laugh. After the accident, she had found that she couldn't bear to play it any more.

Slowly, hesitantly, she placed her fingers on the keys and began to play. She closed her eyes, and the notes came back to her. *Moon River.* One of the first songs she had ever learned.

Music filled the air, surrounding her. When she opened her eyes, the room was still there. Nothing had changed. Except for her.

Annie slid the cover back down over the keys. Rising, she picked up the silver-framed photograph that she kept on the piano. A thin, dark-haired man with sensitive eyes looked back at her. Charlie. The photograph had been taken just a few months after they had gotten engaged. A week before he had died.

Slowly she ran her fingertips along the glass, remembering what it had been like to touch him, remembering how it felt to be near him. The sweetness was still there. The pain had faded.

"I've met someone, Charlie," she said softly to the image she held in her hands. "He's not a thing like you, but I think he needs me. As a matter of fact, I'm sure of it, although he probably thinks otherwise," she added with a laugh.

Turning the frame around, she removed the back. With shaky fingers, she took out the photograph. She set the frame aside and crossed to the coffee table where she kept her album.

"I'll always love you, Charlie. But it's time to get on with my life. I need sunshine." She sat down on the sofa, pulling the photo album onto her lap. "I need love, and most of all, I need to give it." Searching through the book, she found an empty page. "But you always knew that, didn't you?"

Charlie would have understood. Somehow it helped to know that.

Tenderly she placed the photograph on the empty page and smoothed down the clear plastic over it. Then slowly she closed the book.

No, she thought, Marc was nothing like Charlie. Nothing like her, either, but he was someone she could love, someone who could love her. There was something basic within him, something sensitive beneath the surface that spoke to her, moved her.

Sensitivity had been easy to see in Charlie. With Marcus, it wasn't that simple. But she knew it was there. It was in his words. His written words. She felt confident that Marcus Sullivan was every bit as sensitive, as passionate, as his writing. She had had a taste of it in his kisses. He just needed help to release the real man.

And if she couldn't do it, she thought as she rose, leaving the album behind her, no one could.

He didn't want to be stirred up like this. But that was exactly what she was doing. He was used to going along a nice, unemotional, straight path. She had him zigzagging, filling up with emotions, with wants, with needs suddenly exploding within him, with no more cause than the fact that the sun had highlighted her face or a corner of her mouth lifted higher than the other. It all seemed so ridiculous. And yet, Marcus couldn't reason himself out of it even though he knew what the dangers were of following the path he was on.

His childhood had been nothing if not a stark reminder of where emotions, if released, led. To disappointment. To pain. He could remember making a card for his mother. It had been her birthday, and his father was taking her to a party to celebrate. Marcus wasn't included. But he had worked feverishly to make her a card, oblivious to the mess he generated in its creation. When he had handed his mother the card, she had carelessly tossed it aside and then scolded him for the mess he had made. Most of his childhood had been marked with incidents like that, until he had been afraid to reach out.

With the Danridges, it had been different. It had been safer. He was allowed to experience all the warmth, all the love, of a family unit without being completely involved. All the good parts, none of the problems. But when Nathan came to live with him, it made Marcus realize how deficient he was, how unequipped he was to deal with another human being. He still couldn't open up all the way.

And no one made him see his problem more clearly than Annie. He realized how difficult it was to express his feelings, feelings other than anger and annoyance. The easy way she got Nathan to open up simply emphasized his own inability to do so. He was accustomed to repressing his emotions, yet with her there was a strong desire not to. But in order to survive, he knew he had to.

Restless, unable to sort out the jumbled thoughts in his head, Marcus paced around his den. He had seen to Nathan's needs, then left the boy in Holly's care and thrown himself into the script. He thought he'd feel better, calmer, if he worked by himself, without her distracting him.

Methodically he reviewed the work they had completed that morning, fully intending to rework everything they had done. He didn't need to. The pages were still in rough-draft form, certainly not polished enough, but they were good. And they reflected the combination of both their feelings, both their philosophies. The fact that they were good worried him. It meant that the collaboration was working. His world was being dismantled. He had been so certain that a collaboration with Annie wouldn't work. But it seemed to be. Maybe he was wrong about other things, too.

They were good together. The thought throbbed in his brain like the relentless tattoo of the rain beating against a windowpane.

He hadn't wanted to give an inch today, had hung on to every piece, every principle, tenaciously like a junkyard dog. But she had managed, somehow, to temper, to add, to augment. He refused to use the word "change" because she hadn't actually changed anything. She had, God help him, *enhanced* it.

Just as she had somehow managed to enhance his relationship with Nathan. The awkwardness he had felt, that both he and Nathan had felt, was peeling away, layer by layer. They were finding each other in their need to grieve over the same loss, the same emptiness. Annie was the catalyst. He'd like to think that somehow the relationship between Nathan and him would have evolved on its own, but he knew that before Annie had walked into the house, it was going nowhere. He had felt frozen inside. His grief had him sealing himself off from Nathan.

She, either consciously or not, had helped him open up to the boy. She had talked and coaxed and wheedled until a crack within his armor had been found.

And then she had slipped in.

Damn her. Damn her for making him feel. He didn't *want* to feel, not again. Feelings had consequences. With feelings, there was always that awful risk of losing. He didn't think the risk was worth the pain.

Annie. The name made him think of a little girl with frizzy red hair and black dots for eyes. Anne de Witt wasn't quite "Annie" to him. He thought of her as that *woman*, the screenwriter, the hurricane.

A self-deprecating smile came to his lips. That seemed like a lot of titles for such a little woman. A little woman who took up an awful lot of space in his life, he thought, pacing the length of the room with the pages still in his hand. He really didn't want to get involved, not with anyone. He didn't want someone to matter. He didn't want to give her that kind of control over his life. He had worked too hard to become independent and self-sufficient.

And yet the hole, the aching emptiness in his life, demanded it.

It was too jumbled a mess to be straightened out now. Later.

Marcus looked at his watch. She had probably gotten home by now. Impulse overtook him again. Without thinking through his actions and their consequences, he dialed her number. He didn't even realize that he knew it until now.

He almost hung up when he heard her voice on the other end. Bright, soft, sensual, it filled his head like trapped sunshine. "Hello?"

Hang up the phone, you idiot, before you make a fool of yourself, Marcus thought angrily. His hold on the receiver tightened. It got no closer to the cradle than it had been a moment before.

"De Witt?" he fairly snapped out her surname.

The man was a born romantic, she thought. Now what was wrong? "Marcus."

It wasn't a question, he realized. It was a pleased identification. As if she knew all along that he was going to call. "Predictable" she had called him. He was tempted to hang up just to show her she was wrong.

He didn't.

If he was going to do this, it best be done quickly. Wasn't that a line out of *Macbeth*? he wondered. Macbeth died at the end of the play, he reminded himself. He was walking into a trap of his own making. What the hell was the matter with him?

He didn't know. Just as he didn't know what possessed him to ask, "Do you have any plans for tonight?"

Annie thought of the old MGM musical she had found listed in the *TV Guide*. The bowl of potato chips stood waiting by her chair. She felt a smile spread through her. "None."

He knew he had to talk quickly before she jumped in and invited him over. He wanted to be the one doing the asking. The balance of control between them was very delicate at this moment, and she had a penchant for pulling it over in her direction. "All right, dress. I'm taking you to dinner."

"I never eat dinner naked."

It was a teasing line, but it conjured up an image in his mind that was very hard to shake. He could picture her across from him at a table, nude, candlelight playing on her smooth, soft skin, tempting him, making him burn. Making him want.

There was silence at the other end. Had he changed his mind? "Marc, are you still there?"

All too much so, he thought as he glanced down, glad for the distance between them at this particular moment. He was letting his desires run away with him. God knew his mind had already fled. The phone call was evidence of that. "Yes, I'm still here."

She cupped the receiver in her hand, cradling it. Beatrice had waddled by for another scratch. Annie stooped down to oblige the dog. "We're making real progress, you and I."

He knew he was losing ground and that it was of his own making, but he didn't have to give in without some sort of a semblance of a fight. "We're making plans for dinner."

"Yes, we are."

Why did she always have to make everything sound as if it had another meaning behind it? Maybe, he thought, because it did this time. He just wasn't ready to admit it. "How soon can you be ready?"

It had never taken her long to get dressed. Like everything else, she did it quickly. "How soon can you be over?"

Marcus glanced at his watch, gauged his time and heard himself saying, "I'll be by to pick you up in an hour."

More than ample time. "Then I'll be ready in forty-five minutes."

"I'll see you then." He hung up, then caught a reflection of his face in the multipaned window. "You are an idiot, you know that, don't you?"

Yes, he knew that. Muttering, he went off to change.

Annie hung up and grinned broadly. She gave herself two thumbs-up, savoring the moment. "That was him, Beatrice. Think you can entertain yourself for the evening?"

The dog yipped.

"Atta girl." Annie dashed off to do a million things in forty-five minutes.

Marcus showed up exactly fifty-three minutes later. She didn't keep him waiting. The door flew open almost immediately in response to his knock.

She looked the same. Bright, glowing, the speed of light trapped under glass.

She looked entirely different.

It was her hair, swept up from her neck, piled high in a haphazard way, secured by pins, he imagined. What he couldn't fathom was why it looked so terribly appealing.

She wore a hot pink dress that had a halter top and absolutely no back to speak of. If he placed his hand on the small of her back to guide her out the door, she would feel naked. It made his hand burn.

The dress's skirt came around like a sarong. A very short sarong. The woman might be small, but she was very long on leg. A physical impossibility, except that she managed.

"You're staring." She liked the look in his eyes. Dazed. She decided to hunt for a compliment. Just a little one. She needed to hear words. "Is that because I look very good, or very bad?"

Marcus looked away, nonplussed at being caught. "The former."

"Flatterer. You do carry on." Her laugh was low and sexy. His hand tightened on the flowers he was holding. He had made no move to enter her house. "I love flowers. Are those for me?"

Feeling none of the polish he had so painstakingly developed, he thrust the bouquet forward. "These were Nathan's idea."

"They're lovely." He could have brought her a string of pop tops from soda cans and she would have felt the same. Very, very pleased. Hooking an arm through his, she drew him inside. "You told Nathan you were taking me out?"

Nathan had come to his room just as he was leaving. It had seemed natural to tell the boy. He didn't know why the fact pleased her so much. But Nathan made a good topic of conversation. Marcus found himself in need of one. "Yes. He says he thinks you're 'neat.'"

"I think he's neat."

Releasing Marcus, she looked around for a vase. She found one on a shelf on the breakfront. A cut-glass vase that had been a gift from her mother on her last birthday. Deftly she arranged the bouquet and placed the vase on the piano. Perfect.

Annie turned then and looked at Marcus. "What do you think?"

He wished he had a drink to toy with. "I think he's a nice kid."

"He is, but I was asking about me." She took a step forward, then turned slowly around. When she faced him, Marcus was eyeing her warily. "What do you think of me?"

"I try to think of you as little as is humanly possible." The operative word here, he added silently, was "try."

"Are you succeeding?"

He could have lied, but he didn't. She had a way of knowing when he lied. "No."

She tucked her arm through his again. "I'm glad. So, would you like a drink before we leave?"

Several, he thought, wondering again how he could have put himself in this situation of his own free will. *Had* he had a free will where she was concerned? He no longer knew the answer to that.

The drink tempted him, but if he had one here, his control might dissipate permanently. "No, our reservations are for seven-thirty, and I think we'd better be on our way."

"Whatever you say." She handed him a shawl that seemed to be spun out of silvery threads and little else.

"I wish I could believe that."

Since she stood waiting, he draped the shawl around her shoulders. Her skin felt soft, silky. He caught himself lingering there a little longer than he knew was safe. For either of them.

He remembered he was supposed to be the one in charge. It wasn't easy. "By the way—"

"Yes?"

When she looked up at him like that, he could almost believe that she was innocent, sweet, without a contrary bone in her body. Almost. "*This* is a date."

With that, he ushered her out to the car. He didn't look at her, but he knew she was smiling to herself.

In charge? Marcus thought. Who was he kidding? If he was lucky, he'd come out of this alive.

Chapter Eleven

The restaurant was subdued and dimly lit. Conversation around them was discreet enough to be hardly audible. Marcus felt completely alone with her in the booth. Yet it wasn't the kind of isolation he was familiar with. This was different. It was an intimate solitude. Because of the inner reserve he had developed over the years, he had felt alone in the midst of people at parties and at meetings. He had always stood apart from everyone, observing. It was what he was used to.

It had been different, of course, with Jason and Linda, but that had been a very special case.

And this, it seemed, was another.

He knew he couldn't really let himself believe that, not even for a moment. If he did, if he let his guard slip, if he started to believe that he could reach out to someone and not be rebuffed at some point, then he would start believing that perhaps a relationship could actually evolve and last.

But it couldn't. Not for him.

If ever a man had laid the plans for his own self-destruction, Marcus thought, it was he. Why else grab a rubber raft and deliberately run straight for the point where the rapids plummeted?

That was exactly what he was doing, he mused, putting himself into this vulnerable position with a woman who thought taking charge was one of the inalienable rights guaranteed to her by Thomas Jefferson and the other founding fathers. With every passing moment, she continued drawing him to her, pulling him toward her.

Knowing this, knowing what was in store, why had he made this overt move? Why had he asked her out? And why did he find her harder and harder to resist? It was the quicksand principle again, he thought. The more he tugged, the more he strained, the deeper he was being sucked in.

So why was he so stimulated, so excited? What was it about those almond-shaped eyes that made him lose his thoughts? What was this anticipation that kept slicing through him at unexpected moments when she'd look up at him?

People probably faced approaching death the same way, he thought.

"You've been awfully quiet," she observed over dessert. She had hoped, when he had asked her out, to finally get to know him, *really* get to know him.

As always, she seemed to be enjoying her meal. If someone would have asked him at this moment what he was eating, he wouldn't have been able to answer. "So have you. I didn't think that was possible."

Finished, Annie set down her fork. "I have my quiet moments," she told him. "I just happen to like conversation, preferably with someone who's living."

She leaned forward, the single familiar movement signaling privacy, intimacy. Marcus felt himself being drawn to her, slowly, inevitably, like the needle of a compass was destined to be always magnetized to the north.

"Why did you ask me out?"

Because after working with you for over a week, I'm nine-tenths certifiably crazy. The response flashed through his mind, but he didn't give it. Why did she always have to be so direct? Didn't she understand subtlety? Didn't she know when not to probe with embarrassing questions he had no answer to?

Marcus shrugged. "I think there used to be a line in the late sixties that went, 'The devil made me do it.'"

She laughed as she took a sip of wine. He watched the slight movement of her throat as she swallowed and wanted to trace the path the wine took with the tip of his finger. He wanted to press his lips to that throat, lose himself in her scent and her touch and her taste.

More than anything else in the world, Marcus wanted to make love with Annie before speculation about it drove him insane with desire.

Yes, he thought, definitely nine-tenths certifiably crazy. The other tenth wasn't that far off.

"Sometimes," Annie murmured, watching the light shine within her wine glass, "the 'devil' can be a very nice guy." She raised her eyes to his. He had such beautiful eyes. "Talk to me tonight, Marc. Don't waltz around with words. You're so good at that, but—"

She reached for his hand. He turned his palm up, his fingers slipping around hers. It was an action as natural as breathing. "I feel disarmed around you," he said in a moment of honesty.

She shook her head. "Never that. You'd never be disarmed. But that's exactly what I mean. You've got too many words to hide behind."

She understood that, he thought. Understood that he had always used words to shield him, to separate him from others. A cloak, a barrier. Safe, he couldn't be hurt. How much else did she know?

She saw that look entering his eyes. He was distancing himself from her. She didn't want to be shut out, not tonight. "Talk to me, Marc. Really talk to me," she pressed. "As if I'm a woman you want to get to know. A woman who wants to get to know you." A smile curved her generous mouth. "Pretend."

There would be no pretending necessary, he thought. But he wanted to know her reasons. "Why?"

"Because when you pretend, nice things happen and things can end happily ever after."

It wasn't exactly what he had wanted to know, but it would do. This wasn't the time or place for rewrites. She looked so earnest when she spoke. She believed in what she said. He knew better. "There is no happily ever after."

"There is for a while," she insisted.

He thought of his parents. Of the motherless boy waiting for him. He felt his own anger rising at the injustice of that. Didn't she understand? "Are you really that naive?"

"No." There was an unshakable firmness within the quiet tone. "I'm that hopeful. There's no point in cutting yourself off from life because it might end badly. You can't live expecting only the worst."

"Why not?" His words displayed the raw bitterness he felt. "Disappointments don't happen then."

Oh, God, how deeply did his wound run? There had to be more to it than just the loss of his friend. But how could she get him to open up, to trust her enough to tell her what he felt? She bit back an impatient retort.

"Neither does the joy." She saw his expression harden. She beat him to his response. "Are you going to disagree with everything I say?"

He took a long swallow of his own drink. An incurable optimist, that was instinctively what she was. Jason and

Linda would have loved her. His need to back off from her warred with his need to grasp hold of the things she believed in, if only for a little while. "Probably."

Annie felt her annoyance dissipating. She never could manage to maintain it for long. "So long as I know." Annie studied him for a moment over the rim of her glass. "I don't believe you, you know."

When she looked at him like that, he felt as if she could see right through him, see him better than he saw himself. "Believe what?"

A waiter at her elbow swept away their plates. Annie kept her attention focused on Marcus. "That you're the man you're trying to project."

His hand slid over the tray with the check the waiter had left in his wake. "It's not a projection." Marcus placed his credit card on top of the tab.

"I think it is. The real man lives in his books."

She hit too quick, too deep. The lady was as astute about real life as she was about the world of make-believe. And she was truly rattling his cage. But then, he knew she was capable of that. "Those books are just works of fiction."

He wasn't convincing. "The feeling in them isn't. Tell me about you," she asked again.

He couldn't share himself with her. It was too hard, too painful. He didn't know exactly what he had had in mind, coming here, being with her, but it wasn't to talk about himself. "There's a bio on the back cover of every book."

She knew, she had read it. It had said next to nothing. Nothing about his family, his past, except that he had gone to school in the Midwest. Who was he? Why were his eyes so eloquently sad?

"I want to know more."

He said nothing. Annie folded her hands before her. "If you died tomorrow, what would your obituary say?"

She certainly didn't give up easily. He couldn't help the grin. "That I knew there wasn't any happily-ever-after all along."

Annie laughed. She had met her match as far as words were considered. Perhaps as far as everything was concerned. "You're impossible."

He toasted her with his half-empty wine glass. "I try my best."

The waiter took the tray with Marcus's card. Annie looked on as a couple walked by their booth. They were crossing to the area in the back that had been cleared off for dancing. The song that came drifting from there was low and bluesy. Annie had a need to be held in a man's arms. His arms. "Dance with me?"

Marcus knew it would be a mistake. To hold her in his arms would be a mistake right now. He felt particularly vulnerable, particularly in need of her warmth. When the waiter reappeared, he took the diversion gratefully and signed his name to the receipt. "I don't dance."

His body, tall and graceful, was made for dancing, for smooth movements. She couldn't picture him being awkward. "You're kidding."

She never stopped, did she? A lot of people didn't know how to dance. "When have you known me to kid?"

"Well, then, it's high time you learned. To do both." Annie rose and took his hand. The retreating waiter grinned at them.

Marcus stayed where he was. "Even if I was so inclined to let you teach me—and I have absolutely no desire to learn—it wouldn't be in the middle of a crowded floor." Although, if he were to hold her, that probably would be the safest place to do it.

No, touching her was never safe. He knew that.

She prided herself on knowing when to back off. "Sorry." Lifting her hands up in surrender, she sat down again. "I forgot who I was dealing with. Maybe we can find room in your closet.''

He was amused. "It's occupied."

She gave him a knowing look. "I bet it is." With skeletons from his past that he had yet to set free.

His had been a flippant retort. He wasn't about to ask her what she meant by hers if his life depended on it. "Ready to leave?"

"No, but you are." She picked up her clutch purse and rose with a sigh. "I don't know any more about you than I did before. You shadowbox well."

"I've been getting a lot of practice lately," he said as he escorted her out.

Leaving the close, intimate atmosphere of the restaurant didn't help. Filling his lungs with fresh, cool air didn't help. It didn't stop him from wanting her, from knowing that if he had taken her in his arms on the dance floor, he wouldn't have wanted to let go. He would have wanted to take her home with him and make love with her until he had rid himself of his need for her. Or until the twelfth of never, whichever came first.

He was beginning to have a frightening feeling that if nothing else, he knew the answer to that part.

Asking her over to his home was still on the tip of his tongue even as he brought his car down the narrow street to her front door.

Overwhelming things, urges, he thought. But he wouldn't allow himself to be governed by physical wants or emotional cravings.

The light on her front porch was on. Marcus brought his car up to the curb, then cut off the engine. For a moment, he just sat there, silent, watching the pale moonlight filtering through the interior of his car. It bathed half her face in light and half in shadow. He didn't know which he found more alluring.

And which would spell his ultimate defeat.

"We're here," Marcus murmured, his hands still gripping the steering wheel tightly.

"I recognize the house." She wanted him to come in. Why didn't he ask her if he could?

Never say die, she told herself. He had overcome one obstacle and met her part of the way. She could go the rest of the distance. "Want to come in?"

Yes. A great deal. He didn't release the wheel. "It's late."

"I have a watch." She raised her right hand. "I know what time it is. That wasn't what I asked." She saw his brow furrow. He probably thought she was being flippant again. "Okay, I'll ask an easier question. Would you like to take a walk? It's a beautiful night, and I don't want the evening to end yet."

When she looked at him like that, he couldn't say no. Besides, what harm would it do? And he did want to be with her for a little while longer. "All right."

"One point for the home team."

But she smiled softly as she said it so he didn't bother to retort. Instead, he got out and opened her door, then took her hand. She curled her fingers around his and left it there. It seemed natural.

"It's really a very nice neighborhood," she told him. "Grandpa picked it because he loved the ocean. Do you?"

He let her choose the direction, trying not to think how right her hand felt in his. She was only a temporary part of his life. It was senseless to form an attachment. Worse than senseless. It was stupid. "When I get the time to get down."

"Marc," she chided indulgently, "you're in Southern California. There's always beach around somewhere within a few miles. You're shattering our surfboard, sun-bleached image."

The lights in the beach community were muted, just as the restaurant's had been. The night was warm, but the breeze from the ocean kept it from being hot. It was a night made for loving, Marcus thought.

So would Nome, Alaska, have been. With her.

Get a grip, Sullivan, he ordered. "I was never one for images."

"No, I didn't think you would be."

As they walked past the next house, a weather-beaten two-story building, a dog began barking ferociously. Marcus started.

"That's Chauncey, Beatrice's lover," Annie explained. "He's a lot smaller than he sounds."

Marcus looked down at her face. She was being absolutely serious. "Who the hell is Beatrice?"

"My dog. She tempted Chauncey once too often." An affectionate grin spread on her face as she thought of her pet. "She's going to have puppies any day now."

Marcus pitied Chauncey. The dog probably never stood a chance if Beatrice was anything like her mistress. "Fascinating."

"Attraction always is."

He didn't answer. Because she knew he'd prefer it, they walked in silence for a bit.

He discovered another unnerving thing. He felt relaxed with the silence between them. Felt oddly comfortable with her despite the need to possess her, to finally discover the secrets that were waiting for him. But he wasn't ready for a relationship, knowing the pain and disappointment that was involved in caring about someone. He wasn't going to risk rejection.

He never wanted to care about anyone again. Only writing was a constant. It was the only thing he could depend on.

And yet, why couldn't he stop this powerful need rising within him, this need to matter to someone, to make a difference? To connect?

They came to a halt at the end of the long winding block next to a darkened art gallery on the corner. Across the street was a restaurant, brightly lit in contrast. The outdoor tables were filled with people, couples enjoying each other. He didn't want to walk past them. "I think I'd better take you home."

Annie looked across the street. Why did the sight of happiness make him retreat? "My place or yours?" Her eyes were twinkling.

"Your doorstep."

"You are precise." She raised herself up on her toes just before he turned to make his way up the block again and whispered, "Coward," teasingly into his ear.

Her warm breath sent a shiver down his spine, and he reacted before he could stop himself. Forgetting the people at the café, forgetting everything but the woman in front of him, he framed her face in his hands and kissed her.

He felt alive for the first time all day.

The kiss was rougher than she had come to expect from him and all the more thrilling because of it. Anticipation hummed through every pore of her body as she gave herself to the wonderful sensation that Marcus created within her. Without her realizing it, a little moan of pleasure escaped.

Marcus felt her soft gasp vibrate against his lips. The excitement it triggered couldn't be measured by any scale man had created. Sliding his hands along her back, he felt Annie arch her body into his. The feast she offered him was far more sumptuous than anything he had had tonight. Above the passion he detected a trusting innocence that overwhelmed him. She was vulnerable. Dear God, he had never thought of her in that light, not really. It was an awesome responsibility.

With the utmost effort, Marcus regained himself and slowly pulled free of the vortex. He didn't have to look to see the smile of satisfaction on her face. He knew it was there. He *felt* it. "Let's go," he muttered.

"To the ends of the earth if you want."

Her laughter had the same effect on him as her kiss did. How the hell was he going to get through the next few weeks with his soul intact? He walked faster.

She trotted to keep pace. "Why are we jogging, Marc?"

"We're not jogging. I suddenly remembered something I have to do at home." *Like get there.*

They reached her front door in a few minutes. "It was a lovely evening, Marc, even though you had trouble getting out of the phone booth."

He was all set to go. That stopped him. "*Now* what are you talking about?"

She turned her face up to him, amusement in her eyes. "Clark Kent, shedding his disguise and becoming Superman." She lightly placed a fingertip in the center of his chest and tapped it. "I know he's in there somewhere."

He took her hand and elaborately returned it to her side. "Now you're babbling."

"Speaking metaphorically," she corrected him.

"Babbling," he repeated.

She pretended to shiver and ran her hands up and down her arms. "I love it when you're forceful."

"You are an infuriating, exasperating, crazy woman." So why did she reduce the pit of his stomach to a semiliquid consistency every time he kissed her?

"Thank you."

He tried his best to look annoyed, but he knew he really wasn't. "I didn't mean it as a compliment."

She could read the look in his eyes. He was weakening. "Yes you did."

He shook his head. "There you go again, putting words into my mouth."

"If I were to put anything into your mouth—" she raised herself on her toes again "—or near your mouth—" her arms were on his for balance "—it would be this." She tilted her head back, her eyes half shut, her mouth inviting, inches away from his.

It wasn't an invitation he could refuse, especially with the impression of her last kiss still blazing hot on his lips. But he hoped he was in control enough to just kiss her this time and break free quickly.

He was wrong. He would never be able to break free.

The quick, gentle kiss blossomed in proportions until a tiny daisy had evolved into a giant sunflower, startling the planter beyond words. The power and intensity of his passion, of hers meeting his, rocked him. He heard his own blood rushing in his ears, exhilarating him, lifting him to plateaus he would have staunchly maintained did not exist.

Until he scaled them.

He couldn't deny their existence anymore. He was a believer. A shaken, reluctant believer.

Yes, she thought, yes! She arched against him, tangling her fingers in his thick, dark hair.

She hadn't imagined it, hadn't just wished it into being. It was there. She could taste it. The desire, the passion, the need, dark and exciting. All there in proportions that enveloped her and made her feel safe even as it spun her on the rim of a giant top going faster, ever faster.

She felt his hands go up her back as she gripped his arms again. Her hold tightened until the fabric beneath bunched and wrinkled as she clung. She didn't dare let go. If she did, she'd spin out to the edge of the universe and no one would ever find her again.

He felt every inch of her body against his. Hunger burned bright. The sensation in his soul could only be likened to the way he felt standing on the beach after a wave had washed over him and then tried to reclaim the sand beneath his feet. He was being pulled out to sea.

He was going to go under.

When he could finally think clearly enough to stop, he found that he was shaken and struggling for a semblance of balance. For a moment, there were no words, no sounds. His own emotions and hers had rendered him speechless.

Trouble. He was in deep trouble. He didn't want this, couldn't want this. And yet, he wanted nothing more. Yes, he thought, he was in deep trouble.

Marcus took a step back from her. "You'd better get some sleep if we're going to work tomorrow."

"Right." The word was hardly a whisper as she pressed her lips together, sealing in the taste of his.

This was something big, she thought. She was tottering on the brink of something very big. Maybe she should slow down before she burnt up like a meteor plummeting into the earth's atmosphere.

She stood on her doorstep, taking a slow, deep breath as he moved away from her and toward his car. She was still standing there when he pulled away.

He reached home. He wasn't exactly certain of the route, only of the thoughts that were crowding through his brain, falling into one another. Each thought was reinforced with the word *no*.

As Marcus walked into his house, the phone in his den began to ring. Perfect timing, he thought, wondering who would be calling at this time of night.

Holly, her square body wrapped in a sensible beige robe that whispered along the wooden stairs as she descended, was en route to the den to answer. It was his private line and there were no extensions in the house.

"Never mind," Marcus called up to her, slamming the front door behind him, "I'll get it."

Holly changed direction without a word and trudged up the stairs again.

He got to the phone on the seventh ring. Whoever it was, he thought, was persistent. "Hello?" When he heard her voice, he realized he should have known.

"I think it's time," she said, drawing out each word as if it was just occurring to her, "for you to work at my place. We can get started tomorrow."

"I think we already have," he answered, but he was giving his reply to a dial tone.

The sound of her voice vibrated through his brain long after she hung up.

Chapter Twelve

He couldn't sleep.

It wasn't the sudden, unexpected storm that had materialized with its repeated cracks of thunder, threatening the land like an angry fist of God. It was the sound of his blood pounding in his veins that created the restlessness that kept Marcus from finding a place for himself in his bed.

More simply put, it was Annie.

Every time he closed his eyes, he would see her before him: warm, inviting. Making his mouth go dry. A siren on the rocks of destruction, beckoning him on to eventual heartbreak. He had told her the truth. He didn't believe in things continuing "happily ever after." Happiness, if it came at all, came in short, minuscule amounts and then evaporated, leaving devastation and bereavement in its wake. The lesson had been taught to him by his parents' behavior and brought even closer home by Jason and Linda's deaths. That had been the final straw—to venture out, to hope, only to be beaten down and deprived at the end. He didn't want to experience that sense of loss again. He didn't want what she had to offer.

He didn't think he could live without it.

Marcus swore under his breath and sorely wished for once that he was a drinking man. He wanted to numb his senses, douse his brain so that his emotions were doused as well. It wouldn't solve a damn thing, but at least for a little while, it would let him forget. It would let him sleep.

Marcus threw off his sheet and got up. He was too keyed up, too wired, to stay in bed and wait for sleep that refused to come.

And then he heard it.

The sound was faint, almost muffled, but it stood out against the sharp crack of thunder. It was—

Marcus listened closer, turning his head to find the direction the sound was coming from.

It was whimpering. Someone was whimpering.

Nathan.

Forgetting his robe in his haste, Marcus opened the double doors of his bedroom and stepped out into the dark hallway. He inclined his head toward Nathan's room. He heard it again. He'd been right. First came the thunder, then the sound of a frightened whimper.

God, how many nights had he cowered as a child, listening to thunder and not having someone there to tell him that it was all right? Too many to count. Enough to make him always remember.

Marcus placed his hand on the doorknob, then stopped before he could open the door. Not from restraint, but for Nathan's sake.

Instead, he knocked, giving the boy a moment to pull himself together. "Nathan, the storm's got me up and I was wondering if you'd mind keeping me company."

Behind the door, Nathan rubbed away tear stains with the back of his hand, gulping in snatches of air. His father had never told him that it was wrong for a man to cry, but he didn't think that his father's friend shared that belief. He didn't want to displease Mr. Sullivan. Mr. Sullivan was all Nathan had left of his father. "Su-sure."

Marcus opened the door a little at a time, hoping that the boy wouldn't be embarrassed, yet wanting to let him know that he wasn't alone. Being alone at that age was the worst thing in the world.

He remembered how awful it felt.

"Thanks." Marcus walked in and shut the door behind him. "I—um—"

Now what? He was as unsure of how to proceed with the boy as he was with the woman. Except that the boy needed him, and need was something he couldn't turn his back on.

Marcus studied the small, flushed face. Nathan was trying so hard to look unconcerned, but the tension was evident everywhere, in the way he sat, in his eyes. Marcus's heart went out to him.

"Want to come into my room? It's bigger. And we can talk."

Nathan flashed a relieved smile that told Marcus he had made the right move.

"About what?" the boy wanted to know, climbing out to join him. He felt safer next to Mr. Sullivan. Protected. The thunder couldn't get him as long as there was light and someone to talk to.

Guided by instincts that Annie kept telling him she saw in his writing, a fact that she was more convinced of than he, Marcus ran his hand lightly over Nathan's fine, dark brown hair.

"Anything you want to talk about." *And I sincerely hope you've got a subject handy,* he added silently, momentarily wishing that Annie was here. She was better at this than he was. A lot better.

He saw the fear flicker in Nathan's face as they approached his darkened room. Nonchalantly Marcus switched on the light. Nathan relaxed.

Small round eyes looked up at the tall man, half hopefully, half fearfully. "Can we talk about Dad?"

Marcus let half a beat go by because the question had found him unprepared. "If you like."

"I think I would. It'll kinda help." He could put it in no better words than that. But it was enough.

Marcus pulled down the rest of the covers on his bed. "Want to climb in?" He sat down on one edge and pretended to test the mattress. "It's a pretty comfortable bed as far as those things go."

There was nothing Nathan wanted more than to spend the rest of the night beneath Marcus's protective wing. At home, when he had had a home, he'd climb in with his parents whenever a storm or a scary dream had frightened him. His father had always made the monsters go away. They were afraid of him. Monsters were always afraid of football players, his dad had told him. Nathan stared at Marcus, wondering about his powers over monsters.

Marcus saw the question in Nathan's eyes. "What?"

"Are monsters afraid of writers?"

Marcus went with it. "Terrified."

"Really?"

"Absolutely." Without waiting, Marcus got in on his side and left the choice up to Nathan. "Writers can make them disappear into thin air without a trace."

Nathan had pictured his father beating monsters up and knocking them out. This was something new. Carefully the boy climbed into the bed, trying not to pull the sheets out of place. "How can they do that?"

Marcus leaned over, elaborately looked around to make sure that "no one" was listening, and whispered, "We erase them."

Nathan covered his mouth and giggled. It immediately occurred to Marcus that he had never heard a more heartwarming sound. Except, perhaps, the sound of Annie's laughter, but then another part of him had been warmed besides his heart.

He couldn't help thinking of Annie, even now. She would have approved of this, he thought, approved of his letting a frightened boy share his room. Well, he hadn't done it because of her. He had done it because once, a long time ago, he had been terrified of thunder, of the sky suddenly lighting up at night for no reason and making angry sounds. He had wanted to be reassured that it wasn't seeking him out for some boyish wrongdoing. He would have given his soul to have crept into either one of his parents' separate bedrooms, into either one of their beds. But he had been rebuffed by both and told to be a little man. He had been a frightened little man for many long nights.

"That's pretty cool," Nathan commented, in awe of Marcus.

Marcus tucked the sheets around the boy. "I think so." It was getting easier to play along.

"My dad was never afraid of monsters." There was love and longing in each word.

"No," Marcus said, leaning back and remembering, "the only thing your dad was ever afraid of was low grades."

Pencil-thin crescent eyebrows drew together as Nathan tried to understand. "Why?"

"Because then he couldn't play football." Marcus looked at Nathan to see if he was following him. He wasn't. "Colleges have rules. If you have low grades, you can't play on the team."

"Oh."

Marcus thought back to the long, all-night sessions he had spent with Jason, staying up to try to cram enough information into Jason's head to help him through. Jason hadn't been bad in math and science, but English, English was a subject that his brain seemed to retain like a sieve. Marcus would tutor him until Jason could parrot the right phrases, hit the right buzzwords and eventually even distinguish a sonnet from a limerick. It hadn't been easy. But it had been infinitely rewarding to know he had had a hand in giving the university its star quarterback.

And as Jason rose in prominence, he pulled a protesting Marcus along with him for the ride, letting him sample the limelight. Letting him find the people that eventually lived on in his books.

Marcus blinked, realizing that Nathan was asking him something. "What?"

"Was he stupid?" Nathan didn't think so, but then he wasn't as smart as Mr. Sullivan. Maybe he knew better. Adults always thought they did, anyway.

"Your dad?" Marcus shook his head. "No, he wasn't stupid. He was the smartest man I ever knew." As he said the words, he knew that he meant them, had always meant them. "He knew how to enjoy life, how to find that joy and make it work for him."

Nathan's eyes were getting heavy, but he could still see that there was something sad about the man sitting next to him. "Don't you know how to find joy, Mr. Sullivan?"

His laugh was small, self-deprecating. "Not even if you drew me a map."

Nathan looked at Marcus uncertainly. "I don't draw maps very well."

Marcus laughed and ruffled the boy's hair. "Your dad couldn't draw very well, either."

Another peal of thunder and the boy cringed slightly, glancing over his shoulder. Effortlessly, naturally, Marcus gathered him close. "Why, I could remember a time when he had to do this relief map of . . ."

Marcus continued to talk, his voice soft, soothing. Story after story came back to him, and he talked until the boy was asleep. Suddenly he knew the subject of his next book. The last of the writer's block broke apart as if it had never existed. His next book would be about Jason, about them. About the friendship that blossomed between two out-of-state boys on their own for the first time who found something within each other to help them face the world.

Gently Marcus slipped his arm away from Nathan's slight shoulders, taking care not to wake him. Tucking the sheet around the small body again, Marcus was surprised, and gratified, to discover what he was feeling at this moment. He loved Nathan. Really loved him like his own son.

"You don't ever have to be afraid of thunder again," he promised the sleeping boy.

Her house looked smaller in the daylight. Smaller and somehow cozier. The exterior was stark white. Marcus guessed that the house had been painted in the not too distant past. The salty sea air hadn't had a chance to eat away at it.

With conscious effort, he unclenched his hands that hung at his sides.

This was ridiculous. There was absolutely no reason to feel uncomfortable, standing on her front step, like a suitor about to embark on a first date. This wasn't a date, for God's sake. That was last night, and he had gotten through *that* without any bloodshed. Just barely.

This was just another work day.

So why did he feel as if he were about to face the firing squad without having had a chance to have his last wish granted?

He rang the bell. No one answered. He knocked sharply. Nothing. He pictured her in bed, still asleep. Impatiently he knocked again. And again. By the fourth time, he decided that she had forgotten about telling him to come over and had gone to his house. That would have been par for the course. It wasn't as if she was exactly stable.

No, he amended, that was unfair. She was stable. She was just—

Enthusiastic was the only word that he could think of that would even begin to describe what she was, the *way* she was.

He was all set to leave, then he remembered that she loved the sea. Hadn't she mentioned something about a terrace? Knowing her and her regard for punctuality, she was probably sitting there right now.

Picking his way around the white picket fence—it figured, he thought—with scads of colored flowers leaning against it, he circled to the rear of the house. The land sloped so that the back was half a story above him. He shaded his eyes and looked up.

She was there, sitting in a white rattan chair, nursing a steaming mug of something or other.

He felt like throttling her. Why couldn't the woman be more professional? She didn't look the least bit surprised or chagrined to find him glaring at her.

She had lost track of time, thinking about him. It didn't faze her. "Hi."

"Didn't you hear me?" he wanted to know. "I was banging on your door for the last five minutes." The woman was totally irresponsible.

"Sorry." She flashed an apologetic smile and his annoyance vanished immediately. "The ocean tends to drown things out. Why don't you come in?" She indicated a path that led right to the stairs to the terrace.

He looked down. The decorator stones ended abruptly. The "path" was nothing but sand. "I'll get sand in my shoes."

She smiled down at him. "It shakes out."

Right now, he had the urge to shake her out. Out of his life, out of his dreams. Out of his fantasies. He crossed the sand and took the stairs up to her, a disgruntled Romeo approaching his Juliet.

He didn't take the chair she indicated with her eyes. He held the briefcase full of manuscript pages aloft. "Are we going to work out here?"

"No, we're going to drink coffee out here and enjoy the view." She was already pouring coffee into a mug. A scene from a popular cartoon movie danced around the sides of the mug. She'd been waiting for him to join her, he realized. "*Then* we're going to work."

He didn't want to be comfortable with her. It might become a habit. "I don't want to waste time—" There was no heart in his protest.

"Enjoying nature's handiwork is never a waste of time."

Seeing no way out, he sat down and took the mug she pressed on him.

"Sit back, enjoy," she coaxed, her voice as hypnotic as the repetitive rhythm of the sea. She picked up her mug and leaned back. "Isn't it breathtaking?"

Yes. But he was looking at her, not the view. Her lips were slightly parted as she stared out at the ocean endlessly caressing the shore with curled fingers of white foam. She seemed in awe of it, with her hair tied back away from her face, her face bare of makeup, dressed only in the glow of enthusiasm.

"Breathtaking," he agreed.

She looked toward him, aware that he wasn't looking at the ocean. The glint of desire in his eyes made her want, yet there was a part of her that was still fearful, a part that was still the tiniest bit raw.

"Well—" she took a breath "—since we've agreed on something, I think we should get to work. Might as well strike while the moment's promising." She rose and took his hand. "C'mon, I've cleared off a work area for us inside."

She opened the sliding glass door and led the way into the family room. Unaccustomed to the decreased light, Marcus almost tripped over something on the floor. There were several things scattered haphazardly on the floor, he noted. She wasn't exactly a fanatic about housekeeping. But this "something" was shaggy. And moving.

"Careful!" Annie cried, dropping to her knees. "Are you all right?"

"I'm fine." He felt self-conscious. Why was she on her knees? After all, he hadn't fallen. And he knew her well enough to know she wasn't about to start cleaning now. "I regained my bal—"

She looked up, confused, and then amused. "No, not you. I was talking to Beatrice."

The woman talked to mops. It fitted. He looked at her, then at it. "To whom?"

"My dog, remember?" She held the dog in her arms as she rose to her feet. With a light, gentle touch, she stroked the dog, murmuring endearments. "I told you last night. She's going to have pups any day now, and I don't want to upset her."

Maybe that was the answer. Maybe he should pretend to have pups and she'd try not to upset him.

He dragged both hands through his hair. He was beyond "upset" and on his way to a nervous breakdown, total and complete, he judged. If he weren't, he wouldn't have had that insane thought, even cynically.

"Oh yes, the tryst with Chauncey." Because the dog's face was adorable, Marcus petted the animal. Beatrice responded by licking him. He pulled his hand back, then saw Annie looking at him curiously.

"It felt rough," he explained.

"All dogs' tongues are rough." Annie scratched Beatrice behind the ears. "Haven't you ever been licked by a dog before?"

"No."

His dog probably graduated top in his class in obedience school and repressed the urge to lick. Annie looked at the expression on Marcus's face. A thought dawned on her. "Didn't you ever have one?"

"No."

No one should live their life without having a pet at some point. The solution was obvious. "Well, when she has pups—"

He saw the look entering her eyes. He knew how her mind worked. That fact that he did was a sobering thought. "No." He raised his hands as if to ward her off for emphasis. "Absolutely not. Don't even think it. Now can you please put Lassie down so we can get to work?"

Annie obliged, sending Beatrice on her way. "Lassie would be too large for me to hold."

He let the remark pass. And then he looked around, really looked. "How can you work here in all this chaos?" There was too much clutter. It made him feel claustrophobic. She had knickknacks on every conceivable surface.

He felt hemmed in here, trapped. Just as he had suspected he would. He wasn't meant to be with her in such a tiny space. He searched for his temper, because temper was all he had to protect him from her. From himself. It wouldn't come.

"I—" she looked up at him "—can work anywhere, anytime." She thought of his den. "Even under pristine conditions." She felt the electricity crackling between them.

There was no escaping it. "You'd better kiss me and get that out of the way before we get down to work."

It was no longer a surprise to him how correctly she read him and even less of a surprise how much he wanted to kiss her.

"All right, anything to get this screenplay over with," he murmured against her mouth.

He didn't give her a chance to laugh the way she seemed ready to. He was too hungry for her. God, the more he had, the more he wanted. It was like being addicted, like having no say in his life anymore.

He had a say. He could say no. But he didn't want to. Not yet. Soon, but not yet. Slowly his lips moved on a languid, exhilarating journey of her mouth, her cheekbones, her eyes, his own breath catching fast as the beat of his heart increased.

His hands tugged out the final inch of her T-shirt from her jeans, then slipped beneath. He needed to hold her, to touch her, to feel her skin. She moaned and moved closer. He found himself going on instincts alone, instincts that fueled the fire raging within him. Almost reverently, he moved his hands up her body until he cupped the swell of her breasts. He fought to keep the spasm that traveled through his body from seizing him.

She had wanted to let herself drift, to flow with this feeling, to let him mold her. His hands were gentle, warm, possessive, and she wanted him desperately. She found she had to hang on with both hands. Needs slammed through her, making her heart thud against her rib cage. There had been only one other man she had allowed to come so far, both physically and emotionally, and she was hungry to go the distance, to love again.

His mouth was greedy and passionate, and excited so much more than it soothed. She felt his lips framing her face, touching her jawline, her throat. Pulses jumped everywhere he touched. And then his lips were covering hers again.

The kiss was hard and impatient, draining her as much as it drained him. Over and over, his lips slid over hers, challenging, daring, taking, losing and winning.

If he didn't stop now, he'd be beyond the point of no return. He would take her right here and now, in the midst of all this clutter. Something, fear, held him back.

Forcing himself back before he tumbled into the abyss she had cracked open for him, he buried his face in her hair.

It smelled of the sea. And flowers. "I think we've gotten that out of the way," he said into her hair, trying to steady the erratic beating of his heart. "Let's get to work."

Out of the way? she thought, still dazed. *No, my friend, we've gotten more into the way. Much, much more than we bargained for. But have it your way for now.*

"All right." Braced, she took a step back, then tucked her T-shirt back into the waistband of her jeans. "We'll work here, by the window. It's almost the same view as from the terrace."

The same view. The same world. But nothing, he knew, was ever going to be the same again. Not for him, not after her.

He looked at the woman who stimulated him beyond belief and wondered if the devil tended toward disguises of long blond hair and almond-shaped blue eyes. He decided that he must. For Marcus knew that he was surely losing his soul as well as his mind.

Chapter Thirteen

It was progressing.

They were four weeks into the screenplay, and it was going far better than he had initially anticipated. It was actually going according to schedule, no thanks to her, he thought irritably as he glanced at his watch and wondered where she was. Annie argued with him over every point, every scene, every bit of dialogue.

Of course she said *he* argued, but he knew better. If she would only go along with things, there would have been no arguments. After all, it took two to argue.

But she insisted on putting her stamp on things, telling him that *The Treasured Few* needed "the woman's point of view." He had pointed out that it hadn't needed "the woman's point of view" to explode on the bestseller list. She had only smiled that infuriating, inscrutable smile of hers and gone on defending her position like a dog hanging on to a bone until he threw up his hands and surrendered.

With a critical eye, he perused the pages that she had printed on the computer yesterday and was forced to grudgingly admit that, despite his peppered words to the contrary, what was evolving was a piece of quality entertainment fit to captivate even the toughest audience. She brought out the best in him. At least on paper.

They were different, he thought. So different. She wrote with people in mind. He wrote only to please himself. That way, there was no danger of feeling the sting of someone's disapproval. He had told himself that he was above that, that he no longer felt hurt when someone rejected his effort, but deep within his soul, he still did.

He let the pages fall back on his desk and went over to the window.

Where *was* she? It was her idea to work here today. They kept shifting work areas like gypsies moving from camp to camp. He should have insisted that they continue working at her place. At least he'd know where she was.

He let the curtain drop. She was late—again—and he was watching for her like a schoolboy watching for the girl next door. He laughed at his own thought. The only way she could have qualified for that title was if he was living next door to some sort of an amusement park.

The screech of tires on his driveway told him she had finally arrived. The flying figure that passed his den on the way to the front door he identified as Nathan. A Nathan whose cheeks were no longer hollow, whose eyes were no longer haunted and sad. Marcus would have liked to have felt that he alone was responsible for the change, but knew it was only partly because of him. A small part. The main contributor to Nathan's transformation was Annie.

Annie, always Annie.

No, not always, he reminded himself. She'd be gone soon. As soon as the screenplay was wrapped up, she would flow mercurially out of their lives the same way she had flowed into them. It was her nature.

Marcus heard Nathan's voice as the boy greeted Annie and then squealed. "For me?"

Now what? It was obvious that she had brought something for the boy. Again. She had already presented Nathan with a video game system, not to mention a collection of children's videos, both games and movies. By the cry that Nathan uttered, Marcus judged that this was something more exciting than just a game. Nathan sounded completely animated. Like her. It made for a frightening thought.

Maybe she had brought along her niece and nephew. No, Nathan sounded as if whatever it was entitled him to possession. The boy hadn't learned Annie's trick about possessing souls yet.

Okay, so what was it? Consumed with curiosity, Marcus left the sanctuary of his den and walked into the foyer. Nathan and Annie, with Holly hovering close by, were still at the front door.

Holly was clucking and circling Annie and Nathan like a mother hen, her attention, as well as Nathan's, on the contents of the box Annie was carrying. A box that was making noise.

Annie looked his way just as Marcus crossed to them, her eyes wide, smiling. It disarmed him every time even when he thought he was braced for it. "Hi."

He hid the fact that he had been impatiently anticipating her arrival for reasons other than their work. "You're late."

She was used to that tone of voice by now. And immune to the censure. "You're predictable."

"That's one thing no one'll ever accuse you of being." Marcus saw that the pronouncement pleased her. "What did you bring this time?"

"It's a puppy!" Nathan exclaimed just as a wet, pink tongue got him on the cheek and branded him for life. Nathan was instantly and completely in love. The euphoric look abated only a little as the boy looked Marcus's way. "Is it all right, Mr. Sullivan? Can I keep him?"

Nathan still wasn't completely secure here, Marcus realized. He still acted like a guest who expected to be evicted for the smallest transgression.

Marcus reached out and scratched the taffy-colored fur. The puppy twirled about in his small space and eagerly licked his hand as well. "If I said no, I'd feel guilty to my dying day."

Annie laughed, satisfied. "Good. It worked." She pushed the box into Nathan's hands. "I now pronounce you boy and dog."

She had engineered this, just as she did everything else. Marcus knew he could say no, that he *had* said no when she had offered to bring him a puppy. But was control so important to him that he could disappoint Nathan? He knew the answer to that. Establishing and maintaining control around Annie wasn't nearly as important as the radiant smile of a seven-year-old boy.

"Yes," Marcus agreed. "It worked. I take it Beatrice is willing to part with this one?"

Beatrice had had her litter over five weeks ago. It was time to start finding them homes before she grew too attached to all of them. By she, Annie was thinking of herself, not her dog. Annie hated parting with anything that was a piece of her life.

"This one is the runt of the litter and keeps getting pushed out of the way by the others. I thought Nathan might want to lend a hand and help him get his proper nourishment." She ruffled Nathan's hair. He was so involved with the bundle of fluff that he hardly noticed. "How about it, Nathan? Are you up to helping?"

The puppy licked his face again and kept on licking. Nathan laughed with glee. "Yes!"

Annie raised her eyes to the housekeeper. "Holly?" The request went without saying.

Holly's mouth puckered as she pressed her lips together. "It always comes down to that, doesn't it? Let Holly tend to it."

"Well, I—" Holly wasn't fooling her. She was as pleased about Nathan getting a pet as she was in giving him one.

Holly raised a hand to dismiss any further words from Annie. Nice trick, Marcus thought. Maybe he could ask her to teach it to him.

"C'mon," Holly said to Nathan as she put an arm around his shoulders and turned him in the direction of the kitchen. "I think I can rig up a bottle for him."

One down and one to go, Annie thought, turning to Marcus. "Thank you for letting him keep the puppy."

He shrugged away her words carelessly, turning toward the den. "I never had a choice, you know."

Another man might have. A harder man. "Yes, I know. You know, Marc, I've been thinking—"

Marcus stopped in the doorway. "Oh God, should I head for the hills?"

Annie grinned. "Yes."

Someday, if he lived to be that old, he was going to understand her without benefit of explanations. The fact that he was even remotely planning to wait around that long in her company amazed him. "Would you care to elaborate a little on that?"

"Absolutely." She crossed to him, winding her arm through his. He was trapped in every sense of the word and only a little uncomfortable about it. Had he been more alert, he would have been worried. "The second half of this movie takes place near Santa Barbara, right?"

He raised a brow, wondering what she was up to. "You *have* been paying attention."

"Cynic." She laughed. "I just thought that maybe we should go up there for the day, you know, soak up the atmosphere a little and bring the flavor back with us."

The only flavor he really wanted to soak up was the flavor of her mouth. Especially when her lips were so close to his.

With effort, he disentangled his arm from her grasp. "I *was* up there," he informed her. It had been there that the idea for the story had germinated, in a quaint little town that hadn't quite hurried its way into the last quarter of the century.

She wasn't about to let him talk his way out of this. She wanted to go away with him for even just a day. They needed this time together, needed more than just an hour or two shared in a restaurant. She wanted him to herself. "When?"

"When I first started writing it. Three years ago. Maybe four." He switched on his computer and sat down, ready to work.

She said nothing in reply. Instead, when he looked at her, there was that look on her face, that look that said she knew she had made her point.

He leaned back in his chair, staring at the empty screen thoughtfully. It had been a long time since he had been up there last. Too long. He thought back. It had been a peaceful time. A good time. Suddenly he wanted to show it to her, share it with her, and though he knew he was probably making an error, he went with it as if, like with the puppy, he had no choice. Because as far as he was concerned, he hadn't.

"All right, we'll go."

"When?"

The woman was never satisfied. "I suppose you'd like to go today." He did know her. It was scary. And strangely exhilarating.

Unsuccessfully she attempted to appear submissive and patient. "If it's all right with you."

He gave a short laugh and switched off his computer. There was no use pretending that any work was going to get done today. "As if my opinion mattered."

Annie stood in the doorway. Suddenly there was nothing and no one. "But it does," she said quietly. And more than anything else, she wanted his opinion to meld with hers.

God, he could almost believe her. If he let himself. Shaking his head to clear it, he picked up the telephone receiver. "I need to make a few arrangements," he muttered, turning so that he couldn't look at her. If he didn't see her, he couldn't want her.

And the river only flowed when you watched it. He *was* a fool, and he was quickly getting past the point where he cared.

With determination, he jabbed at several numbers on the telephone. There was an appointment he had to cancel. And a redwood he had to see.

He had just ended his phone conversation and hung up when Annie walked back into the den, a large basket slung over her arm.

They really were on the road to Oz, he thought, and she was carrying Toto in her hamper.

"What's this?" He tapped the hamper as Annie set it down on his desk. "Did you bring another dog you wanted to get rid of?"

He didn't really understand her yet, did he? she thought. "I didn't really want to get rid of the first one."

But she had brought it to Nathan. "Then why—?"

"I thought that Nathan needed a friend—besides you," she added pointedly.

Her statement made him self-conscious. "I'm not—" He was about to say that he didn't think that Nathan saw him in that light.

She was quick to stop his denial. "Nathan thinks you are."

"Does he?"

He sounded almost eager when he asked, Annie thought. No, she hadn't been wrong about the man. She had been very, very right. "Yes. He does."

Marcus cleared his throat, embarrassed by his own show of emotion. "Okay, now what's that?" He nodded at the basket.

She let him retreat. "That's lunch. Holly packed a picnic lunch for us."

Marcus could only stare at the hamper. "Holly? A short, squat woman in orthopedic shoes? The one who gives lectures about the importance of having hot meals? The woman who wants to outlaw fast-food places?"

"The very same." For his benefit, Annie lifted the lid. "You'll note the abundance of fruits and nuts." She moved aside the linen napkins. "No cold cuts. Only pieces of cold fried chicken."

Only Annie could have managed this, he thought. Holly believed in decorum, in meals served on time and at the table. His respect for Annie's powers of persuasion went up another notch. But then, look at the hoops she had him jumping through.

He ran his fingers over the woven hamper. "I didn't even know we had a picnic basket."

Annie let the lid fall again and picked up the basket. "You don't. I do."

"And you brought it." She was running true to form. She might act as if she were scattered, but he was beginning to believe that she left very little to chance.

Delicate shoulders lifted and fell in an innocent shrug. "Just in case."

Right. He'd just bet.

She was already ushering him to the door, one arm linked through his. Marcus looked around for Nathan. "What about Nathan?"

"He's opted to stay with the puppy." Annie opened the front door.

Marcus eyed her as he stepped over the threshold. "Is this a planned seduction?" Not that he had any objections to one. Another clear sign that he was losing his grip and his mind.

The innocent expression on her face made her look like an angel. "We're only going to see trees and recapture a mood. Besides, you're the one who made the decision to go today."

The front door closed behind him. Now that he noticed it, it was a perfect day for a picnic. His first picnic, he realized. There were a lot of firsts with her. "As if I had a choice."

"Why, Mr. Sullivan." Annie fluttered her lashes at him and her voice took on a slow, southern lilt. "I thought that you above all people had a choice." She grinned at him, the lilt fading. "You're not a man to be bullied into anything. You wouldn't be doing this if you didn't want to." She wanted him to know that. She stood next to the car, waiting for him to unlock the door.

She was right. He *did* want to. Which, he supposed, made it all the worse. It was something he was going to have to ponder.

Later.

It was a three-hour drive, much of it through sparsely populated country. In a subtle way, it renewed his faith in nature, in life, in the importance of using his senses to take in beauty. When they finally reached their destination, a hundred and fifty miles later, Marcus had lost some of his hard-edged cynicism. It seemed that it had been unraveling steadily as the miles registered on the odometer. The farther away they were from the hub of the city, from L.A. and his home, the more approachable and relaxed he became.

He let her pick the place where they stopped. It was too beautiful a day to try to win bits and pieces of victories that he didn't care about. It was nice to agree about something for a change.

"What, no camera?" he asked as they wandered, hand in hand, down an isolated, scenic path that seemed to highlight nature at its best. "I would have thought you'd be taking tons of pictures." It was the kind of thing she'd do. He'd seen the photo album on her coffee table, crammed full of photographs, of memories. He envied her that.

"I am." When he looked at her quizzically, she touched a finger to her temple. "Up here. It's all being stored up here."

He looked amused as he brushed a hair away from her temple. "How will you ever find it again?"

"Very funny." She tightened her fingers around his. "You know, you're coming along, Sullivan. You're really coming along."

"Please, don't depress me."

She lifted herself up on her toes to lightly brush a kiss on his lips. A butterfly landing on a flower was heavier. The impression it made on his soul couldn't begin to be measured. "Not a chance, Marc."

He was enjoying himself, enjoying her. He felt, as they wandered around the tall redwood giants that had been there before man had felt a need to communicate with others of his species, as if he were seeing all this for the first time.

The afternoon was a joyous celebration of life itself. She had taken his hand easily and never released it. He found that there was a certain warmth, a certain feeling of well-being because her hand was curled in his. It felt, he realized, as if this was the way it was meant to be.

For the day, just for today, he could pretend to believe that.

Maybe he was getting too caught up in the romance of his story. He knew the danger in that. On paper, he could control the situation, could fix anything that got out of hand. If something didn't turn out the way he wanted it to, there was a delete button on his computer to press. Life didn't quite work like that. The only way to avoid having something turn sour was not to have it happen in the first place.

That meant having choices, implementing them, sticking to them once they were made. He had made his when she walked into his life, but he hadn't stuck to it. And now, as he sat cross-legged beneath a tree, watching her unwrap lunch, he had a feeling that the condemned man was having a last hearty lunch before the trap beneath his feet was sprung.

There was no way out.

Like a man gripping the sides of a toboggan that was poised on the very top of a snow-covered peak, Marcus knew his fate. He was about to go plummeting down. And all he could do was hang on.

Unless, of course, he thought as he sipped the wine, watching her every movement, he somehow managed to get up off the toboggan before it took that first plunge.

Fat chance.

She had been talking all this while, steadily and without more than a few seconds' pause between observations and thoughts. It didn't seem to disturb her, he noted, that he made little response.

"Do you realize that you talk while you chew? I didn't think a person could do that without choking." She didn't look the slightest bit chagrined when he pointed that fact out to her. "You talk incessantly."

She wiped her fingers slowly on a linen napkin. He couldn't help wondering what those fingers would feel like, moving that slowly along his flesh. "That's because you don't talk at all. Natures balances things out."

"Nature has nothing in its bag of tricks to balance you out." He paused, studying her. "Are you afraid of being alone with your thoughts?"

The slight wince told him that he had hit the mark, even though he hadn't really meant to. He hadn't meant to hurt her. He was just being philosophical.

"Sometimes."

His thoughts about being a condemned man faded as he stepped further into the trap. "Why?"

She shrugged, looking off into the distance. "Long story."

"And you're not up to it?" An incredulous note came into his voice. "This from a woman who just talked over a hundred and fifty miles? I find that rather hard to believe."

She smiled, but it was a smile tinged in sadness. A squirrel darted between two trees, then stopped, frozen, to stare. Annie pretended to be engrossed with it. "Some thoughts are private." She tossed the animal a bit of her bread.

The tables were turned. He found that incredible. "Mine aren't to you."

Nervously she tore off another bit of bread and threw it. "That's because I want to get to know you, the real you. The man I met in your books." The squirrel darted away, frightened, but scrub jays flew down to make off with what he had left behind.

Marcus placed his hand over hers, covering it. "Suppose I want to get to know you?"

She felt her heart beat harder. "Do you? Do you really?"

Yes, he thought, he did. He waited, but the sinking sensation did not come. "I don't say things I don't mean. There's not enough time in life for lies."

She liked that, liked that honesty in him. Whatever else he might be, he was a good man. An honest man.

For a moment, she said nothing. The fabric of the napkin seemed to hold her mesmerized. Just as he was about to say something, he heard her voice, low and still, as if she were afraid to let go of the emotion bound up within her. "I was in love once."

He felt a spasmodic tightening in his midsection and wondered hotly why that fact should bother him so much. But it did. Selfishly he hadn't wanted her to have loved someone else.

Nonsense, all nonsense, he told himself.

She had no idea what was running through his mind. "I thought that Charlie was my happily-ever-after person, like in the stories. I guess I was a product of my environment." A bittersweet smile creased her lips. "Movies."

"He left you?" Though he had voiced sentiments to the contrary, he couldn't picture anyone walking out on her. Not permanently. Except, of course, for him, but that was another matter. It didn't have anything to do with her. Just with him. And survival.

She closed her eyes, remembering. "Not of his own free will," she said softly.

"Then why?"

He wasn't prepared for the hurt in her eyes when she opened them again.

"He died. A little over a year ago. Very suddenly." Her words were short and rushed, pushed out in small staccato bursts as if she couldn't manage to say them any other way. "One of those stupid boat races. He hadn't even wanted to go, but his buddies talked him into it. One of them needed a first mate, or whatever those people are called who help steer." She looked up at him, tears shining in her eyes. Tears for the horrible waste it had all been. "It doesn't matter what they're called, I guess." She gestured helplessly. "I just like being accurate around you."

The smile she had on her face was brave and sad and wounded him. He grieved for her hurt even as he was jealous of the man who had created it.

"This time, you don't have to be. I don't know what they're called, either."

Because there was nothing else he could do, Marcus gathered her into his arms and kissed her. To wipe away her pain and to share it with her.

Chapter Fourteen

It was a soft, gentle kiss, with only the barest hint of what existed hidden beyond the barrier he was struggling to keep in place. It was all he could allow himself to do against the fear of exposing his emotions without having the certainty of being accepted. If he let the kiss deepen even the slightest bit, this time she would see the force of the emotions that he held in check. Emotions that even surprised him.

Her mouth was sweet, pliant. He had only to let himself go. Only to—

There were no happily-ever-afters. Believing in them was for fools.

He felt she wanted him, but did she? She was so different, so unpredictable. Maybe what he interpreted as interest in him was just her way of maintaining a friendly business relationship and nothing more. He created complex people on the page, but there he could control them. In real life, he found complexity overwhelming. He gravitated to order, predictability.

There was a faint rumble in the distance and the sun retreated, leaving only shadows in its wake, across the land, across his soul.

There was a storm approaching.

He pressed a kiss to her temple. "I think perhaps we'd better be getting back."

She sighed as he released her, trying to hide the deep frustration and the annoyance that was building up within her. For a moment, he had been kind, tender, and she had hoped that he might cross the imaginary line that separated them. It couldn't all be up to her. Not if it was to matter.

Each time that they were like this, each time he held her, kissed her, he'd bring her that much closer to the brink. This last time, she knew she was about to tumble over. But it had to be with him, not alone. And at the last moment, he had pulled away, leaving her emotionally stranded, as he sought refuge in that haven only he occupied.

For the first time, desperation clawed at her. She wanted to beat on him with both fists. To yell at him. To demand to know what it was that had rendered him an emotional cripple.

But what good would it do? He'd just look at her with those intense eyes of his, making her feel as if there was something the matter with her instead of the other way around.

What was she doing to herself, anyway, hitching a ride on this emotional yo-yo?

There was no way around it. She had to be crazy. And yet . . .

And yet, he *wanted* her, she knew it. She could taste it in his kiss, feel it in his touch, see it in his eyes. He was too straightforward a person to be pretending to care. Damn him, anyway.

Antsy, uncertain, Annie started placing the dishes into the hamper, although she would have rather thrown them at him. Maybe that would have gotten a rise out of the man. "I guess we've absorbed enough atmosphere for one day."

She leaned forward to pack what was left of the picnic into the basket. Her blouse fell forward, exposing the swell of her breast above her bra. She could see his reflection in the bottle. Without moving she glanced up at him and could see the desire on his face. Was it just a physical reaction? Or more? God, he had her so confused.

Marcus watched her as she cleared the blanket, saw the tension in her shoulders and knew it was because of him. He shoved his hands deep into his pockets and stared into the distance. "More than enough."

Now what was that supposed to mean? It was about time he did some explaining. She stopped packing and rocked back on her heels. "You seem interested, yet you back off as soon as things get started. Are you just playing some sort of a game with me? Is this your idea of fun?"

The hurt, angry tone in her voice surprised him. He wanted to protect himself, not wound her. "No, it's not any kind of a game." He swung around to look at her. "Look, I won't deny that I'm attracted to you, that I don't feel some—some kind of pull every time I kiss you."

She wasn't satisfied with that. She wanted more. She wanted reasons. "But?"

He blew out a sigh. "But I'm just not in the market for a relationship."

Annie jerked the blanket and pounded it into quarters as she folded it. She wished that it was him instead. "I didn't know you could find those kinds of things in a market, although laundromats seem to be up-and-coming among single people." With a thrust, she shoved the blanket on top of the hamper. "They say they might even take the place of a singles' bar."

He was trying to explain his feelings, a difficult thing for him at best, and she was talking about socks bringing people together. "Is everything a joke to you?" Grabbing the blanket, he held it in one hand and took the hamper in the other.

"Consider yourself lucky. If I wasn't making a joke, I'd be hitting you in the teeth. Take your choice. Lose them or use them."

He had never cared for her flippant remarks less. "You're right. We've absorbed enough atmosphere for today." The convertible was parked on the road a short distance away. He made for it. "Look, I've got enough in my life right now."

Annie walked behind him, mentally counting to ten. "It's just brimming to the top."

He had had just about enough of her high-handed opinions. The world did not operate according to her rules no matter what she thought. In addition, he was getting frustrated with his inability to express himself around her. "I've got my work."

She stared at the back of his head. It didn't look thicker than anyone else's. But it was. "Dandy substitute for living life firsthand."

Marcus tossed the hamper and blanket into the back seat of the convertible. The hamper tilted as it fell and the contents threatened to spill out. He left it where it was. "And a boy I'm not too sure what to do with yet." Wasn't that enough for her? How could he take on more now, no matter what his emotions said to the contrary?

"Do with?" she repeated, incredulously. Tired of looking at the back of his head, she placed a hand on his shoulder and made him turn around. "You make him sound like an erector set. You don't *do* anything with a boy like Nathan. You love him."

He was trying, but it wasn't that easy for him. "I have trouble relating to people." He had no idea why he was even bothering to explain himself.

Annie leaned against the car. "Why doesn't that surprise me?"

He raised his hands in exasperation. What did she want, blood? "I've already decided not to send him to military school—"

Her eyes wide. "Military school?" Was he out of his mind? Nathan would shrivel up and die in a military school. "You were actually considering sending him to military school?"

"Yes." Although he had rejected the idea, he grew defensive in the face of her attack. After all, he had only considered it because he thought it would help Nathan. "What's so wrong with that?"

If he didn't know, she didn't know how to tell him. Maybe she had been wrong about him after all. "You have no heart, Marc."

That was exactly his problem. He did. And it could feel pain. "Yes I do."

Then why are you always backing away from me? "Who says?"

"My doctor. It showed up in the X ray." My God, he was beginning to talk like her. His condition was getting serious.

She stared at him. How could he have even contemplated flushing the boy from his life like that? Easy, wasn't he trying to do the same with her? "Well, that's probably the only place it showed up."

Marcus clenched his hands at his sides. She was pushing him. "For two cents I'd—I'd—"

Annie raised her chin. "Yes?"

It was a tempting target. A very tempting target. He clenched his hands harder. "Nothing."

There were oaths she had heard her brother use once when he had lost a championship tennis match that would fit this occasion, but she kept them to herself. She was crazy, absolutely crazy to have thought that she was falling in love with this man. She was just fascinated by insanity, that was all, nothing more. Tall, dark and handsome only went so far. And in this case, not nearly far enough.

Annie surrendered. Maybe she had been wrong all along. It had been known to happen once or twice.

Feeling dejected, Annie climbed into the car on the passenger side. "Okay, let's go home." There was a note of resignation in her voice.

It was better this way, he told himself. They'd keep their relationship strictly professional. He'd been a fool to even entertain the idea that anything else was possible. Marcus got in and shoved the key into the ignition. When he turned it, nothing happened. He swore as he tried again.

The silence was ominous. "What's the matter?"

He didn't even look her way. "It won't start."

It's not the only thing, she thought. "Jiggle the key." Annie leaned over, her hand raised, ready to do it herself.

One dark look from Marcus had her withdrawing her hand. "I could jiggle the damn key until my hand fell off," he told her, "the car still won't start."

A fat drop fell on her face, followed immediately by another of equal size. Within a minute, a steady rhythm had begun. *Perfect, just perfect.* She glanced up, then down again quickly, as the rain increased. "Doesn't it know that it's not supposed to rain in July?"

Rain was beginning to plaster her hair to her face. She looked exactly the same way she had the first day she had burst into his life. Wet. Why was that so damn appealing? How could he feel drawn to her at the same time he wanted to strangle her?

"Maybe it's never read the California handbook." He really *was* beginning to talk like her.

But there was no time to contemplate the fatal consequences of that. Rain began falling with alarming force. Marcus looked at the top of his convertible neatly folded at the rear. He and Annie were already soaked, as was the interior of the car. He remembered seeing a house not too far back. "There was a house back on the road. Want to make a run for it?"

"What about your car?"

The interior would get soaked, but that could be remedied. Right now, he wanted to get her safe, out of the storm. "We'll worry about that later." The storm was getting worse. "Let's go!"

Annie was already out of the car. "Sounds good to me. I never cared too much for drowning."

Without thinking, he grabbed her hand and they made a dash for shelter.

The house, a modest one-story, wood-frame building, was further away than he remembered. By the time they got to it, they were both soaked to the skin. Marcus knocked on the door several times, but there was no answer.

They couldn't just stand out here all night. There were lights coming from within, but those could have been set on timers. "We give them one more chance," Annie decided, "and then we break in."

Marcus stared at her, trying to make sense out of what she was saying. She probably thought of this as an enactment of "Goldilocks and the Three Bears". He knew how her mind worked. "We can't just break in."

She rubbed her nose. It tickled, which meant there was a cold in the making. "Breaking in sounds a whole lot better than pneumonia."

She was definitely one of a kind. "But not better than jail," he pointed out.

The door swung open, ending the debate. The elderly woman inside the house took one look at them and then immediately stepped back. "Come in, come in," she urged, taking hold of Annie and ushering her inside. She was totally unfazed by the fact that a good deal of rain came in with them. "Henry," she called, "we have guests."

"More like drowned rats," Annie laughed, pushing wet bangs out of her eyes. "Hello." She extended her hand to the woman. "I'm Annie de Witt and this is Marc—"

The woman enveloped Annie's hand in both of hers. Her hands felt warm, inviting, as did her smile. "Your husband?" the woman supplied, beaming at Marcus. She looked down at Annie's hand, which was still cradled in hers. Annie's ring gleamed in the lamp light.

"Yes." If he was interrogated for the rest of his life, Marcus would never be able to explain what had possessed him to voice that lie. It had just come out, perhaps because it was a lot simpler than explaining. He put his hand out and shook hers.

"I'm Polly Flynn and this is Henry." She beckoned to the man who was just stepping into the living room.

The man was tall and loose-limbed and looked as if his bones jiggled with each step he took. His wife was short and round, with a wide face that seemed to naturally fill out with a smile. They made Annie think of the nursery rhyme about Jack Spratt and his wife. Annie liked them both instantly.

"Hello." Annie nodded toward the man. "We're awfully sorry to barge in on you like this."

Marcus hooked an arm around her waist as if the action could somehow keep her anchored. He had an uneasy feeling that she'd be off and running any second. "I'm afraid our car broke down about half a mile from here," he explained to the older man.

Marcus looked into the living room and tried to see if there was a telephone. There was none visible from his vantage point. "If we could use your phone to call a garage, we'll be out of your hair as soon as possible."

The man scratched the few remaining hairs that stubbornly clung to his head. "Only garage in the area closes at five." Henry's brows raised up high on his wide forehead as he looked at his watch. "It's half past that now. 'Fraid you're out of luck."

"You're welcome to spend the night here." The invitation was genuine, one look at Polly's eyes told them that. "We have a spare bedroom."

"We couldn't possibly put you out, Mrs. Flynn," Annie began.

"Polly," the woman corrected her, a finely wrinkled hand patting Annie's shoulder. "If you're going to spend the night under my roof, you'll have to call me Polly."

"All right, Polly." Annie grinned. "Thank you both. We appreciate your generosity."

Annie seemed to take this all in stride, but for Marcus this was all much harder to comprehend. "You'd take us in? Just like that?" He looked from the man to his wife. "But you don't know us."

"Of course we do," Polly smiled at his confusion and spoke slowly, the way one did to a dim-witted child. "You just introduced yourselves." Polly turned on her heel and beckoned for them to follow. "Now come with me and I'll get you each something dry to put on."

"Could we use your phone first?" Annie asked before Polly could lead them to the laundry room. Annie saw the confused look Marcus gave her over the request. "We have to call Nathan," she told him.

He didn't understand her reasoning. The boy was safe with the housekeeper. "Why?"

Impatience highlighted her face. How could he be so thick-headed? "So he won't worry."

"Is Nathan your son?" Polly asked. "Children do get frightened," she went on, assuming the answer to her question was yes, "if their parents don't come home when they're supposed to."

Marcus thought of the way Nathan must have felt when he waited for his parents to return and they never did. Annoyed, he upbraided himself for his own stupidity. He saw the look on Annie's face. Trust her to think of it. This time he was grateful that she had.

"We'd like to call him as soon as possible," Marcus put in. "I'll reverse the charges."

"Never gave it a thought," Polly clucked, pointing out the phone in the corner of the living room.

"I didn't think people like that existed outside of fantasies," Marcus said to Annie after Polly had brought them to their room for the night. Gingerly he closed the door behind them. She seemed to be making herself right at home, he thought, watching Annie.

He hiked up one drooping suspender. He was wearing a pair of baggy, faded, cuffed, gray trousers that were a size too large. The trousers and his plaid shirt were a loan from Henry until his own clothes had dried. They had spent a far more pleasant evening than he would have anticipated learning about the woman's family and Henry's career as a carpenter over dinner. They had been born, met and married in a small town in Kansas. After forty years, they had moved to California and settled in Santa Barbara.

Annie tightened the huge pink robe that Polly had pressed on her. It gave new meaning to the word roomy. "People aren't as dark and horrid as you'd like to believe."

He watched her as she crossed to the only bed in the room. Her body was hidden in the folds of the robe, her outline was not. He looked away. That sort of thing wasn't going to help get him through the night. "It's not something I'd like to believe, Annie, it just is."

Annie sat down on the bed. The robe parted and one long limb was exposed before she pulled the robe over it. Marcus paced the room restlessly.

The man was utterly hopeless. "Right. Then how do you explain those people we spent the evening with?"

"Easy," he said dryly. "They're a figment of your imagination." He tried to block out the sound of her laugh and the effect it had on him.

He looked around the room. It was small and cozy, just like the rest of the house. The furniture was worn, but looked comfortable. Rather than illuminate it, the light from the single lamp by the bed made the room appear that much more intimate. The double bed dominated the room. There was a bureau and a stuffed armchair that didn't seem to match anything but somehow just belonged.

He moved toward the chair. This, he supposed, would be his bed for the night. The idea of successfully sharing a bed with Annie didn't even remotely present itself as having a snowball's chance in hell. "You don't have to worry."

Outside, the wind howled. The rain was still falling in sheets. She was grateful to be on this side of the window. "About what?"

He lowered himself into the armchair. "I intend to be a perfect gentleman about the situation."

Their definition of gentleman differed. A gentleman wasn't supposed to cut up your heart. "I never had any doubts."

Why did her voice sound so distant when she said that, so frosty? Didn't she realize what a struggle it was for him not to take what he wanted so desperately? What a struggle it was for him not to give in to the storm that raged within him, more violent than the one outside the house?

"Just as long as we understand each other."

"I don't think that'll happen in a million years," Annie murmured. She looked down at the huge robe she was wearing. "Actually I was going to ask you if you wanted to share my robe. There's room enough here for two, possibly three." She laughed softly, disparagingly. "Never mind, I've probably shocked you again."

He didn't care for her sarcasm. He didn't care for the situation, not any of it. Least of all, he didn't care for the fact that he couldn't let go like any other man and take advantage of the opportunity. But he didn't believe in taking advantage. There was too much at stake.

"Look, I—" He glanced over toward Annie. She had gotten into bed. The robe lay on the flowered circular rug, a soft pool of pink. Marcus felt every inch of his body tighten. He licked his lips, trying to raise a little moisture for a mouth that had suddenly gone very dry. "What are you doing?"

She turned toward him. "I thought it was obvious."

He tried not to think about the fact that she was several feet away from him, dressed in a smile and percale sheets. "The robe—"

"Would probably smother me in my sleep during the night. Besides, it's hot tonight." The rain had only succeeded in making the air sticky.

And it was getting hotter all the time, Marcus thought. He tried not to think about what she was like underneath the sheets.

He couldn't think of anything else.

"I'll take the chair," he mumbled needlessly.

"Fine."

It wasn't fine. It was torture. If ever a piece of furniture had been deceptively presented, it was the armchair. There wasn't a comfortable position to be found on it.

Annie listened to him move restlessly around for ten minutes. Finally she raised herself up on her elbows, tucking the sheet around her breasts. He was an idiot, but she felt sorry for him.

"There's room enough for two in this bed, Marc." With a nod of her head, she indicated the other side. "And we can still stay very adult about it. People share beds all the time without anything happening." A smile twisted her lips as she thought of their screenplay. "If it makes you feel any better, you can pretend it's a foxhole during the war."

It felt like war, all right, he thought as he rose. A war that he was losing no matter what the outcome.

Annie turned away and faced the window. She had extended the offer because if she didn't neither one of them would get any sleep. He was thrashing around in that chair like a fish out of water. If he thought there was something more to the invitation, he was mistaken. She had decided to let him retreat behind his barriers. She wasn't going to let her feelings run away with her any longer. She had been rebuffed by him enough times to qualify her as a volleyball. Any moves whatsoever were all going to be his from here on in. If he was made of stone, that was his problem, not hers.

The hell it was. Annie gathered the sheet to her and prayed for sleep.

He knew he had made a mistake as soon as his body touched the mattress. He stripped off his shirt and let it drop on the floor, then laid down on top of the bed, purposely keeping the sheet between them as a barrier.

It didn't help. Even at a distance of a good nine inches and with a sheet between them, he could swear he felt the heat of her body searing up toward his. There was only so much a man could humanly withstand.

Marcus raised himself up on his elbow and turned in her direction. The light from the lamp was playing on her hair, creating scattered shafts of blazing gold through it. Hesitating for a moment, he touched it, letting it shimmer through his fingers like golden rain. The desire only grew. "This isn't going to work, you know."

Her breath caught in her throat, Annie turned toward him slowly. His fingers skimmed along the hollow of her cheek. She fought to keep her eyes from fluttering shut as anticipation vibrated through her.

"That depends." Her voice was husky as she felt her heart beating wildly in her throat. So much for promises about not letting her feelings surface.

"On what?"

Her eyes never left his face. She was searching for signs of a retreat. There were none. "On what you mean by working."

"I haven't the vaguest idea what I mean. I can't seem to think straight around you."

"Why is that?" she heard herself ask. He traced his fingers along one smooth, bare shoulder, dipping down to the planes of her breasts. Slowly he tugged the sheet loose. She shuddered. And so did he.

"Because I want you." There was no use in denying it any longer. No point in denying it. Softly he kissed her temple. "I want to hold you, to kiss you until I can't make my lips form a whistle."

Her laughter warmed him. "A fate worse than death," she agreed.

She was impossible. Totally and utterly impossible. And he had never wanted a woman more. "I want to make love to you until you can't make wisecracks anymore."

The suspender sagged again and Annie slipped it all the way from his shoulder, her fingertips splaying across his chest. She felt the muscle there tighten beneath her palm. "That might take some time."

He gathered her close to him. The outline of her body thrilled him, aroused him until he knew he couldn't bear any more. "That's what I'm counting on."

Annie framed his face with her hands. "Countdown," she whispered, pressing her lips to his throat, "begins now." She felt his pulse there jump.

She was brazen and she knew it, but she had never wanted like this, never felt like this, not even with Charlie. It was as if everything within her had caught on fire and she was going to die if he didn't make love with her. With hands that felt oddly steady, even as everything else within her shook, she undid his trousers.

Marcus shucked them off with a sure, swift motion, kicking them to the foot of the bed. Every inch of his body was as taut, as ready, as a finely tuned instrument about to be played.

But it still didn't change anything. He ran his hand slowly along her body until his outstretched fingers touched her breast. He watched her lids lower as he cupped his hand around it. "This is all wrong, you know."

She focused on his face. For now, despite his words, there were no doubts in his eyes, only desire. "We'll argue about this later."

"Fine with me." His hands slid down her body, tangling in the sheets and then tossing them aside. They fell on the floor, covering the robe.

It was a night of passion that matched nothing in his memory. Her body, so small, so sleek, had been created for loving. Senses swimming, he explored it with the awe of man discovering a place where no one had ever been before. It delighted him to make her arch toward him, to moan when he pressed a kiss to the back of her knee, to the inside of her elbow, to the hollow of her throat.

With his heart beating in his ears, he took more, reveled in taking more. Each kiss built, flowered, exploded into a wondrous stepping-stone that took them both higher and higher, past a point of no return.

Annie loved the feel of his nude body against hers. She couldn't get enough of touching him, of feeling it grow harder in its desire for her. The heat was almost overpowering.

"I knew it," she whispered hoarsely.

His tongue poised over the swell of her breast, Marcus looked up. "Knew what?"

She tangled her fingers in his hair. It felt silky. "That it'd be like this with you."

He ran his tongue slowly along her nipple, watching it tighten. "How did you know?"

She smiled, her breath growing shorter. "Read your books."

"Later. I'm a little busy right now." He closed over the other nipple and Annie arched, muffling a cry.

It was a series of volleys fired and returned. He wasn't in control but it no longer mattered. What mattered was this sensation that traveled through his veins like trapped lightning. He wanted it to go on forever.

He wanted to take her now.

Somehow, he managed to hold back a little longer, long enough to let his hands memorize every line, every curve, to know the feel of her smooth skin. Long enough to only begin to satiate his longing for the taste of her. But when she touched him, when her long delicate fingers began to stroke, to possess, his control thinned out to barely a thread. Groaning her name, he raised himself over her and entered. He felt her body tense, then her legs wrap around him possessively. Slowly he began to move, his hands on her hips. There was no need to guide her. She anticipated his every rhythm, his every movement, hurrying with him to the summit. Once and then again. And again.

And somewhere in the heat of the long, endless night, Marcus found what he so desperately sought.

Pleasure took on a whole new meaning for him, an entire new scope. Life, he thought as he lost himself in her flavor, in the very scent of her, had picked him up and thrown him into the eye of a hurricane.

And he was going willingly.

Chapter Fifteen

Marcus lay in bed with his arm tucked under his head, staring at fading shadows stretching across the bedroom wall in the early dawn light. He recognized the sweet sensation blossoming in the center of his soul. Recognized it, cherished it. And feared it.

Happiness. Such a wonderful, frightening thing. So fleeting.

Annie stirred next to him, her body curving into his. It seemed so natural, having her sleep next to him. She snuggled against him. Trying to move into his space, he thought, smiling as he looked at her. Just like she did when she was awake.

He needed to get a grip on himself, on his feelings that threatened to burst free.

Threatened to? He laughed silently. They already had. There was no point in closing the barn door anymore. The horses had escaped. The only option he had now was to round them up before they were lost or hurt. That was the bottom line. First happiness, then sorrow. An even, eternal balance. He couldn't logically expect more. He had never had more.

Yet at this moment, even when he was trying to summon the melancholy numbness, he couldn't shake this feeling of happiness. Not with her beside him like this.

But it wouldn't last. He knew that. It was a given. Happiness was always transitory. And the greater the feeling of well-being, the greater the sense of loss at the end. He had learned to approach life like that, had learned at an early age that only sadness was dependable. Emptiness always won out in the end. If there was nothing to compare the emptiness to, then it wasn't so bad. He had accepted living in a gray world.

But Marcus couldn't force himself to retreat, not just yet.

Oh God, he wanted to savor this, wanted to believe with his whole heart and soul that what he felt at this very moment, what had spread through him in the night like silvery threads of tenacious nylon cord, would last. Would go on until there was no more life and breath left within him.

She was having too profound an influence on him. He was beginning to think like her. The lady held only disappointment for him in the end, nothing but pure disappointment, even if she didn't know it.

So why did disappointment have to come packaged so sensuously?

He sifted her hair through his fingers, watching the first rays of the morning sun nudge away the shadows in the room. That's what he had felt like inside when he had finally made love with her. Like the shadows in his soul were being nudged away by a force stronger than they were. Light always seemed stronger than dark. At least at dawn, he thought as a small smile quirked his lips. Midnight was another story.

And they were heading for midnight. It was only a matter of time.

He almost wished he had managed to retain that paralysis of the soul he had been living with for so long. At least then he had an excuse not to feel. There had been a certain amount of security in his gray, non-feeling world. This kaleidoscope world Annie had opened for him was fraught with uncertainty. No, he thought, the end result was certain, only the trip there would be a maze.

She stirred and reached out to him even in her sleep. Her hand fell over his chest. He felt his heartbeat quicken. Slowly he ran the back of his fingers along her cheek and watched as her eyes fluttered open. There was no dazed look, no single moment where orientation escaped her. She knew exactly where she was and why. Her smile was warm and just for him.

Annie touched her lips to his; just the slightest of kisses passed between them. It was enough to start him again. "'Morning."

He sighed, but for now it was a sigh of contentment. "Yes, it is."

Annie shifted closer and rested her head on his chest. She liked the sound of his heart beating beneath her cheek. It was a warm, comforting sound. A special excitement wafted through her as she felt his fingers glide along her shoulder. "So, that really was you last night. I thought I had dreamed it."

He could feel her lips form a smile along his skin. "It was me."

Annie laughed. "Talkative as always."

He tried not to react as her fingertips feathered along his waist slowly. He would have had more success bench-pressing a five-hundred-pound weight. "I'm not sure I know what to say."

She wondered if that meant that there hadn't been that many women in his life. She would have liked to think so. She wanted this to be special to him. " 'You were magnificent' would be nice."

He laughed. "You were magnificent."

Annie raised her head. He was just parroting the words. "With feeling."

"With feeling," he echoed.

Laughing, she shook her head, her hair falling about her shoulders in golden, tangled waves. "You are impossible." She pulled herself up on her elbow until her lips were a whisper away from his. She searched his face, but there was none of that wariness that she had come to expect. Instead, there was an innocent confusion. She could work with that, she thought, relieved. "You're going to have to go the rest of the distance on your own, Sullivan."

"I think," he murmured as he cupped the back of her head and tilted her face so that his mouth came down on hers, "I already have."

Not yet, Marc, not yet. But soon, she thought, hoped, prayed. *Soon.*

She was impossible to resist. One kiss was like one bit of chocolate, one potato chip. There was no such thing as just one and he knew it. But knowing that didn't stop him. He couldn't deny himself another taste of her mouth in this strange, cozy little room, one more sampling of a paradise that couldn't be allowed to exist beyond this place, these walls.

It all seemed unreal. The place, the woman, the time. An adventure out of spun sugar. Something she might have conjured up. And since it was unreal, he could indulge and let his wildest fantasies come to fruition.

He could have her, love her.

Fantasizing hadn't been something he had done on any sort of a regular basis. Until Annie. It seemed that until she had burst into his life, everything had stayed on more or less an even keel. There had been Jason and his wife, but they had never disturbed his life the way she had. They had enhanced his life. Annie set it on its ear. Now he was in turbulent waters, holding on for dear life and loving every breathtaking second of it.

He had never felt so alive.

His mouth slid over hers, down to her throat. The moan that vibrated beneath his lips aroused and excited him, but this time, he forced himself to hold back, really hold himself back.

There was no need to grasp things with both hands quickly, or to be stunned by the intensity, the passion. This time, he knew, or thought he knew, the pleasures that were ahead for both of them. Pleasures he had never fully sampled before there was Annie. She had brought this wonder to him. Making love was an adventure, not a simple, pleasing event that left no imprint on his soul and didn't linger on the mind.

Every detail of last night lingered now, every movement burned into his brain with the hot branding iron of passion. As it came rushing back to him, he suddenly wanted the exhilaration he had experienced last night. He wanted to thrust himself into her, to feel her legs wrap around him again and ride, hell-bent for leather, to the top.

No, he wanted to hold back. Anticipation enriched the end reward.

It wasn't easy holding back. Not when she touched him like that, skimming her fingertips lightly over his skin, making it blaze. It wasn't easy holding back when he knew that she gave so much more than he thought he was taking, than he was giving. He was in awe of her, totally and utterly in awe. In awe of her body, in awe of the gift she gave him. She made love with him as if he were the only man she had ever done this with.

But he had seen the tears shining in her eyes when she had mentioned her other lover. This had happened before. Had the other man been her first? Was Marcus now her second? He didn't want to be the second. He wanted to be the first. He wanted to blot out the memory of every other man from her mind, the imprint of every other man from her body. He wanted to make love with her until there was nothing and no one but him.

It was important to Marcus. He didn't want to explore why. Not yet. The implications were far too earthshaking and numbing.

He stroked her until both their bodies hummed, found all her secret places again, first with his hands, then with his lips and tongue. Annie twisted and moaned, away from him when the pleasure was too great to bear, toward him as soon as the lack of it penetrated her consciousness and left her bereft.

The ground beneath her feet opened up, and suddenly she had nothing to grab on to except him. Her lips parted, inviting him to sample, to take, to possess. Because he did. He possessed her without ever wanting to enslave her. She was his for as long as he wanted her. Longer. She was his forever.

Annie's mind spun madly, yet she saw everything clearly, felt everything as if it were trapped beneath crystal for her to see and hear and touch. She reveled in the fact that he shuddered when she touched him. Just as she did with him. It magnified her own arousal.

There were no techniques, no him, no her, just an intense whirlwind of passion that engulfed them both. Each wanting to give the other pleasure.

Annie withered and arched as his mouth claimed all of her, marking a slow, maddening path to the core of her being, reminding her how much she needed to be loved, held, cherished, reduced to this pulsating mass of wants and desires. She grabbed fistfuls of the sheet beneath her as he explored the most secret part of her, bringing her up to thunderous peaks. Each time she fell to earth, spent, only to be lifted up again.

The lovemaking made her feel one with him. To her, it was special, private, a wondrous gift she had only given one other man, shared with only one other human being. And now she was sharing it with Marcus. She had a feeling that it was the same with him. He hadn't talked about women, but she sensed that they had drifted nameless, faceless, through his life, touching his body but not his soul. She had it just within her reach. Whether he knew it or not, he was offering it to her. And she wanted it.

It made her want to cry. It made her want to laugh. Above all, it made her want to hold on to this feeling with the last breath that was in her.

His body slick with sweat that belonged to both of them, Marcus raised himself on his elbows, his body hovering over hers. He loved the look in her eyes when they made love. Dark, smoky, only for him. This much he could believe, here and now. Only for him. For now, it was enough.

As they joined together, his hands tangling in her hair, framing her face with powerful fingers, his body arched over hers, she stifled the cry that rose to her lips. Euphoria and warmth laid claim to her in a fast, climaxing, fever pitch. She tightened her arms around him as the spiral twirled her faster and faster, the rhythm they achieved already in harmony. A blending. It was a blending of thoughts, of styles, of beings. Whether he believed it or not, Annie thought, whether he admitted it or not, he was her soulmate for all eternity. Annie opened her heart and let him in.

He held her against his heart, knowing it was dangerous, knowing he couldn't help himself.

Let me hang on to this feeling a little longer, he prayed, loving her, *just a little longer.*

"What," he whispered softly into her hair, hardly knowing he was saying the words aloud, "am I going to do about you?"

She raised her head slightly, her cheek brushing against the dark stubble on his chin. Slowly she ran her fingertip along his lips. "For the time being, I'd say you've done it."

She saw the desire still shining in his eyes. And the perimeter of fear bordering it. Why? What was there to be afraid of? This was the most natural thing in the world. The very best part.

Marcus pressed her fingers to his lips and kissed them one by one. Who would have ever thought that someone so overbearingly pushy would have held such appeal for him? "No, I meant—"

Annie sighed. Reality was already intruding. There were times she hated reality. "I know what you meant." She pulled the sheet back up around them, making a show of tucking it about her breasts primly. "You're going to look into that thesaurus you carry around in your brain and find another word for all this. Maybe 'coupling' will suit you," she suggested, wondering how long her patience would hold. "Or mindless melding, or something else, but whatever words you use, Marcus Sullivan—" she jabbed a finger into his chest "—I know the right ones."

For once, temper made her look adorable. He tried not to grin. "Which are?"

"We made love here."

He raised a brow. "And there's a difference?"

"Yes, there's a difference." Exasperation tinged her words. Why was he pretending to be so obtuse? He *knew* there was a difference. "I don't think either one of us take things like this lightly. I know I don't." She raised her eyes to his face. "I don't think you do, either."

She didn't take it lightly. It was something he wanted to know, wanted to hear, and yet hearing it had such grave implications, such huge consequences. Did she know? Could she possibly know what it would do to him when the time came and she left?

She had told him that she had loved once. She had to know what doing without it meant.

"And that's the word you're running from," she concluded, her voice dropping. "Love."

He was all set to argue with her. After all, that was what they were best at, arguing. But then she smiled at him with that damn inviting smile and he felt his flesh rebelling against his thoughts, against all thoughts. He felt himself wanting her, needing her again. It amazed him almost as much as she did.

Gathering her into his arms again, he shrugged in answer to the question in her eyes. "What the hell, I might as well have more of a reason to run."

The smile within her flowered to fill all the corners of her being. "By all means, let's have more of a reason."

With practiced ease, they both slipped back into ecstasy.

"I think," Annie said as she dragged a brush through her tangled hair, "that we should leave the Flynns some money."

Tucking his freshly laundered shirt into his jeans, Marcus looked at her curiously. That was a very practical statement for someone like Annie.

No, he amended, there *was* no one else like Annie.

"To buy new sheets," she explained. "These—" she held up a corner of one for his inspection "—are just about worn out." Her eyes full of mischief, she rubbed the section she was holding against her cheek and looked up at Marcus affectionately. "I wonder if they'd think I was strange if I asked to keep them as a souvenir."

He had been watching her get ready, fascinated by the intimacies of the act. He had made love to women before, enjoyed their company and then gone on his way. Try as he might, Marcus couldn't remember seeing a single one of those women getting dressed. He couldn't remember wanting to watch any of them comb their hair, or ache to undress them again once they *were* dressed.

He ran his hands though his own hair and tried his best to look nonchalant. "No stranger than they probably already think you are."

Annie dropped her comb into her purse. "I'm glad to see that nothing has changed on the cerebral front." She brushed a quick kiss on his cheek. "I like matching words with you, Sullivan. It keeps me on my toes."

"No, nothing's changed," he echoed, but saying it didn't make it true. Things had changed, changed drastically, and would never be the same again. Not for him, not emotionally. And not ever again.

The overall picture, though, was still the same. Things ultimately would still be the way they were. He would grasp happiness only to have it slip through his fingers. And he was now trapped inside where he had sworn never to be.

Annie heard the sounds of a household starting a new day. "I think I hear the Flynns." She left the robe neatly folded on the bed and picked up her purse. "Want to go see about getting that mechanic to come up here and hopefully get your car going?"

He took her arm and she smiled to herself at the change, but said nothing. The old Marcus would have never taken that initiative. He would have instinctively backed away from contact.

You're coming along, Marc Sullivan. And you're taking me with you whether you like it or not.

Not only were Mr. and Mrs. Flynn up, but Henry Flynn had put in a call to his son Andy. Andy and Henry, Polly Flynn told them with pride she didn't bother hiding, were undoubtedly already working on the car even as they spoke, and more than likely, repairing it.

"There isn't a thing that man has made that my Andy can't fix," Polly told Annie and Marcus matter-of-factly as she served them breakfast in the tiny kitchen. There was just enough room for four at the table. "I expect he'll be done by the time you two finish breakfast."

Marcus discovered that he had an appetite. Breakfast was usually restricted by choice to black coffee. Now a hunger gnawed at his belly that made him look upon the pancakes, sausages and eggs that Polly pushed toward him as a blessing.

Must be all that lovemaking, he thought. It sapped a man's energy and built up his appetite—for more things than one, he added mentally, looking at Annie over the table.

Annie merely grinned, digging in as heartily as he was. But then, he remembered, she could always eat.

True to Polly's prediction, Annie heard the sound of a car pulling up just as Polly swept away the last of the dishes.

Shooing away Annie's offer of help, Polly deposited them into the old-fashioned sink she had told them she preferred to a dishwasher. "I'm too old to try new things," she had explained cheerfully. Annie had thought that she had never seen a woman look more youthful.

Henry and a younger, taller and rangier version of the old man walked in. "This is my boy, Andy," Henry said, nodding in the youth's direction as he cleaned his shoes on the worn mat just within the door. "Our youngest."

Annie judged the young man to be around twenty or so. A love child, she guessed, gauging the older couple's age.

Andy said nothing, just ducked his head in a quick, shy greeting. Annie put out her hand, and he was forced to take it, after first rubbing his own on the back of his jeans.

She was drawn to shyness like a magnet. Andy didn't stand a chance, Marcus thought with a touch of amusement.

"Were you able to figure out what was wrong with the car?" Annie asked the two men.

That was his line, Marcus thought, but for once it didn't bother him that she had jumped in and beaten him to the punch. Maybe making love with her anesthetized certain parts of his brain, he mused.

"Yes," Andy mumbled in reply, not looking at either one of them.

"Your battery was dead," Henry explained. "Andy here recharged it for you. It'll get you to where you're going and then some. Andy helps out part-time at the garage. Kirby keeps him on as an apprentice." It was evident that Henry shared his wife's pride in his last born. "It seems to me, Kirby could stand to learn a few things from our boy."

"Dad." The single word, tinged in embarrassment, was deep and resonant as Andy flushed.

Marcus dug into his back pocket and took out his wallet. "What do we owe you?"

Speaking for both of them, Polly placed a wide, surprisingly soft hand over the wallet and pushed it back toward Marcus. "Keep your money, Marcus. It's the neighborly thing to do." The women winked at him.

She must have been a hell-raiser in her youth, Marcus thought. The wink gave her a flirtatious air.

"Maybe you can dedicate a book or movie to us someday." It was apparent that Polly Flynn was in awe of what he did for a living. Conversely Marcus was in awe over anyone who could fix machinery so easily.

"The very next one," Annie promised, taking Marcus's arm. "And now, we'd better hurry off. There's a screenplay waiting for us back home."

And once it's done, everything will be over, Marcus thought.

She tried to pretend she didn't see the frown that crossed Marcus's face before he hid it.

Now what had she said?

Chapter Sixteen

Dammit, why didn't she say something?

Marcus's hands tightened on the wheel. She had been sitting next to him, silent now, for the last hour, ever since they had gotten into the car. Was she having second thoughts? he wondered, trying to stave off nervousness. Was she sorry about what had happened last night? He hadn't forced himself on her. She had seemed willing, receptive. Had he misread her reaction? If not, why was she so quiet now?

Annie looked at his profile. Marcus was staring straight ahead, his eyes on the road. Over an hour had gone by and the only sound she had heard was the sound of the tires against the road.

Why didn't he say something to her? Anything. She didn't want to be the first to speak. She was always the first. She wanted him to take the lead, to make her feel that this situation between them was going to be all right. This wasn't just a game anymore.

Maybe it never had been.

But the closer they got to the city, the more distant he became. She hadn't expected reams of words from him or protestations of undying love. But after last night and this morning, she *had* expected something from him, a change, perhaps a small aura of romance, or at least some kindness. Instead, he was just the way he had been before. He was acting as if nothing had happened last night. Or worse, as if he was regretting what had happened between them.

She felt a horrible pang seize the center of her stomach.

The silence was driving him crazy. He had never thought he'd feel that way, but right now, he wanted her to say something, anything. He had made the first move last night. He would have thought that would have shown her how he felt, would have made her happy. But she obviously wasn't happy or else she'd be talking. He had made a mistake. He shouldn't have let last night happen.

Annie looked down at her hands. She was twisting the hem of her shirt. Dropping it, she sighed. Muhammad was going to have to pay another visit to the mountain before he twisted off his clothing. She wet her lips. "A dollar ninety-five, taking inflation into consideration, for your thoughts."

Vaguely her voice penetrated his thoughts. She sounded the way she always did. Nothing had changed for her. He had been right. Last night didn't mean to her what it had for him. When they returned to the city, they'd be writing partners again, nothing more. Last night had been a lovely aberration, brought on by circumstances, by rain and wind and redwoods. These things happen. There was no more to it than that.

Oh, but there was. And after last night, how could he just go on working with her side by side, and not touch her? Not make love with her again? He didn't see how that was possible. "Did you say something?"

Annie blew out an angry breath, telling herself *not* to get angry until he had had time to plead his case—as if he *had* a case. There was no excuse to treat her so shabbily. "Would it matter if I did?"

He tried to concentrate on what she was saying and make sense out of it. He never did have much luck at that, he thought wryly. "What?"

She turned on the radio, hoping that the lively music would break this mood she felt consuming her. "You seem to be off in your own little world. Is it a private planet, or can anyone journey there?"

"What are you talking about?"

"About being left out."

He glanced at her, then looked back at the road. Why the hell was he feeling guilty? There wasn't anything to feel guilty about. He slowed as the car took a curve. "Left out of what?"

Out of your life, you idiot, she answered silently. "You haven't said two words since we left the Flynns' house."

Neither have you, he thought. But maybe it was just as well. The time they had spent in Santa Barbara had been idyllic, wonderful. It had nothing to do, he tried to convince himself, with the people they were in their day-to-day lives. And they were returning to that world. They couldn't stay in that little house, enjoying each other, indefinitely. It would have been wonderful, but utterly impossible. That episode had been nothing more than a fantastic interlude. Now it was back to the real world. Back to reality. And reality meant that their project would end soon and their lives would go on. Separately. He couldn't believe in anything else, couldn't let newly flexed, raw emotions lead him into making mistaken assumptions.

Because they wouldn't be true.

But even if they weren't, he knew that he needed her. Already he could feel that terrible, overwhelming loneliness envelop him as he anticipated her leaving. There wasn't that much of the script left to work on. And then what? He could ask her to stay, to explore this relationship with him. But what if she said no? He couldn't risk that. It was better not to put his feelings into words than have his feelings thrown back at him. Her silence on the trip back was enough of an indication that she probably thought the whole thing had been a mistake. She *always* talked. The fact that she didn't was a dead giveaway. Right now, the relationship hadn't progressed very far, and though he felt hurt, it was just a wound. He was strong. He could regain his composure. It wasn't as bad as it could be. Like a recovering alcoholic who had slipped, he had managed to stop himself in time before the damage was too great.

He could see impatience on her face. Why? Was she annoyed with him? With herself? Maybe he was wrong. Maybe he had hurt her in some way. Maybe there was a chance for them—no, dammit, what was wrong with him? "I've been thinking," he said slowly, trying to find an excuse for his own silence.

"About what?" she prodded, desperately wanting him to go on talking. If they talked, the truth would come out and then maybe she'd know what was troubling him.

She kept hoping that if she said the right words, set up the right situation, she'd hear what she needed to hear. Make him say things she felt were in his heart. Or prayed that they were.

Words eluded him. He grasped at the thing that was closest at hand. "About the screenplay."

Annie leaned back against the seat, disappointed. *What else did you expect him to say?* They were collaborating, for heaven's sake.

She rested her arm on the open window. The wind played havoc with her hair, whipping it around. She didn't bother trying to tie it back. "I think the screenplay is going well."

She didn't want to talk about the damned screenplay. They almost always argued when they discussed it. She didn't want to argue. Not now. She wanted to talk about what had happened between them last night. She wanted to hold on to that sweetness.

The expression on his face told her that now was not the time to explore the significance of last night. She tried a different approach. "Sure you don't want me to drive?"

"No, I'm fine." Besides, if he didn't drive, he'd have more time to look at her. It wasn't a good idea.

Liar, Annie thought. *You are not fine, and I wish I could beat you about the head and shoulders and get you to admit it. Talk to me, damn you.* She blew out a frustrated breath. *Patience, Annie.* She wasn't so sure that she could follow her own advice.

He glanced at her and was captivated by the simple way the wind played with her hair, the way the sun seemed to be reflected in it. He found himself, despite all his well-thought-out arguments, wanting her again. Right here. Right now.

He drove past a sign announcing a motel just a couple of miles down the road. Impulsively he toyed with the idea of stopping. Why not turn off here? What was so important about reaching home within the next hour or so? He had time, time enough to make love with her until the stars blanketed the sky.

Marcus gripped the steering wheel. *Drive,* he told himself. *Just drive.*

Another lapse into silence. Dammit, he was going to drive her crazy. She was almost hungry for the sound of his voice, even if it was raised in argument.

"So," she said suddenly, "do you really think it's coming along well, Marc?" Not waiting for him to answer, she lowered her voice and pretended to be him. "Well, I think it'd be coming along a lot better if you stopped trying to change lines and passages that are perfectly acceptable."

Out of the corner of her eye, Annie saw Marcus looking at her as if she had lost her mind. She kept going. "Marc, you have to learn how to bend. Things work in books that don't on screen." Again her voice dropped. "I guess you're right, de Witt. Maybe it's time for a change. But don't let it go to your head."

Signs proclaiming that L.A. was fifty miles away popped up on the road. Not soon enough for him, he decided. "Are you feeling all right?" he finally asked.

Annie wiggled her feet, trying to get comfortable. "Sure," she said tersely, "why?"

A crazy woman—he was emotionally hooked on a crazy woman. "You're talking to yourself."

"It's a dirty job, but someone has to do it."

He started to laugh and shook his head. Life, he knew, was going to seem empty without her.

Life *was* empty, he reminded himself. There were only occasional disturbances to make it seem otherwise. "You know, you really are crazy, absolutely crazy."

Pleased to hear him laugh, she grinned. "It's one of my better qualities."

He thought of last night. The way she'd felt in his arms. The way her body seemed to meld with his. "No, I wouldn't say that."

Annie turned, tucking her feet under her, her expression eager. "What would you say?" Her hand was on his arm, coaxing. "Anything, I'll settle for anything. I've had more spirited conversations with my shoes than I've had in this car in the last hour."

"Annie." Marcus felt almost helpless with the situation, with himself. "I don't know what to say."

"That hasn't stopped you from criticizing me before." She stopped, then looked at him. "Do you realize that that's the first time you've called me by my name of your own free will without my prodding you?"

That was impossible. They'd spent over a month together. He had to have used her name in all that time. Hadn't he? "No, it's not."

"Yes it is. Trust me, I've been listening."

"With all your rhetoric?" he scoffed, turning the car down the serpentine road that twisted and curved. "When did you have time to hear?"

She winked. "I'm gifted."

There was no point in arguing with her. She'd win. She always seemed to.

A straight stretch of road gave Marcus the opportunity to look at her again. She was grinning. He wanted to kiss that impish expression until it changed into one of desire. He wanted her in his arms the way she had been last night by dim light, this morning by the first rays of dawn.

He wanted her forever.

Forever was a word in a dictionary. Nothing more.

"So you are," he agreed softly. She had gotten under his skin, hadn't she? Somehow gotten to him the way no other woman ever had. Gotten to him and dug in despite his best efforts to eradicate her. That made her unique. "Gifted" was stretching it, perhaps, but somehow it fitted.

"Say it again."

"Say what again?"

"My name." She propped her head up with her hand, leaning it against the headrest. Okay, so she was settling for crumbs. She'd work it up into a feast somehow later on. "I have a feeling I won't hear it once we're back at work. At least, not said that softly."

Feeling silly, he obliged. It wasn't that much to ask. "Annie." She had closed her eyes, he realized, and seemed to be savoring the sound.

Annie let the sound of his voice wash over her like a warm caress. No, she decided, she wasn't going to give up. Determination had always been her mainstay. When Charlie had died, it had been what she had clung to to dig herself out and live again. She wasn't about to let it slip through her fingers now. Marcus might have a problem, but it was no longer his alone. She was going to help.

She glanced at him now, her green eyes widening. *If you're going to try to retreat, Marcus Sullivan, you're going to have one hell of a fight on your hands,* she promised herself. And him.

A motorcycle suddenly came up behind them and then whooshed off around them, disappearing down the road. Marcus realized that he was about ten miles under the speed limit and pressed down harder on the gas pedal. He saw her smile as he did so.

"Am I rubbing off on you?" He had told her before that she drove too fast.

Perhaps she was. But nothing was going to rub off the impression she had made on his life, he thought. It was now a matter of how much damage would be left in her wake once she was gone.

"No, I just wanted to get back. Why don't I drop you off at your place first?"

When he retreated, he did it quickly, she thought. "My car's at your place."

He had forgotten about that. "I can have someone drop that off later."

She wasn't about to be obliging. "No need," she said cheerfully. "It'll still be early. We can get some more work done. That should make you happy."

He didn't know what would make him happy anymore. Certainly not the future. He tried to concentrate on the present. For she was in it.

Marcus had scarcely managed to pull his convertible up into the driveway and park it before the front door flew open. Holly, her hands on her ample hips, stood in the doorway glaring at him the way his mother had never been moved to do. His mother hadn't cared enough about his activities to take notice of his comings and goings. Holly, it seemed, did.

"So, you're back."

"Yes," Marcus answered, wondering what had gotten into his placid housekeeper, "we are. What's the matter with you, Holly?"

Annie was out of the car in a heartbeat and at the woman's side. "Has something happened to Nathan?"

The possibility hadn't even occurred to him. "Has it?" he demanded.

Seeing Marcus's concern, Holly relented a bit. "I'm not sure he can walk anymore," she sniffed.

"What?" Had he been in some sort of an accident? Annie looked toward the house, then grabbed Holly by the shoulders. "What happened? Where is he?"

In reply, Holly turned on her heel and stalked back into the house.

"Holly," Marcus demanded, hurrying after her, his hand on Annie's arm, "what the hell are all these dramatics? Has the boy been hurt?"

Holly didn't answer. Instead, she pointed toward the front room like an avenging angel. "He's over there on the window seat, where he's been since early this morning. Probably," she amended, her expression accusing, "since last night after I went to bed."

Marcus walked into the living room quickly, but Annie was faster. Her heart almost broke when she saw the boy, his back to them, his slight shoulders moving as if trying to silence a sob. The puppy dozed at his feet.

She knelt by Nathan's side, but he kept his face averted. He didn't want them guessing that he had been crying.

"Nathan, honey." He wouldn't look at her. Annie put her hand on his arm and felt it stiffen slightly. "What's wrong?"

"My guess is that he's been waiting for you to come home." There was no mistaking the censure in Holly's voice, or whose side she was on. Marcus might pay her salary, but it was the motherless boy at the window seat who had won her heart.

Marcus didn't care for being on the defensive. Lately that was all he seemed to be doing. "We called you last night," he pointed out.

"Yes, about something being wrong with the car," Holly recalled. "You were in a car, Mr. Sullivan." She emphasized the word car and neither one of them needed a diagram as to what went on in the boy's mind.

Marcus looked at Nathan, not knowing what to say. It was all well and good to talk about logic, but what place did logic have in the mind of a small boy who had already lived through one tragedy that had turned his entire life upside down?

Slowly Annie stroked the boy's hair. She felt the stiffness abating. "Honey, I told you last night we'd be back today."

Nathan sniffled hard, determined not to cry. He passed the back of his hand over his damp cheeks. Somehow, the gentleness in Annie's voice made it worse. He shifted around in his seat to look at her. The sleeping puppy at his feet yelped a little before settling back down. "My mom and dad said the same thing before—" His lower lip trembled. The words wouldn't come out. "Before—"

She had enjoyed a night of passion while a small boy had gone through hell. Her feeling of contrition was almost insurmountable. "Oh, darling, I'm so sorry." Annie's heart ached as she took Nathan in her arms and held him to her. "I'm so very, very sorry if we made you worry."

For a moment, there was only the sound of Nathan sobbing against her shoulder. Annie stroked his head, shedding silent tears while Marcus wrestled with guilt he felt was unreasonable.

But beneath the guilt was the realization that the boy had transferred his affections, his love, to him. It took Marcus's breath away. More than that, Nathan had encompassed Annie in this transfer. Marcus knew that for however long it took, he would be there for Nathan. But as far as Annie went, that was another matter. The boy shouldn't count on her. It wouldn't be fair to either of them.

Marcus regretted the day he had agreed to this damn screenplay.

But if he hadn't, a small voice whispered, he wouldn't have had last night. And last night had been worth all the agony that hell had to offer.

"I thought you were never coming back again," Nathan sobbed.

Annie kissed Nathan's forehead. "We'll always be here for you." It was a promise she intended keeping.

Nathan blinked back tears. The puppy, awake, wagged his tail and jumped into his lap. "Promise?" He looked at her hopefully. If she said yes, he knew he could believe her. She wouldn't break her word to him.

Annie raised her hand and said solemnly, "Promise." Elaborately she crossed her heart. "If you ever need me, all you ever have to do is call." She looked back at Marcus and saw that he was watching her. "Marc has my number."

Yes, Marcus thought, I have your number.

Her very answer reinforced his thoughts. If Nathan needed her, he would have to call her. At her house. Because after they finished the screenplay, that's where she would be. It was her way of saying that she would go on with her life and it would be a life separate from his.

It was what he expected. Yet he couldn't help the angry feeling that sprang up in its wake. He had known that all along, told himself that all along. But when the words were out of her mouth, they stung.

She saw Marcus stiffen and hadn't the vaguest notion why. Was he annoyed at the boy's attachment to her? Jealous of it? Threatened by it? What?

You are a damn hard man to love, and I should have my head examined for it. But, God help me, I do love you. And on my tombstone they shall write, she thought wryly, *that 'she loved not wisely, but all too well.'*

With a resigned sigh, Annie rose to her feet. It wasn't easy to put these feelings aside, but she gave it her best shot. "Why don't we go out for a soda and celebrate our homecoming? And after that, Marc and I are going to have to settle back down in front of our computers and make up for lost time." She looked at Marcus, daring him to say something different, daring him to send her home. "That all right with you, Sullivan?"

She was taking charge again, Marcus thought, but it didn't really matter, did it? She'd be gone soon. Too soon.

He looked at Nathan. An emotion that he could only identify as paternal and which fascinated him, tugged at his heart. "As long as the puppy stays here."

"Here," Holly gathered up the squirming mass. She was licked for her trouble and pretended to scowl. "I'll take him." She gave Annie a sharp look. "You might have at least housebroken him before you dropped him off."

Annie linked an arm through Marcus's elbow and placed a hand on Nathan's shoulder. "And have Sullivan here miss the fun? Not on your life, Holly."

"Fun?" he echoed, then found that he was smiling. "Is that what we call it?"

Annie lifted her chin. "That is precisely what we call it." Her eyes danced at she looked down at Nathan. "Right, Nathan?"

"Right." The boy beamed.

Who was he to argue? Marcus thought. At least for the time being.

Chapter Seventeen

The sun was shining and the world outside the den window looked bright and cheery. Annie shivered and ran her hands up and down her arms. The sunshine hadn't managed to penetrate the interior of the room. At least, not in the way that counted. Feeling oddly out of sorts, Annie watched a bluebird soar up in the sky until he faded into nothingness.

Was that all that there had been between them that night? Just a glimmer of a moment, a flash of feeling, and then fading away like a bird soaring out of sight?

Maybe it was her fault for wanting too much. She smiled sadly to herself. It seemed as if instead of her endless optimism rubbing off on him, his dark view of life had rubbed off on her.

How had he engineered it? she wondered. How had he managed to work beside her day after day and still reconstruct those damn walls of his? Except when Nathan was around, for all intents and purposes, Marcus had withdrawn into himself right after they had returned from their outing. That had been over a week ago. Eight days. Eight days of hell to endure, eight days of being shut out.

He hadn't changed. He was still the same removed, antiseptic man. Although not totally. Every now and then, he'd slip. But, like a well-trained tightrope walker, he always regained his balance. That night together, she had shaken his rope and yet he *still* regained his balance. What did it take to shake him up?

She didn't understand. It was as if that wonderful man who had brought her to the brink of ecstasy and beyond hadn't really existed, had been only a figment of her overactive imagination.

Annie pressed her fingers into her palms until her nails dug in. But he had been real, she thought as a fragment of a memory skimmed over the outskirts of her mind. Marcus, his dark, manly scent seeping into her, filling her senses as he kissed her. Involuntarily Annie's body tightened like the strings of a violin that needed playing, that ached to make music but couldn't on its own. *He* made the music within her, his hands had strummed the right chords, had found the right notes.

Annie leaned her forehead against the window. She needed him, the big idiot. And he needed her. Didn't he see that?

They were alone in the big house. She had brought Stevie and Erin with her, and Holly had taken the lot out to Knott's Berry Farm, bless her, after the "joyful noise" had proven to be too much to creatively compete with.

Alone. It should have been an ideal time to recapture what they had discovered a week ago. She had secretly hoped they might. But he had only grown more distant.

She looked at him. He was bent over the computer, pecking out words. It never ceased to amaze her that the man who produced such wonderful books was a three-fingered typist who couldn't seem to commit the keyboard to memory.

Annie dragged her hands through her hair and then let them fall again. They might as well have been on separate islands for all the good being left alone did. They were alone all right. Together, they were very much alone. She ached from the loneliness.

It made her angry.

She left the shelter of the window seat and crossed to his side of the desk. Looking over his shoulder for a minute, Annie contemplated her options. She could beat him on his thick skull. She rather liked that option. No court in the world, once it knew him, would convict her.

Or she could forget about her hurt self-respect and try again.

Once more with feeling. "Looks like another wonderful day in paradise."

"What?" He glanced at her, slightly bewildered. It always took him a moment to refocus when he left the dimensions of the world he was creating.

He sounded as if he was snapping at her, she thought. He had been snapping at her constantly this past week. Maybe she was turning into one of those masochists, she mused, who thrived on adversity.

"I said it's a beautiful day." She sat down on his desk and slid back, her hands braced on either side. His pages were neatly stacked to her left and she saw him eye them protectively, as if he were afraid she'd knock them over. "You haven't smiled lately, Marcus."

He wished she'd just concentrate on doing the job they were supposed to be doing. It was hard enough trying to re-fortify the boundaries of his life without her pushing at them every time he turned around. "I didn't know that smiling was in our contract.'' He pecked out another three words.

She deliberated shutting off his computer to get his full attention, but since he was working, that was too drastic a measure. Not, she thought, that he didn't deserve it. ''It's right after the paragraph that allows you to bite off my head only twice per session.''

It was no use. He stopped typing. ''Are you trying to tell me something?''

''Desperately.'' She leaned over, and he put a protective hand over the off switch on his computer. ''I'm not going to shut anything off,'' she said tersely. ''That's your department.''

''You'll get to the point, I trust, before I apply for social security.''

''Security?'' she echoed angrily, her emotions finally erupting. ''You have so much damned security in that high-walled life of yours, I sincerely doubt that you'll ever need any more.''

A lot you know, he thought. Trust her to pick up on the one word that would send her verbally off and running. ''Annie—''

But she was in no mood to listen to a formal tirade. ''Where *are* you, Sullivan?'' She jabbed an impatient finger at his chest, her eyes smoldering. ''And I warn you, if you give me some pat answer with your address in it, I won't be held responsible for what I do to you.''

He was having trouble curbing his own temper. ''I don't know what you're talking about.'' So what else was new?

She felt like hurling things, hurling expletives, but what good would it do? She couldn't make him leave that world he had retreated to. Not if he didn't want to. But she'd be damned if she was going to take the insult lying down.

With more temper than she had ever displayed in her life, she shoved the pages they had been working on aside with the back of her hand, sending a shower of white onto the carpet.

"What the—?" He pushed back his chair, ready to scoop the pages up.

"Leave them there!" she ordered.

It was a side of her he hadn't seen before. He rose to his feet, concern warring with anger. "What's come over you?"

She lifted up her chin. "Maybe a belated attack of pride."

He saw the fire in her eyes. He saw the hurt as well. Had he caused that? He didn't want to hurt her, just to get out before there *was* no getting out. It was a mess all right. "Annie, I—"

She had had enough of excuses. "Damn you." Annie doubled her fists and punched him in the chest, frustrated beyond words.

He grabbed her wrists. She was *not* as fragile as she looked. He had to exert effort to hold on to her. "Stop it!"

But she went on struggling, trying to get free. She wanted to land just one more blow to make up for all the blows that he had given her. "I'm not just some one-night stand," she cried.

My God, was that what she thought? That he saw her as someone on whom to exercise his rutting libido? "Annie, I know that."

Annie yanked at her wrists, but he wouldn't let go of them. "Then why do you treat me like one?" She could see he didn't understand. He was so enmeshed in his own problems that he didn't know what she was talking about. "Why don't you just let things evolve? Why won't you let them go on the way they started?"

She wasn't going to cry. She wasn't going to give him the satisfaction of crying in front of him. She'd deck him and then cry her eyes out in the privacy of her own home, if he'd only let go of her hands.

He didn't know when her struggling burned away his anger and formed a new crack in his armor, he only knew it did. He wanted to hold her, to make love with her until he was too exhausted to breathe. At night, she haunted his dreams. By day, she haunted his mind, not to mention his house. But the consequences of giving in were so great, so painful. "Because one day, you'll walk away."

That was it? He didn't want it to start because he didn't want it to end? She stared at him, dazed. How could he think that way? What had happened to him to make him this wary, this skeptical?

"Only if you tell me to." She relaxed her hands and he released them. Annie reached out to touch his cheek. She saw him watch her hand warily. "Trust me, Marc. I don't know what happened in your life to make you like this, but trust me," she whispered the words, a plea in them. "Let me in."

"Let you in?" he repeated incredulously. "Let you in?" Didn't she see? Didn't she know that she was going to be his undoing? He surrendered to the battle that raged within him and took hold of her. "Damn you, you already *are* in." Marcus covered her mouth with his own, his lips hot, demanding, extracting her soul from the depths of her very being.

Annie twisted against him, wanting to savor every moment, every sensation he created within her.

Oh God, if she died now, Annie thought, threading her fingers in his hair, it would be all right. She wanted to go on a rising crest of happiness, and she didn't want to hear any words that would rob her of this later. She stood high on her toes, bending her body into his like a flower trying to absorb all the sunlight it could before darkness enveloped it.

Breathless, Marcus drew away from her. Her eyes had a dazed, unfocused look, her pupils wide, disoriented. But her mind, he knew, was clear. It was always clear. The woman would never feel desire to the extent he did. He doubted that anyone ever could. She had had love in her life. There had been her family, her fiancé. For Marcus, there had been no family, only three people beneath a roof, united by a common last name. It had sapped his ability to love, beating it back. But no one could have hungered for love the way he had.

"Tell me," she said in a whisper that was barely audible. "Tell me everything."

He didn't know what she wanted from him or if it was in his power to give it. "What?"

"I have to know about you, Marc. You're a good, decent man who's trying so hard to hide the sensitivity inside him with harsh words and barbed-wire retorts." Her eyes held him, asking him for the truth. "Why?"

"Annie, don't—" He turned away, unable to face the look in her eyes.

He was always turning away from her. And this time, it hurt more than she could bear. She was far too vulnerable to rally. "Don't what? Love you? Too late for that, I'm afraid." The words were tinged with sarcasm. He had no way of knowing it was aimed at herself. "I won't tax you with it. It's my burden, not yours."

She wouldn't have believed that she was susceptible to pride, but something stung now. Pride? Hurt feelings? She didn't know the right term, she didn't care. She just wanted the pain to go away.

Pressing her lips together, she forced the tears back and bent down to pick up the pages she had scattered. "Look." Her breath hitched. She tried again more slowly. "This is our last scene. Maybe—" *Don't cry, darn you, don't cry.* "Maybe I can just take it home and work on it and then send it to you."

Running. By God, she was running for the first time in her life. She hated him for doing this to her.

He saw the pain, the vulnerability as she was stripped bare before him. "Annie." Taking her free hand in his, he brought her up to her feet. "I never meant to hurt you."

"Funny thing for a man holding a bloodied spear in his hands to be saying." She was clinging to quips when everything inside of her was suddenly going dead. He didn't trust her. She couldn't force him to. A tear she couldn't stop seeped out of the corner of her eye.

Fascinated, Marcus touched the teardrop and let it melt onto his fingertip. She was crying because of him. And last week, Nathan had done the same. He had never meant enough to anyone before to cause tears.

Gently he took the pages from her hand. Annie stared at him, numb, striving to rally, striving to keep in mind who and what she was. She'd been a person before she had fallen in love with him. She had to recover that person. "I need those pages, Sullivan, if I'm to fix them."

He let them drop on his desk without looking to see if he had hit the mark. He hadn't. They fell to the floor and he made no effort to retrieve them. "Later."

Hope snapped up its head. Annie smiled. Just a little. "Want to wrestle me for them?"

"No." His hands skimmed along her arms. He felt her shiver and felt her fight to keep her crumbling composure. "I don't want to wrestle at all."

"What do you want to do?"

He surrendered. If there had been a white flag handy, he would have waved it. Later he would gather his protective shield back around him, do what he knew was right, what he had to do. But for now, fighting off this feeling that had him in a death grip didn't even make sense. Nothing made sense except holding her, kissing her, making love with her.

What she had said was true. This was the last scene left for them to work out in the screenplay. After this, there would be no more work sessions, no more reasons to have her here. He knew what she had said about not walking away, but he wouldn't hold her to that. She would move on to another project, taking her sunshine with her and he would move about in the darkness that was his lot. He accepted that.

But right now, he wanted the light. Her light. He wanted to bask in her sunshine just one more time.

What did he want to do? he repeated her question in his mind. "Guess."

His eyes held her captive. He was unbuttoning her blouse, and Annie thought she had never felt anything so sensuous in her life. The man blew hot and cold and drove her mad, but she didn't care how he blew, as long as he was here, with her. As long as he wanted her half as fiercely as she wanted him.

"I dunno." She kept her expression innocent as he pulled her blouse from her waistband. His fingers slipped beneath it, to the small thing she wore that served as a bra. "Give me another clue." She felt the clasp release at her back and the bra slip forward. His hands cupped her breasts. "I haven't got it yet," she murmured as her pulses scrambled. She braced her hands on his forearms. "But I know I'm getting warmer. Definitely warmer." Her head dropped back as he lowered his mouth across her cheek, down to her neck. Her breath quickened, becoming rapid and shallow as he found an erotic point on her throat. Annie moaned.

"Do you ever stop talking?"

"Multiple questions. I don't think—" she tugged at the bottom of his shirt, pulling it free "—that I'm up to functioning on two levels."

"You," he murmured, feeling his excitement pulsate through his loins, his belly, his very being, "can function on *all* levels."

She had to concentrate to look at him and not give in to the flood of emotions threatening to drown her. "That's the nicest thing you ever said to me. So far."

With hands that were suddenly clumsy, she worked the buttons on his shirt loose, wanting to feel his chest against hers. She caught her breath as his arms enveloped her, stroking her back. The soft, dark hairs on his chest tickled her. She arched her back as his kisses lowered to her breasts. He moved his face against them, rubbing his cheek along the sensitive skin as his hands cupped her hips.

Slowly he sank to his knees in front of her.

Annie braced her hands on his shoulders, gripping hard in anticipation. "You don't have to beg for forgiveness. I accept your apology."

He chuckled softly to himself as he undid her shorts and let them sink unnoticed to the floor. She was truly something else.

Annie's stomach quivered as Marcus languidly trailed his tongue lower and lower. She felt his moist tongue through the delicate fabric of her panties as he reached journey's end. She wanted to rip away the barrier, but her hands couldn't move. Her arms were limp, too heavy to lift.

"I think I'm beginning to figure it out," she rasped, her throat dry as words were getting harder to say. His hands were stroking the sensitive part inside her thigh until a fever pitch raged all through her.

Holding her, he lowered Annie to the floor, then loomed over her, his body so close that shafts of heat passed between them. "Annie."

She struggled to think within the thick cloud forming in her brain. "Yes?"

"Shut up."

"Gladly." She pulled his head down to her and kissed him as if her very life depended on it. Because, at this moment in time, it did.

Hours passed. Holly had called to say that she and the children were staying a little longer at Knott's Berry Farm than anticipated. Perhaps until seven. There was no threat of being interrupted. They had time to enjoy each other in peace and in excitement. And they did. But during it all, Annie had the feeling that there was something final happening. It was as if he were saying goodbye.

She wasn't about to let him.

"You know," Annie said teasingly as she shut the door behind the courier who was hand-carrying their finished product to Addison, "for a stuffed shirt, you've come a long way." Not far enough to share what troubled his soul, but that would come. She hoped.

He told himself that it would do him no good to try to memorize her every movement. It would only make matters worse in the long run. "This is just an interlude."

If he had taken a knife and plunged it into her, it wouldn't have hurt any more.

She took a deep breath, telling herself to calm down and not say anything that she would be sorry for. They had made love, then, inspired, had rewritten the last scene. The script was finished. Addison would be reading it before the evening was out. Everything should have been perfect.

Should have been.

Was she going to have to go through this with him each and every time? Make love with him, then watch him rebuild his barriers? Were they on some kind of tumblers that he could pull them up so quickly? Or didn't she matter to him? Didn't what was happening here count?

Holly was due back at any time now. Annie busied herself with getting her things together. The children would be tired and there was no reason to hang around tonight. Not if he was going to be like this. She was suddenly much too tired to fight.

"I don't know what I'm going to do, Marc," she said tersely, "not having you around to properly label things for me."

Not having him around. It was her way of saying that things were over, with no more meaning than he should have attached to them. He had given her an opportunity to deny it, but she hadn't. He had known all along.

Knowing didn't help. "I suspect you'll manage," he said quietly.

"I always have." The words were cheerfully said. Her throat felt hollow. He was pushing her out of his life, sweeping her away neatly. She wanted to say something to him, but couldn't summon the words. She wasn't going to beg, and she had come as far as she could on her own.

The noise in the hallway and the slam of the front door told her that Holly had returned with Nathan and her niece and nephew. "Right on cue," she said brightly. "I'd better collect what's mine and leave."

Before I do something that's everlastingly stupid, she thought, willing her tears to stay in place until she had driven off.

The tears nearly came when she said goodbye to Nathan, who seemed to sense that this was more than just the usual leave-taking, despite the smile on her face.

"You won't be back?" he asked.

She heard the fear in his voice. "Sure." She tousled his hair. "But you have to invite me. I can't just barge in." She looked over his head toward Marcus. "I don't do things like that."

"Ha." The single sound escaped his lips.

She rose and took a step back toward the sleepy boy and girl waiting for her. "Well, kids, I'd better get you back to your mother before she thinks I sold you off to the gypsies." She looked at Marcus, but didn't trust herself to say anything to him. Instead, she looked back to Nathan. "Take care of him, Nathan. He has trouble telling his left foot from his right—unless he's chewing on them."

He wanted to stop her. He didn't know how. Pride wouldn't let him. Marcus leaned against the wall, his arms crossed before him. "Charming, as always."

"I try not to disappoint," Annie tossed off. "Goodbye, Holly," she said in a voice that was oddly hoarse. "And thank you."

Holly waited until after the door was closed to glare at Marcus. She took Nathan's hand and walked out of the room to the kitchen. "I doubt, Nathan," she said in a voice that carried quite well, "if you'll ever see two stupider, more stubborn people in your life than you just saw now."

Chapter Eighteen

The mug warmed her hands even as the early morning breeze from the sea drifted over her in waves, making Annie shiver beneath the heavy sweatshirt she wore.

Warm hands, cold heart.

The singsong refrain kept echoing through her head. She watched two sea gulls disappear into the haze that hung over the ocean. She doubted that anything would ever warm her heart again.

Two weeks. Two whole, long, endless weeks that restlessly fed into each other, forming a chain that was about to drive her mad. Two weeks had passed. Not a word. Not a damn word. No messages, no notes, no pretexts. Nothing. He had totally and effectively evaporated from her life like a pool of water beneath the desert sun.

She took a sip of coffee, trying to find it in her heart to hate him. There was anger and hurt in overwhelming proportions, but hatred wouldn't come.

He had physically disappeared out of her life, but he still lived and breathed and haunted her every move. In her mind. She kept finding excuses not to leave the house for fear she'd miss him if he showed up. She was just now beginning to realize that he wasn't going to show up.

It was a bitter pill for a die-hard optimist to swallow. She stared down into the mug, feeling the steam rise and curl around her face. Cold. She felt so cold, so alone. This time, she wasn't sure if she could regroup. She didn't know if she had the strength.

And for what? To go on alone? Whoever it was who had said that it was better to have loved and lost than never to have loved at all was a raving maniac and should have been put away.

The sharp cry of two more sea gulls pierced the air. For a moment, she watched them as they swooped down, intent on some prey that they saw from their lofty positions. They came away empty.

She lifted her mug in a toast. "Welcome to the club, fellas."

"Always talk to sea gulls?"

Her hand tightened on the mug as she told her heart it had no business leaping up that high in her body. People didn't function with hearts lodged in their throats.

She wanted to laugh; she wanted to cry. She wanted to beat on him until he gave her answers. "What kept you?" she murmured, not trusting herself to look his way.

She hadn't skipped a beat, he marveled. It was as if she had been expecting him. But then, she had always known him better than he knew himself.

All the way here, he had rehearsed what he was going to say. He was going to explain things to her, make her understand that, difficult as it was to admit, he was terrified of getting close to a person. Close enough to be locked out. But he *had* gotten close to a person despite his resolutions. He had gotten close to her.

Now his mind was blank. As blank as his soul had been these last two weeks without her. He had tried to hold out. Lord knew he had tried, until it had finally hit him. Hold out against what? Against grabbing on to a little bit of happiness? Was he crazy?

Probably.

There were no guarantees in life, but that didn't mean he had to accept living in a void. Some people went their entire lives without having anything to show for it but mundane routines. There was no overwhelming love in their lives, no bombs bursting in the air. No hurricanes with blond manes blowing through their day-to-day existences. He found he had a weakness for hurricanes that started with the letter *A*. He suddenly realized that if he was backing away from a relationship because he was afraid of losing her, well, then, he was just going to have to learn how to fight to keep her *in* his life. It was as simple and as complex as that.

The plague he had once thought was descending upon his life was nothing short of a blessing in disguise.

Why was he just standing there, looking at her like that? Why wasn't he saying anything? she wondered. Suddenly she felt awkward and shy. A first.

"Talkative as ever, I see." She nodded at the chair next to her. "Sit down. I still don't bite."

I don't know about that, he thought, sitting down. "That is a matter of opinion."

She allowed herself a tentative smile. At least they were back on some sort of a footing.

Stop dreaming, she thought. Dreaming was what had started the problem in the first place.

He's here, isn't he? an argumentative voice rose within her, fiercely holding on to this newest scrap of hope. With extreme control, she looked out at the sea. The sea gulls were gone. "How's Nathan?"

"He's fine. Still adjusting." Marcus thought of the talk he and the boy had had last night, the words that had clinched what Marcus was going to do with his future. With both their futures. Strange how sometimes a seven-year-old could see things more clearly than an adult. "He misses you."

She smiled and then sighed. "I miss him." And she did. Missed him terribly. It was funny how quickly some people became a part of her life. A part of her.

The ocean breeze whipped her hair about her face. She didn't bother pushing it aside. It would only fly around again. One didn't win against the wind. Annie glanced at him. Or against set natures.

God, she was beautiful, he thought, looking at her profile. He *had* been crazy to run from her, from himself. Everything in life had a price. If there was a price for this, he'd pay it later. Whatever it was, he knew now that it would be worth it. He found that he couldn't live in his empty world any longer. Not another moment.

He only hoped it wasn't too late.

But how to tell her, how to make her see that he had changed? Maybe he should have brought Nathan with him. The boy somehow always managed to break the ice. Marcus looked down at his clasped hands. Perhaps he should have written her instead. He was eloquent on paper. Thoughts, feelings, always flowed on paper. It was in his mouth that the words seemed to die.

"So." She moved the mug back and forth between her hands. It was cooling rapidly. She tried not to shiver. "Everything's all right with Nathan?"

"Yes."

Any second now, she was going to start pounding on him with her fists. *Talk to me, darn you.* "Is this a social call?"

"Not exactly."

"Then what, exactly?" She tried, unsuccessfully, to keep the growing edginess out of her voice.

"I've, um, come about a rewrite." He felt positively tongue-tied again and was annoyed with himself for it, but it didn't ease the situation.

She looked at him, her eyes narrowing. Business? This was about business? Of course, why should she have thought differently? *Because you're an idiot, that's why.*

"A rewrite?" Annie shook her head and banged down the mug against the small patio table in front of her with such force that it had her wondering if she had cracked the glass. "That's absolutely impossible."

He wanted to kiss her, to hold her. He sat where he was, watching fury build in her eyes and thinking that she looked utterly magnificent. He had been running from *this?* No wonder she kept losing patience with him. "Why?"

She threw up her hands. "Addison can't possibly want a rewrite. The movie is into production. They're shooting next week. Besides, he would have called me about it. He would have—"

She didn't finish. Instead, she got up, ready to go call Addison at his house.

Marcus caught her by the wrist. She was getting a full head of steam and that always seemed to help spur him on. The survival instinct kicking in, he realized. "Actually," he began, his voice softening, "Addison doesn't want the rewrite—"

Annie swung around. "Then who?" she asked suspiciously.

He spread his hands wide. "Me."

"You?" Annie slid back into her chair, staring at him. "That's doesn't make sense."

"Oh yes it does." He leaned forward and took her hands in his. "It makes perfect sense."

She blew out an exasperated breath, catching her bangs in the gust. "Sullivan, I know you're a perfectionist, but once the movie is filming and the producer is happy, it's time to back off, sharpen your pencils and work on something else." She wished he'd let go of her hands. She was having trouble keeping control of her emotions when he touched her. Shoe on the other foot, she thought.

"I'm not talking about the script."

Now he had lost her. The only path open was one she refused to entertain. She'd been hurt enough by him, and she'd think twice before leaping forward to impale herself again.

"Then what are you talking about?"

"I want a rewrite of my life."

"Oh?" There was her heart, back in her throat again. She had to squeeze the words out. "What sort of a rewrite do you have in mind?"

He didn't answer right away. He wanted to touch her, to feel her face in his hands, to trace the slope of those delicate cheekbones, to reassure himself that this, unlike what he had conjured up these past two weeks, was not an apparition.

He watched in fascination as a faint trace of pink rose to her cheeks. "Something along the lines of a permanent collaboration." She parted her lips. He placed his finger across them. "You don't have to give me an answer right away."

But she wanted to. She knew if she didn't strike now, an opportunity would be lost. "In order to do a rewrite, Marc, I have to know what was there before." She looked into his eyes, searching. He was offering her himself and she knew that she should snatch this moment, snatch this emotion and run, but what if it faded? What if there was trouble down the line? She couldn't fight, she couldn't hold her own against something she didn't understand. She'd learned that once. "Tell me."

She didn't have to say any more than that. He knew what she wanted. He knew he owed it to her. Yet he didn't know if he could bare his soul. "There was nothing before."

No, no, there was no longer time for evasions. A hand to his shoulder, she tried to coax it from him, for both their sakes. "Marcus," she whispered.

"Now you get formal on me." A cryptic smile lifted his lips for a fleeting second. "I mean it, Annie. There was *nothing*. I wish there was. It would have given me a foundation for what was happening here between us. I never saw any love between my parents, never felt any from them. I was just an extension of what they were, like their cars and their clothes." He paused, trying to thrust aside the memories that suddenly came flooding back, drenching him. "I think it hurt...a lot...to feel what I did for them and not to feel anything in return." Marcus ran his hands through his hair, struggling with his ghosts. "I'm not making any sense."

Now she understood everything, his distance, his fatalistic philosophy. It was all to hide the hurt he kept locked up inside. She ached for the boy he must have been, like Nathan, yet not like him. Nathan had had parents who cared. She wanted desperately to make it up to Marcus. To spend her life making it up to him. "You're making perfect sense."

He looked at her, surprised. She understood. He had rambled and she had understood.

"Only you could say that." He stood up and went to the railing. Now that he had opened up, he had trouble looking at her, afraid of what he would see in her eyes. Would she pity him? Back away? More than anything, he was afraid that she would turn him down. It would serve him right. He had waited too long. But he had needed time to sort things through, time to see that for him, there could no longer be another way. Not if he wanted to be more than just half alive. "Did I tell you that I'm adopting Nathan?"

"No," she said, joining him at the railing. She noticed that the haze was lifting from the ocean. It was going to be another beautiful day. A very beautiful day. "When did you decide?"

"Last night. We discussed it." He turned to look at her. There was nothing but love in her eyes. "He has no objections."

She fell in love all over again, her heart full. "No, I don't see how he could."

He framed her face with his hands. "No barbs?"

She shook her head slowly from side to side, savoring the feel of his hands. "None come to mind."

It gave him hope. "We did a lot of talking last night, about his parents, about how it was all right to miss them and still find things to be happy about. I think he's going to be just fine. Nathan's promised to teach me football."

She laughed. "Brave of him."

"And we need a wide receiver."

Her eyes widened as she pretended offense. "Is that a crack about my bottom?"

"No," he said softly, "that's an observation about your heart."

"Poetry, Marc? That's not like you."

Slowly he let his hand slide down to her shoulders, his anticipation, hopes, heightening as he did so. "I'm not like me when I'm around you. You've changed me."

But she knew better. Annie placed her hands on his chest, absorbing the heat. She'd been wrong about her heart never feeling warm again. "No one changes a person. I just brought things out in you that you've kept hidden."

"You bring out a lot of things." Softly he kissed her forehead. "There's been no sunshine since you left, Annie. And no inspiration. I can't write. Not a word. It's hopeless." The desolation had been utterly overwhelming for him. He had gained nothing by trying to keep her at arm's length and had lost everything. "Marry me, Annie. I love you. You've got to come back."

She entwined her arms around his neck, her heart brimming over. "Twist my arm."

"I'd rather kiss you."

Annie pressed her lips together, pretending to consider that. "You drive a hard bargain, but I'm a magnanimous woman." She grinned broadly. "The answer's yes. It's always been yes."

Marcus kissed her then, stopping any further words. It made her head swim, made the entire world slip away, sea gulls, mist, ocean and all. She shut her eyes tight to keep the tears of joy from falling.

When she opened them again, they were shining, but with a radiance that gave Marcus his final answer.

"I'd like to get to work on the inspiration part as soon as possible, Sullivan."

He swept her up into his arms and nudged the terrace door aside with his shoulder before lightly brushing his lips against hers. "It's about time we started blending our styles again. Let's get to work, partner."

For once, Annie couldn't think of a single argument against that.

* * * * *

Silhouette Special Edition

presents

SONNY'S GIRLS

by Emilie Richards, Celeste Hamilton and Erica Spindler

They had been Sonny's girls, irresistibly drawn to the charismatic high school football hero. Ten years later, none could forget the night that changed their lives forever.

In July—
ALL THOSE YEARS AGO by Emilie Richards (SSE #684)
Meredith Robbins had left town in shame. Could she ever banish the past and reach for love again?

In August—
DON'T LOOK BACK by Celeste Hamilton (SSE #690)
Cyndi Saint was Sonny's steady. Ten years later, she remembered only his hurtful parting words....

In September—
LONGER THAN . . . by Erica Spindler (SSE #696)
Bubbly Jennifer Joyce was everybody's friend. But nobody knew the secret longings she felt for bad boy Ryder Hayes....   SSESG-1

Silhouette Special Edition®

proudly hails

WOMEN OF GLORY

from Lindsay McKenna

Soar with Dana Coulter, Molly Rutledge and Maggie Donovan—Lindsay McKenna's WOMEN OF GLORY. On land, sea or air, these three Annapolis grads challenge danger head-on, risking life and limb for the glory of their country—and for the men they love!

May: NO QUARTER GIVEN (SE #667) Dana Coulter is on the brink of achieving her lifelong dream of flying—and of meeting the man who would love to take her to new heights!

June: THE GAUNTLET (SE #673) Molly Rutledge is determined to excel on her own merit, but Captain Cameron Sinclair is equally determined to take gentle Molly under his wing....

July: UNDER FIRE (SE #679) Indomitable Maggie never thought her career—or her heart—would come under fire. But all that changes when she teams up with Lieutenant Wes Bishop!